Seascape with Body

Seascape with Body

Raymond Flynn

NEW ENGLISH LIBRARY
Hodder and Stoughton

First published in Great Britain in 1995
by Hodder and Stoughton
A division of Hodder Headline PLC
First published in paperback in 1996
by Hodder and Stoughton
A New English Library paperback

British Library Cataloguing in Publication Data

Flynn, Raymond
Seascape with Body
I. Title
823 [F]

ISBN 0 340 64973 9

Typeset by Palimpsest Book Production Limited,
Polmont, Stirlingshire
Printed and bound in Great Britain by
Cox & Wyman Ltd, Reading, Berkshire

Hodder and Stoughton
A division of Hodder Headline PLC
338 Euston Road
London NW1 3BH

TO KATE

and

If it's cold and it's dark and it's raining,
and you're out there doing the Job.

1

I drove slowly from the Pirate's Haven and the Fun Castle at the north end of the Esplanade to the Jolly Fisherman and the autumnal remains of the floral clock at the south. I saw everything from the sand dunes to the shuttered cafés and empty amusement arcades and I counted five people in half a mile of wet promenade. Inside the car, neither of us were impressed.

I stopped directly opposite the sign. No parking between the first of May and the thirtieth of September. It was the third week of wet, windy, semi-deserted November, and, depressingly, there were no immediate laws to break. At that moment I could have done with an officious traffic warden, a yellow-banded black nasty, just for the sake of variety. I would probably have introduced him to Stalin.

Not his real name, of course. Angie had called him Joe, and what with his moustache, his expression of false amiability and his penchant for unexpected violence, he soon became Uncle Joe, finally graduating to Stalin whenever he went over the top. And I'd ended up with him when it came to the parting of the ways. Just the sort of companion I needed, she'd said. In any case, he'd always been more my dog than hers.

A Lakeland; eighteen pounds of curled, uptilted tail and cute, well-cocked ears: black and grizzle-red. As pretty as a picture, as smart as paint, the old ladies' favourite; the lapdog from hell.

Prudently, I slipped the lead over his head, wriggled across to the nearside of my elderly Volvo estate and, keeping a firm grip on the little bastard, slid out of the passenger door. He snarled appreciatively and made a dive for the gap in the iron railings, eager to sample the beach. I was ready for that. Hauling him back, I examined the potential battle area with care: it was apparently empty, apart from a couple of sub-teenagers at the edge of a far-out German Ocean throwing stones at the waves. It seemed a suitably stark, unfriendly title for today's North Sea; field-grey where it met the clouds on the horizon, massing for the attack.

All clear. Stalin has nothing against kids; they probably share his wholly anarchistic view of life. I released him; he bounced down the slipway on to the hard-packed sand and raved through a couple of puddles with a view to improving the upholstery on his return to the car.

I watched as he flew, yipping madly, at a couple of strutting, sullen seagulls, just to let them know who was boss right from the start. Never one to let the weather – or exile – depress him; a sort of canine Marine, prepared for battle anywhere, anytime, by land or sea, the lad. The gulls, recognising the quality of the opposition, swore and took to the air, circling, making threats, before they finally sloped off.

Exile. I turned up the collar of my wax jacket and wished I was wearing over-trousers as well. The Eddathorpe sky was a universal dirty grey; a thin, soaking rain swept in from the sea. A hundred and fifty yards away the disgusting brownish breakers were slurping flotsam, or even jetsam for all I cared – chip papers, fast-food cartons, and possibly the redeposited contents of the town sewage system – upon the sand.

I picked up a stick and threw it morosely after the dog. He loves sticks; I hated the town, the weather, the hired wooden bungalow, my new force and my new job. Not necessarily in that order.

I'd known it was coming, of course. You don't disrupt the social event of the Constabulary year and walk away scot-free; not in my old force, you don't. The annual Ladies Night of the Senior Officers' Mess, with an entirely unnecessary emphasis on *Senior*. God knows why we didn't have an ordinary officers' mess like the Army, the Navy, the Air Force, or, just possibly, the Salvationists, the refuse collectors and the RSPCA.

Anyway, it had turned out to be the mess-dressed, dinner-jacketed and entirely scandalous occasion when Superintendent Clive Jones, BSc, had been decked by Detective Inspector Robert Graham, Regional Crime Squad, for having it off with his wife. Whizz-bang! And a quick trip to casualty for Casanova amidst one or two muted cries of encouragement from the uncivilised elements within the CID, and a very convincing bout of hysteria on the part of Angie, my erring spouse.

Like many an idiot before me, I'd been among the last to know.

Not done. And lucky not to be starring in a script winging its way in the direction of the DPP. Luckier still, no Star Chamber, no disciplinary proceedings in front of the Chief. Just a rapid exit from the Regional Crime Squad, a return to duty with my own force, the break-up of the happy home, gentle advice on the subject of applying for jobs elsewhere, followed by a swift transfer of forces to a frontier province. Another naughty legionary sent off to keep the barbarians in check on the distant Saxon Shore.

I was grateful; well, fairly grateful would be closer to the truth. No need to go over the top. Sweet charity, unsullied altruism, had a pretty low priority in official circles. Buckets of whitewash, and an earnest desire to save a flourishing career (not mine), had been the order of the day. And, I suspected, a nifty shuffle around the old-boy network to ensure I got a suitably distant post.

So here I was, six months later, wallowing in the wages of sin: sand, sea, but with minimal possibilities so far as sun and sex were concerned in the immediate future.

Divorce . . . money . . . the Job . . . money . . . that bloody wooden shack. What on earth had possessed me, taking a lease on that cedarwood, verandahed monstrosity? I knew the answer to that too: money again. I was, I suspected, going to need it. Unless Superhero was going to keep Angie in a style to which she'd very much like to become accustomed.

I was so far gone in self-pity I didn't hear the shouts at first. It was only gradually that I became aware that some sort of disturbance was going on two or three hundred yards away.

Stalin had to all intents and purposes emigrated, but there was a fair amount of excitement going on amidst the piles of boulders set as sea defences further down the beach. A substantial, broad-hatted figure appeared to be lashing out and screaming something pretty rich. Two tiny dots were dancing: one, a master of tactics, was keeping well out of range. As I watched, experiencing a familiar sinking feeling, rehearsing an over-worn series of apologies, the two dots joined, and the shrieks reached a crescendo of fury and despair. I am, I admit it, lazy by nature, unfit; I don't believe in violent exercise, but I lumbered into a reluctant jog.

'Stal – Joe!' I howled diplomatically for the sake of form. 'Come, Joe!'

I knew I had about as much chance as a United Nations peace mission in Bosnia, but I wanted to show a measure of goodwill. Fellow dog-owners can get very het-up about their first experience of Joe.

I approached the scene of the action at a speed which, while showing willing, gave me ample time to assess the situation. The shrieking figure was female, expensively belted, Burberried, and sporting a pair of green wellies. Her hat was one of those flat-crowned, broad-brimmed country favourites much in evidence at game fairs.

Late thirties, Junoesque and furious. I had her pegged: middle- to upper-middle-class. Things were not looking good. It wasn't a dog fight, mind.

'Does this animal belong to you?' The voice carried well in the wind.

'Sorry. Yes.' I was tempted, but.

'That mongrel is trying to rape Sophie!'

I looked at the grinning Hunt terrier bitch; some would have described her, inaccurately, as a Jack Russell. It was, however, far from rape. Attempted Unlawful Sexual Intercourse, depending on her age, perhaps.

'He's not a mongrel; he's a pedigree Lakeland terrier from a championship strain.'

Me and my big mouth. It was not exactly the moment to leap to Stalin's defence.

She took a deep breath and fixed me with a cold, appraising eye.

'That', she snapped, 'is rather like saying everything's all right, providing the rapist is a member of the House of Lords.'

She was, I decided inconsequentially, a good-looking woman; what I would call a big, healthy girl. Right. I don't really live in the nineties. It's quite true, I am a male chauvinist pig.

'I'll try and call him off,' I muttered weakly. 'Joe! Joe!!'

I advanced. The woman stopped yelling, and stared thoughtfully at the dogs. My aristocrat had not quite succeeded – yet.

'He'll probably take your hand off if you upset him. They're awkward little devils!' She was obviously more interested than worried by the prospect.

He had never, ever, made a pass at me. Biting the hand that fed him was not, I hoped he'd realise, a smart move.

'Joe, Joe – Gerroff!!' I flourished his lead.

Miraculously, he left his girlfriend to her own salvation, and backed away snarling, cursing, and giving me an understanding of precisely how ungentlemanly and unpopular I was. Then he ran away.

The little bitch took one look at her mistress, bestowed a bare, contemptuous glance on me, and shot off like a rocket after her new-found love. Given a straight contest between lust and loyalty, lust is likely to secure the first prize every time.

'You – you *bloody* man. Sophie! Sophie, darling!'

She turned and followed her animal, Burberry flapping, Wellingtons thumping clumsily along the sands. Dog and mistress were obviously in perfect accord so far as my character was concerned.

I followed at a fairly brisk walk, making preparations for a silent personal poll: an electorate, since Angie's defection, of one. Stalin and I were fast approaching a permanent, and probably violent, parting. All those in favour of catching that beast and giving him a one-way ticket to the dogs' home, say Aye!

I was only too aware, however, that all my previous self-deluding election promises had produced a series of identical, wholly nugatory results. Just like his namesake,

Joe could afford to ignore the democratic process. I was never going to summon up the courage to kick him out. *Bloody man*; obscurely, I felt I belonged to that equally bloody dog.

I tramped the beach in the wake of that female fury for a good twenty minutes. I must admit I let her do most of the calling. 'Sophie! Sophie!!', I figured, would probably produce more effect than 'Joe!', or even, 'Stalin, you evil little sod, come here!'

She didn't see it quite that way. Occasionally she halted, turned her head and shouted, 'Go on, you fool; call that damned dog of yours back!' And I would give a couple of half-hearted shouts, then, once again, I'd give up.

The rain intensified. We got wet. We both covered a lot of sand; we checked boulder piles and breakwaters, water pipes and the backs of shabby bathing huts on the edge of the dunes at the bottom end of the beach. No dogs.

Finally, but not companionably, we tramped the length of the Esplanade – the Grand Esplanade – searching for the escapees. I was, despite her opinion of me and mine, sorry for her. The woman obviously loved her dog and she was worried about traffic. Fortunately, it was practically non-existent. Eddathorpe; November; Saturday; wind and rain – a recipe for keeping death off the roads.

Eventually, we got as far as my car. Joe had returned. He sat, cocky as ever, his paramour pressed against him, next to the front nearside door. I looked at Sophie, a panting, self-satisfied little bitch: whatever was going to happen had happened, I decided.

So had the broad-brimmed hat. By this time she'd acquired a definite Clint Eastwood look. Fortunately, she wasn't armed.

She reached out and clipped the little bitch to her lead.

Then she looked at me, my dog, the occasional spot of rust on the estate, and she positively snarled.

'I've a good mind', she said, dragging her reluctant animal away, 'to report both you and that dangerous dog to the police.'

I had, for once, the perfect answer. *But, madam, I am the police.*

No. No smart-alec remarks; not twice in one afternoon. Stupid, yes; pig-headed at times, but not quite so stupid as that.

2

'Are you much of a church-goer, boss?'

'What?'

'Do you go to church?'

I stared disbelievingly at the huge, greying bulk of my Detective Sergeant. Comfortable, fiftyish, wearing a rumpled grey suit, he didn't look the type to go in for a wind-up within half an hour of meeting the new DI. A joker, then, George Caunt.

'Yes,' I said. 'Mormon – and I go around in a long fawn mac making converts: what's your home address?'

He grinned. 'Nah,' he said. 'Seriously; don't you know about Teddy Bear?'

Superintendent Edward Baring; a light began to glow at the back of my mind. Hadn't somebody, somewhere, mentioned this back home? The strangest rumours – true, exaggerated, totally unfounded – trickle across force boundaries, but I'd never met Baring in my life.

I'd heard a bit of gossip on my visit to Headquarters after I'd been appointed. Lunch in the canteen, and they'd marked my card about him and his town. The Chief Constable of Eddathorpe, they called him; independent, unaccountable, a law unto himself. They were trying to scare me, or so I thought: according to them I was about to fall victim to a medieval robber baron, isolated in his own dreary little fief. One road in, one road out. See Eddathorpe and die.

'Tell me, George. I can bear it.'

'He's a bit of an . . . enthusiast. Lay preacher, that sort of thing.'

'And?'

'He's likely to have a word with you about your religious convictions. He quotes scripture from time to time.'

'In other words he's cracked?'

'No-o, he's not a bad bloke in his way. But he's been around since Adam was a lad: he's a bit set in his ways. And he's had a hard time, one way and another.' He was giving me a message, but I missed it at the time.

'Thanks!'

It was all I needed; a geriatric. One of Cromwell's russet-coated captains; a soldier of the Lord with his Bible and his sword. It was a punishment posting, all right.

I stared around the cluttered CID office; a bank of filing cabinets on a parquet floor, an oak-cased wall clock, a noticeboard, photocopier, paper-shredder, an open cupboard with untidy, overspilling piles of forms, five overloaded desks. One for George and four belonging to the absent Eddathorpe Detective Constables.

The calendar, our one splash of colour, featured an outstanding example of the politically and sexually incorrect. I didn't need to be much of a detective to work out the absence of women DCs. The blatant sexual stereotype on the wall hadn't got much to grin about, either. Not in our particular seaside November weather.

Half past eight on Monday morning; the two eight o'clock men were out already, examining the overnight breaks. There were criminals everywhere: burglaries at the end of the world. Gas meters broken open. A Ford Escort stolen. Assaults.

Still, it was, in all probability, better than working for a living. Removal leave was over: time to get down to work.

I walked into my glass-partitioned rabbit hutch at the far end of the room, and unpacked. To be honest the police station itself wasn't bad. It had been built at the turn of the century; red brick, riveted impressively with stone. Huge, high-ceilinged offices with covered-over fireplaces containing gas fires, a vast parade room, interview rooms, a superabundance of cells; a sort of barrack yard at the back.

Unfortunately, the town had never grown; if anything it had shrunk since the days of its brief Edwardian boom. The building was too big for Eddathorpe except in summer, when, for a couple of months, the population doubled.

An uncommon complaint for a police station: too much space. We rattled around in the place like peas in a can, yet my office had been tacked on to the end of an existing room. I can only assume that some previous incumbent of the Detective Inspector's spot had been lonely, or he liked to spy on his men. Hence the glass-fronted hutch.

I unloaded the junk of years into my desk drawers, into the filing cabinet and the massive steel cupboard which looked as if it should have contained a rocket launcher, at least.

I had not been selective, exactly, when I'd cleared out my stuff at the other end. My copy of the Offences Against The Person Act, passed in Queen Victoria's heyday, was still going strong; but the Forgery Act, 1913? And where on earth had I acquired the old Larceny Act, dead for more than twenty-five years? I'd still been at school the last time they'd used it, in 1968.

11

I leafed idly through its curling pages; on conviction the culprit could be once privately whipped (and that bit repealed another twenty years before). Wastepaper basket, or should I send an urgent fax to Conservative Central Office? They could reintroduce the legislation; cheer next year's conference up.

A place for everything, and everything jumbled up. A few specimen files, an old Civil Defence manual, stated cases, police promotion handbooks, a copy of my new Force Orders, Archibald's *Criminal Pleading and Evidence*, and a year-old *Stone's Justices Manual*, contributed by a friendly Crown Prosecutor. A *Handbook of Police Discipline*, my personal version of a train-spotters' guide; I could have ticked off quite a few of the juicier bits over the past few months – been there, done that!

Pens, pencils, paperclips, old pocket books – I wasn't going to let my previous employers get their sticky fingers on some of those. I selected, filed, or binned my past as I went along. Two pictures: one, unframed, of Joe, the other, Angie smiling out at me, blonde, sexy and self-assured, from her silver frame. I remembered her giving it to me.

Instant promotion: a silver-framed devil-dog. In any case, I'd never felt comfortable with pictures of nearest and dearest on the desk. Too many oily brass-hats displayed the images of the wife and kids in the office, covering up their multitudinous sins with unctuous family smarm. Stalin, all circumstances considered, would do just as well.

I'd completed my first chore·and I was turning my attention to the Current Crime State when one of my two telephones rang.

'Good morning, Inspector. Mrs Kelly here, Mr Baring's secretary: he sends his compliments, and wonders if it would be convenient for you to visit him now, before he goes out? He's got an appointment.

'Yes? Thank you so much.'

Nothing like getting off on the right foot: old-world courtesy. My morale went up a notch or two; I was quite surprised.

Initiative test; where did the boss hang out? George gave me directions, but I wandered around the corridors of an under-used first floor for four or five minutes before I found him. He merited a massive oaken-doored sanctuary with a glittering brass door-plate and a set of miniature traffic lights in red, amber and green – *Engaged; Wait; Enter* – on the corridor wall.

Middle-aged Mrs Kelly smiled through the open door opposite his room. 'Don't worry about the silly lights,' she said. 'They haven't worked for years. Knock, and go straight in.'

The room was impressive; Edwardian wood panelling, a massive old-fashioned glass-fronted bookcase packed with leather-backed *Law Report*s and bound volumes of the *Police Gazette*. A mahogany corner cupboard, a free-standing safe with a brass coat of arms, a dark green carpet, venerable curve-backed chairs, and a partner's desk gleaming with polish. Not your usual shabby cop-shop pit.

Teddy Baring watched my reaction with the merest hint of a down-turned smile. Contrary bugger. I got that right from the start.

Seated behind his desk, he still looked lanky, hunched, too narrow-shouldered for the Job. His head was abnormally small for his size, balding, close-cropped, while the slightly protuberant grey eyes, set in a thin, sallow face, added nothing to his charm. It was the sort of face that went with a big axe, a block and a pool of blood. He wore a solitary blue and white ribbon for long service and good conduct – or twenty-two years of undetected crime – on his tunic.

Instant assessment: this one could be a totally inflexible bastard; a bad enemy; one of those. Immediate question: did he ever make any friends?

'Good morning, Mr Graham; welcome to Eddathorpe.'

'Thank you, sir.' Well, well.

He waved me into a seat. 'May I say from the start . . .' He turned his lips upward, his voice precise, Midlands-flat, with a touch of the BBCs. '. . . this is not the Derbyshire Constabulary; I am not a relation of poor Mr Parrish, and this room, apart from the carpet, was furnished long before you and I were born.'

And that was the only joke I ever heard him make. If you can call it a joke, and an old one at that. Alf Parrish, Chief Constable of Derbyshire; suspended by his loony-left Police Authority, resigning (dying shortly afterwards) for refurbishing his office without their highnesses' permission.

'This was once . . .' He waved one hand comprehensively over the office, the building, the whole town. '. . . the Chief Constable's office of a borough police force. One Chief, one Superintendent, two Inspectors, five sergeants and forty-one constables. What do you think of that?'

'Er, very cosy,' I said.

'Incestuous.' He rolled the word around in his mouth. 'Too cosy, Mr Graham. Too close by half. They abolished the borough force nearly fifty years ago, but the locals still carry on as if the police were part of their family business. Very close, very clannish around here. Hence the little pleasantry about me, the Chief Constable of Eddathorpe; you've heard?'

'Yes, sir.'

'Well, they're right. I run this place with the minimum

of interference from the top. Self-proclaimed UDI.'
For an instant his eyes acquired the authentic robber
baron look.

'We're isolated: sea that way, and six miles along the
main road before you get to Retton, an even smaller town.
That's my responsibility too – and yours. After that, it's
villages, dykes and reclaimed fen for another ten miles.
But – and I want you to take note of my big but, Mr
Graham – I'm in nobody's pocket. You're going to hear
things, tales; even as a stranger around here. Do your job;
judge for yourself. Don't let anybody put you off. You
don't have to back away from anything; you'll have my
support, all right?'

He was leaning forward, the hint of a flush on his
sallow face. Eccentric; crazy as they come? Or was he
talking round something he thought I already knew?
Some scandal. Was I supposed to have heard he was
in somebody's pocket – bent? It was neither the time
nor the place for a swift interrogation of the new
boss. No enemies at the start. Time was going to
have to tell.

'Well . . .' He stretched a smile. 'You'll find you've
got some good people in the CID; George Caunt, for one.
There's Paula Baily over at Retton; a very sharp young
woman. You've got one idle man. Needs a bomb up him,
but you'll find him out for yourself.'

We spent a quick ten minutes on my previous career,
his expectations, a bit more about the Division, current
crime. He had my file open in front of him, but there
wasn't a word about my reasons for moving; my past.
Not a murmur, thank goodness, on the subject of the old
Senior Officer's chestnut; about his door being ever open
for advice.

Eventually, he looked at his watch; I rose to leave,
thanked him for his time; almost got to the door.

'One thing,' he said. 'I don't know whether you are a practising Christian, Mr Graham?'

I muttered something about church: Christmas, Easter, Remembrance Sunday.

'Well, this may be a comfort to you in your trouble: God will punish the unrepentant sinner, in the midst of his sins.'

Wow! So much, then, for Superintendent Clive Jones. I could hardly wait. What could I say but 'Thanks'?

One way or another, I seemed to have been saying it quite a lot.

3

The first morning rattled by. Coffee with Derek Paget, the expanding, expansive uniform Chief Inspector, who made it perfectly clear that the CID members were all mine: exotica; little or nothing to do with him. Friendly, though; recommended the Links Hotel. Police work apparently came a poor second to an active social life; he enjoyed his pint and a game of golf on the municipal course.

The Duty Inspector said something trite about co-operation between the Uniforms and CID, and the office man and the civvy clerk gave me a conducted tour of the oven in the kitchen: hot sausage rolls, Cornish pasties, steak and kidney pies; put your money in the tin. Oh, yes; and the contents of the big control room drawer: discount Mars bars, Kit Kats, chewing gum, sweets, and two kinds of contraceptives for sale. I got the message; a nice little, tight little, let's-not-bust-a-gut nick.

The two morning Detective Constables, Andy Spriggs and a looming, silent man, Malcolm Cartwright, came back with an eighteen-year-old in tow, straight into the custody suite. Everything by the book: arrested for burglary, empty your pockets, these are your rights, who do you want informing, what's your solicitor's name, then? Sign here.

17

Police and Criminal Evidence Act; exactly the same procedure, the same forms, the same stupid tattoos, and similar, half-scared obscenities from the suspect. Apart from the Custody Sergeant, and his bored, semi-rural courtesy to the moronic little slag, I could have been back home with three hundred thousand, instead of forty-five in the town.

We had a quick whip through the admin – the way they presented their crime files to the Crown Prosecutor – and it was time for lunch.

'Want to visit Paula Baily?' asked George. 'Good pub just outside Retton.'

'Great; but I wouldn't mind exercising my dog on the way.'

George raised his eyebrows. 'The sex machine?'

'Word gets around, then?'

The beginnings of a sly grin faded from his face. 'Believe me, boss. They don't miss anything in this burgh. Your bungalow, now: leased semi-furnished, but you brought a double bed with a pine headboard, a drop-leaf dining table and four chairs, a carpet, a leather chesterfield, two bookcases, a load of kitchen and house-hold nick-nacks, and eight boxes of books.'

'Nine, actually. I'm going to need some more shelves. It's some comfort to know the long-nosed buggers can't count.'

'Yeah; well, nobody's perfect. But snooping's their hobby round here. They've been at it for generations; spying on strangers, gossiping about each other. The railway line closed a couple of years ago; the summer visitors are getting scarcer and that makes 'em worse. Nothing else to do but mind each other's business on the sly.'

'And the lady with the dog?'

'She's not so bad: Mrs Mary Todd – Councillor Mrs

Mary Todd. She's an incomer too; a bit of a queen bee. Enterprising. Got a bob or two and one lot here hate her for it.'

'And that's how you get hated, is it?'

'An outsider with money and a mind of her own? Yep, that's one way. And she divorced Dicky Todd a few years ago. Prominent local family – garage, amusement park, bingo, gift shops; that sort of thing. He's got the garage, and a caff. Left Mary and married a later model: tits like chapel hat-pegs. Mistake; not a bad lass, but she's having this love affair with a big vodka bottle.'

Never mind the ecclesiastical fixtures; I can do without the big vodka bottle, pal. Big was expensively dressed and beautiful, and Richard Todd was probably an undiscerning fool. Maybe I could develop ambitions as a rich girl's plaything; might even get Joe to ingratiate himself, given time.

Mind wandering, ignoring the task in hand, I devoted a quick ten seconds to the charms of Councillor Mrs Mary Todd. Then I pulled up short: me; another woman? Right now? I must be ready for the funny farm. Bring on the strait-jacket, and the little men in white coats!

'You seem to have your finger on the pulse.' I returned, reluctantly, back to reality and George's slightly curious gaze.

'Been here twenty years; married a local girl. But they still don't trust me as far as they'd like to kick me, boss. They stick together like shit to a blanket!'

Bang on cue, Andy Spriggs poked his head round the office door, and grinned sheepishly at George.

'Trouble with Perry Mason again!' he said.

'I've told you; he's got his living to earn, just like us.'

'Yeah; well, you know what he's like, he's your cousin-in-law. Do us a favour, George, and sort him

19

out. We've got this little toe-rag bang to rights, and Charlie's doing his civil liberties stuff.'

George levered himself reluctantly to his feet. 'Case in point, boss: everybody's pissing in the same pot in this town, even me. Two firms doing crime and Legal Aid and me wife's cousin gets a job with one of 'em. Charlie Pringle, assistant solicitor and poor man's friend. Jesus wept!'

Detective Sergeant George Caunt, your man for a colourful turn of phrase; empathising like mad with his fellow citizens, I don't think.

'Like that, is he?'

'Only when he gets ideas above his station; a thirty-five-year-old baby. He'll grow up, I hope. Like to go on without me, boss? I'll give Paula a bell if you like; tell her you're on the way?'

'Thanks. Don't suppose I can get lost on a straight road.'

He made as if to go, then he hesitated and turned back, groping for the right words. I got the impression he'd been working round to it; had probably wanted to break it to me over a pint.

'One thing, boss – Teddy hasn't told you; otherwise you'd have said something.'

'What?'

'An old, old job; nasty, though. Can I tell you later?'

I nodded and George clumped sourly down the stairs, his complaint growing more virulent as his voice grew fainter; 'Andy, my son; why don't you and your oppo tell Charlie to . . .'

Small town: incestuous, even the cops. George, I noticed, had made no effort to introduce me to his awkward relation. I thought of upsetting his apple-cart; having a little heart to heart with the people's friend. Second thoughts: do not unnecessarily poke the nose;

plenty of time for that. I picked up my coat and made my way down into the yard to collect my car.

First impressions: I liked George, he'd been quick to put me wise to the place. Nevertheless, he probably had his reasons; and that cousin-in-law of his . . . Having a solicitor in the family; something of a two-edged sword, all right . . .

Detective Sergeant Paula Baily, Retton CID; thirtyish, dark brown hair, good figure, too much make-up, and a ribald grin. She bought me a pint: nothing to do with sucking up to the boss. She too had her own agenda; was making a different point. Something to do with being as good, as independent as any other member of the team. Standing her corner; buying her round. Just in case I had prejudices against women in the CID.

She smiled at me over her large gin and slimline. 'Well, this is it, sir. Retton equals civilisation. This is the border-post. Cheers!'

'Everybody', I said, 'seems to have a down on Eddathorpe; what's your version?'

'Nothing wrong with the town; just some of the people in it.'

'And Retton?'

'Market town; twenty-odd villages around. Farmers, a trading estate, small businesses – agricultural supplies, that sort of thing. Cattle market on Tuesdays.'

'What's your theory, then; why is it different from Eddathorpe?'

Her smile widened into a derisive grin. 'The Paula Baily psychological theory of towns,' she said. 'In a word: crossroads.'

'Yes?'

'We've got roads going north to Humberside and the motorway, south-west, and eventually to the A1,

21

as well as that glorified country lane to Eddathorpe.
Apart from one minor road, meandering to God knows
where, Eddathorpe is stuck on the edge of the sea with one
way out. Nobody ever goes there, unless they want to –
wrinklies in coaches; caravanners; the bed-and-breakfast
crowd. Hardly anybody ever gets out. The residents are
stuck with each other for eight months of the year.'

'What about wonderful Retton, then?' I teased. 'Fifty
shops, four pubs and a petrol station, all on the way to
somewhere else?'

She leaned forward. 'Shhhh! Keep your voice down,
boss. They'll make you Chairman of the Eddathorpe
Chamber of Commerce, if they catch you praising it up!'

I laughed, and took swift note of the beginnings of
a substantial cleavage on the other side of the table.
Sexy, witty, independent. In other circumstances I'd
have wanted to get to know her a lot better. But the
Angie problem hadn't gone away; and as for the police
force, a relationship with your female Detective Sergeant
– that would be really, really great.

The landlord came over with the plates containing
a massive hunk of French bread, butter, pickles and
substantial slices of beef and ham. I ordered the next
round; a single gin and a half. Neither of us were inclined
to show out as lunchtime boozer-drivers.

'Want to beat the bounds afterwards?' she said through
a mouthful of ham.

'Sorry?'

'Show you the patch? All the cute little villages; the
ones they'd have under ten feet of water, if it wasn't for
the sea defences.'

'Yeah, why not; we'll use my . . .' and I stopped.
Mrs Mary Todd; the big, healthy girl. She sailed past,
her expensive Donegal tweeds brushing the back of
Paula's chair.

'Hello, Inspector; no dog today?' She gave me a smile, half patronising, half friendly. The lady had identified me in one. News obviously travelled fast around here.

'Imprisoned,' I said, 'for the moment; in the car.'

She smiled again, a purely social widening of the lips. She made her way to a table by the oversized fake inglenook and the pseudo log fire where a man, blazered, badged and in his early fifties with carefully coiffured grey hair, was awaiting her. He sprang to his feet as if fitted with springs, bared his teeth and ostentatiously supported the chair while she sat down. The Sir Walter Raleigh of the Four Ale Bar.

'I heard what Joe did, but I think he's a nice little thing,' said Paula.

'So do I,' I admitted, 'so long as he keeps his teeth – and other parts of his anatomy – to himself.' I'd given her a lift to the pub. Joe had been in one of his wag-your-stern-and-be-a-gentleman moods, panting happily on the back seat.

'Who's the boyfriend?'

She glanced across towards Mrs Todd and her companion; they were laughing together, the man casting occasional glances in our direction.

'Julian MacMillan,' she said. 'Major Julian MacMillan, so he says; Superbarg Cash and Carry, would you believe.'

'If I was a major I wouldn't like the way you said that.'

'I don't like him. Professionally speaking, boss.'

'Go on.'

'He's only been around for six or seven months. He bought out the cash and carry warehouse down the road. Previous owner was getting on; glad to unload it – not doing too well, so I hear. Nothing much against MacMillan. Nothing much known about him, either.'

'New boy on the block; so you've checked?'

'The bank: "Good for his engagements; cheques honoured regularly to £5,000".'

I pulled a face. 'That could mean anything.'

'Dun and Bradstreet, the Credit Reference Agency: "informants report prompt payment of accounts. Subject has apparently resided abroad for considerable periods. References appear respectable."' She looked at me levelly, reciting her lesson in an expressionless voice. She might have been giving me a quick overview of her efficiency, but she'd obviously done some graft.

'Anything else?'

'I went round to see him; nothing heavy. New local businessman, a social call, crime prevention; that sort of thing. He welcomed me with open arms. Gave me coffee and biscuits. Told me he used to be in the Rhodesian Army; something called the Selous Scouts. Knocked around the world a bit since the – er – natives took over. South Africa; Hong Kong. Put his arm round my shoulders, and called me "girlie".'

'Yeah,' I said. 'Criminal offence: you ought to lock him up for that alone. What did he call the – er – *natives?*'

'Bunts.'

'A real liberal, then? He's got the jargon right.' A nasty old word denoting a nasty old attitude, that.

'Songs, too: he's palled up with one or two of the rugby club types. Singing this song about good ole Smiffy, and forty thousand heroes holding back the Russian tide, one night.'

'Rhodesia,' I muttered thoughtfully. 'Selous Scouts. That was a long time ago.'

'Fifteen, sixteen years on and still shouting his mouth off. He can't seem to leave it alone. And there he is, flashing his dentures at Mary Todd. Wonder what he's after, boss.'

'The obvious?' I suggested, a trifle sour.

'She must be crackers, then: one scum-bag in a lifetime should be enough for any woman.' Ouch! That's our Paula, the soft, caring face of Britain's modern CID.

Nevertheless, as we got up to leave, with me smiling at Mary Todd and Paula returning the Major's wave with spurious geniality, something vaguely stirred.

It didn't ring true, somehow; the legend of the Old Colonial Hand. A niggling little memory involving Rhodesian Special Forces, tales of long-dead Frederick Courtenay Selous and his disbanded ruddy Scouts gnawed away at the back of my mind.

Nothing to do with heroic majors and military history: common, sordid police work intruded; confidence tricksters, fraud. The more I thought about it, the more insubstantial it became. Nothing I'd ever dealt with, that was for sure. Something I'd read?

Then again, I could be indulging in a spot of wishful thinking: a middle-aged fantasy of a particularly obnoxious kind. It was one way of disposing of a potential rival: lock the bugger up. After which a separated, lonesome and barely eligible Detective Inspector might possibly take his chances with toothsome Mary Todd.

However hard and often I'd been bitten, I couldn't seem to get females off my brain.

4

It hadn't been a bad afternoon, I reflected, as I drove through the country lanes. Apart from Uncle Joe, who was by this time snoring innocently away, wrapped in his blanket, on the luggage platform right at the back. But it had been business as usual, earlier, as soon as I'd let him out of the car. A four-field chase after a rabbit, with all vulgar human abuse, pleas and threats of violence totally ignored.

Eventually, in his own good time, he'd reappeared, as cocky as ever and plastered with mud.

'You're not funny,' I snarled, bundling him into the car. 'One public-spirited farmer, and you could have been shot.'

'Not likely, boss. Arable, not sheep.' Paula grinned her derisive grin. Funny urban man; hilarious little dog. No animosity, but I think she preferred the dog.

We'd done a tour of the rural patch, chatted with one or two local wheels and sized each other up. She was competent all right and she knew how to get her own way. No feminine wiles; straight John Bull. The nominal strength of Retton CID was a sergeant and four: she'd only got three Detective Constables. Somebody had got her entitlement and she wanted him back. Or a her.

She gave me population, acreage and crime statistics, then she geed me up with the possibility that somebody was taking advantage of me; pinching one off my strength. I'd ended up putting myself down for a minor political scrap with Headquarters CID on her behalf.

By the time I got back to Division I was looking forward to a swift run-down of the day's events, an introduction to the two–ten shift, a read through my in-tray and cheers. Life in the unstressed sticks: not a bleep from my paging unit in three and a half hours. I could definitely get used to that.

I met the two till ten, all right. Detective Constables John Robey and Roy Lamb, both in their twenties, both apparently enthusiastic, and each pulling his weight in terms of work-load and detected crime. I was beginning to make up my mind as to my idle man.

We chatted for about twenty minutes over mugs of tea and all the time George Caunt seemed about as happy as a vicar at an orgy. He took little or no part in the conversation. It was only too obvious he wanted them gone. I caught young Robey signalling to his mate; a quick glance in George's direction, followed by a jerk of the chin and a ceilingward roll of the eyes. *Sergeant with bee in his bonnet*, as plain as day.

They exited cheerfully enough, a statement-taking session for an assault, and I waited, a bit unhelpfully, while George hovered. I was itching a bit; the guy wasn't quite as straightforward as he'd seemed.

He picked up the mugs and placed them on the tray; he fiddled with the teapot, rolled up the top of the sugar bag, replaced the top on the milk.

'This morning,' he said finally, 'I was going to tell you about this job.'

'I remember; old, but nasty.'

'Alice Draper; aged twenty-three. Found dead on the Dune Café car park, a few years ago.'

'And she didn't die from natural causes?'

He was wriggling like a worm on a hook, contrary to every impression I'd got of the man. I intended to let this run.

'She was strangled. Murder, undetected.'

'OK. It happens.'

'Her parents would like to see you.'

'Fine: the file's still open; no doubt we get further enquiries from time to time. I'm not being funny, George, but so what?'

He gave me a long, level look. Then he took a deep breath, a man fencing with a stranger and choosing his words.

'Teddy Baring's son, Matthew, was interviewed by the murder team. He joined the Army a few months after and left the area, boss; but the poison's been flowing around here ever since.'

You get the bad news; it always sounds spectacular and it gives you a thump in the gut. Then it's back to common sense. Sure, coppers' children aren't immune from trouble. I knew an old Detective Constable once, who used to volunteer to arrest his vicious, violent son. Poor bugger, he was the only one who could bring him in without a fight.

Divisional Superintendents do not, however, remain in the post if their nearest and dearest are in the front line on a murder enquiry. Not even if they come close. It would tend, I should think, to produce symptoms of acute heartburn up there in the top corridor, never mind destroying public confidence in the system. A media-led burst of guilt by association, and that's understating the case.

Bye-bye, Teddy, so far as Eddathorpe was concerned, if anybody worthwhile had genuine doubts about his lad. So, the Serious Rumour Squad had been at work. On a scale of one to ten I was inclined to award George about two and a half for objectivity and tact.

Even so, if there was a police scandal in a close, interrelated community, I was surprised Superintendent Edward Baring hadn't been issued with his furniture van, anyway. A finely balanced argument for the Headquarters policy-makers to sort out: the damage if he stays, against the gossip if he goes. Teddy must have fought hard to stay. It said something for my new Chief, too; he'd taken Teddy's part. Hard men, both of them. Or stubborn-daft.

'I assume', I said carefully, 'that young Baring could not be connected with the crime?'

'That's right, boss. He went out with her a few times, but he was clean. Volunteered a blood test which is more than you can say for some.'

'So why are you standing there trying to lay an egg?'

He flushed painfully, adopting his self-pitying expression. A chap doing his best and the bosses crapping down on him from a very great height. I knew what he was doing; there were times when I'd tried it out myself.

'I suppose a lot of 'em will have forgotten it by now,' he said, 'but there's some who still make cracks about it; some who knew her.'

'Yes?'

'People who run things round here.'

'I thought that was us!' I was fed up with George's convoluted hints. Nothing like a spot of provocation to stir things up.

'Factions,' he said. 'The Todd family and their hangers-on. Then there's another business group who don't like the Todds; then the hoteliers and boarding-house lot, and one or two others.'

'The Buffaloes, the Rotarians, the Left-Handed Trouser Rollers and the Pope, no doubt. But it all comes down to the same thing, Sergeant. Sticks and stones – I'm sure you know the rest.'

'It's just – just whenever you start looking at things – not only tinpot burglaries and stuff. Well, the Alice Draper murder comes to the surface, and they throw mud at the police.'

'At Teddy Baring's son?'

'Yeah, but not entirely – the whole investigation. Skimming over the surface; incompetence, or worse.'

'Anything in it, in your opinion?'

'It wasn't a good enquiry; the team never got it together. Silver did it.'

'Silver?'

'Detective Superintendent Hacker. They started out by calling him the Lone Ranger: when he was a DI he used to steal other people's jobs and never gave anybody else any credit. Now they call him Silver 'cos he's turned out to be about as bright as the Lone Ranger's horse.'

'So, if anything worthwhile does come up, we report back to him?'

'Yeah; but he won't thank you. He's got less than a year to do. Wants a quiet life.'

'OK, George.' I grinned at him. 'Let me put it another way: if we find anything worthwhile, we report back to him *very slowly*. Right?'

'Right.' He began to lose his hang-dog air; he almost cheered up. A bit of a crusader, George. He didn't like the greyish-greenish, tacky stuff; loose ends, criticism, mess. He wanted goodies and baddies and a black and white world. A familiar attitude among cops. Useful too, in a limited sort of way.

5

—◄—

'When did you say the Drapers were coming?'

I looked at the Alice Draper murder file. It occupied a room to itself; well, an eight-by-six cubbyhole, anyway. Most of it was tripe; message pads, copy computer print-outs, files of completed actions, descriptive forms, negative statements, reports. The usual snowstorm of paper a murder enquiry engenders in its wake. The gear that nobody ever weeds or throws away. But the typed-up nitty-gritty occupied six green filing boxes, a good two feet of space on a shelf.

'Ten o'clock in the morning, boss.'

'You're joking. What do you expect me to do, stay here all night?'

'I've done a briefing sheet, boss. For anybody new. The job isn't dead; we still get bits and pieces, so I've done a résumé of the salient points.'

A résumé of the salient points; he was obviously proud of that, and our first meeting so recent that I didn't have the heart to mock. In any case, credit where credit's due. You could come to the enquiry cold without looking a bloody fool, thanks to George.

My predecessor, an elderly, reputedly idle Detective Inspector, hadn't shown a lot of interest. Sleepy, seedy

Eddathorpe had suited him fine. He'd plodded through the last couple of years of his service, retired, and failed to leave so much as an anecdote behind him, good or bad. None of his business; he'd left an old, embarrassing murder enquiry to gather dust. Now, within a month of his departure, nobody even bothered to mention his name.

George handed me a slim buff folder. 'I could give you a chance to read it. Come back, go over anything you want, after I've had me tea.'

'Great. Fancy a pint, afterwards?'

He left briskly, inspired by thoughts of food. I settled down to read.

Briefing Notes: Murder of Alice Margaret Draper, 23 years, Late of 'Tintagel', 23, Selby Avenue, Eddathorpe. Night of 12/13 December 1989.

1. Alice Margaret Draper (born Derby, 19.6.1966) lived with her parents, Albert Mark Draper, 71 years, retired British Rail employee, and her mother, Ruth Draper, 58 years, housewife, at the above address. (Ages given as at time of offence.) The family have lived in Eddathorpe since the father's retirement on health grounds in 1983. The deceased has one brother, Michael Draper, aged 30 years, married, a Clerical Officer (DSS) residing in Carlisle.

Not what you'd call a scintillating start; like most police reports it lacked immediacy, drama, zip. George, however, was not a man to let a fact shuffle off and hide.

Carefully, in language from which emotion had been almost entirely purged, he plugged away at the job. Impressive in its way, the report eventually conjured up its own picture: grey, winter afternoons; stolid men with clipboards slamming car doors, tramping up and down garden paths and ringing doorbells. Getting it all on paper; grinding on.

On her arrival in this town Miss Draper first secured employment at the Dune Café as a waitress, where she was employed for the 1983 season – Manager-ess, Doreen Simpson, Statement file V2–38. Proprietor Richard Todd**. Statement File Volume 2/39 & Inter-view File 3.

A great man for the cross-reference was George.

The list of employments dragged on: shop assistant, Campion's News; receptionist at Carter's Dentists, then back to shop assistant, something called Quality Gifts, proprietor Victor Todd, another man with an interview reference and a two-star rating in the notes. Back to Richard Todd, as a garage receptionist this time, with a manager listed as E. Goodwin, and doubling as a part-time barmaid for a while. Finally, she'd left the garage but she'd continued to serve behind the bar.

Sept. 89 to decease. Barmaid – Part time – Links Hotel. Landlord – K. Baker **. Interview File 1.

The double-star rating denoted a suspect, and I soon found out why. In George's stiff, perhaps disapproving phrase, the victim enjoyed male company.

Fond of a kiss, and fond of a guinea?

Not exactly; no gems of Victorian verse in police reports. Besides, there hadn't been any guineas from men in Alice's case; the odd present, maybe. A free spirit, in both senses of the word; and two stars for a lover and a suspect, as assessed by Detective Sergeant Caunt. But the unconscious irony was in the whole tone of the briefing. He was setting it all out in terms of a one-star, or one-star-minus, life.

In addition to Richard and Victor Todd, the following male associates were interviewed under caution during the enquiry:

**Matthew Roy Baring.	Int. 5.
**Ian Richards.	Int. 6.
**Alexander Buchanan	Int. 7.
**Keith Baker.	Int. 8.

Other interviews under caution:

**Andrew & Paul Reynolds Ints. 1 & 2.
(Discovered body)

Not brothers, nor lovers either in their case; a pair of workmen, father and son. Suspects nevertheless, if only because they'd been first on the scene. An old police tradition; whoever finds the body draws the short straw. A mean-minded approach on the part of the cops, but it's almost embarrassing, the number of times we're right . . .

I went through the meticulously recorded, painfully long-winded *Circumstances of Death*. Apparently she'd left her job at the garage early in September 1989, increasing her hours at the Links, but never achieving full-time work.

On her final evening, Tuesday, 12 December 1989, she'd gone to work in her battered old Mini, arriving at about 6.55 p.m. She had, in the words of George, agreed to work late on the occasion of the ESP (Eddathorpe Singers & Players – amateur Opera and Theatrical Society) Annual Buffet and Dance. The vast majority of the 180 guests have no connection with the Society and the event is open and one of many run in the town during the winter.

I had this picture of her, turning up for the last time in her grotty little car for five hours' work at £2.95 an hour (George again). However had she managed to keep her crate on the road on that sort of wage?

Funny, how interested I became; she'd been dead for years, and reading on, I soon got the message: we were talking internal police politics. Inexpedient, probably damaging, to rummage into this sort of enquiry: hints of a botch-up by a senior officer who would not take kindly to some clever-clogs coming along and digging up the past. Good old George – not so dry as dust, after all. Reading between the lines, he was telling the next investigator to watch his step.

He was tiptoeing over the sort of job that tainted the career of whoever it touched. I could practically see the signs glaring out at me in big red letters: *Somebody else's balls-up! If you want to get on, just go through the motions, and Keep Out!* But somehow, I could feel myself getting engaged. Ancient, messy, exceedingly incorrect; just the thing for a bored pariah, exiled to a sea-lashed dump beyond the edge of the civilised world.

Poor Alice; they'd gone through the details of her last evening step by step. She'd worked in the Concert Room Bar at the Links, dispensing beer and doubles and chaff to the small-town bloods. She'd been assisted by a friend, Sandra Carter, aged nineteen.

Meticulously, George had cross-referenced her; the daughter of the local dentist, and Alice's former employer.

He'd even updated the file to cover her subsequent marriage and her new name – Sandra Lawrence. Married to Roger, council labourer; still living in town.

> Approximately 120 persons were present in the other bars of the Hotel during the evening (118 statements – traced) and eight resident guests have been traced and interviewed ... 3,170 items of information have been actioned in the course of the enquiry ...

Terrific: not just stolid men with clipboards; more like an army on the march. Information from the public, action files. Statements and more statements; galloping overtime and a budget running madly out of control. Somebody, somewhere, eventually applying the financial brake. Inadequate or not, I didn't envy the original investigator his job.

> Licensing hours were extended to midnight; the dance ended at 1 a.m. Miss Draper was engaged in washing glasses until 12.30 a.m., when she saw the landlord, Keith Baker, with a view to leaving prior to the ending of the event ... She engaged in a minor dispute with Baker, who instructed her to remain until closure ... She was last seen on the premises, in outdoor clothing, at approximately 1.20 a.m., Wednesday, 13 December 1989. She was not, however, seen by anyone on the car park. Her abandoned car was discovered there by police/Baker at 9.45 a.m. the following morning.

I kept on skipping, losing the chronology, going back. Finally, I had most of it in my head.

The body of Alice Margaret Draper had been discovered by the Reynolds, father and son, Painters and Decorators, just before 8 a.m., Wednesday, 13 December, in a patch of sand and grass at the side of the Dune Café, near the beach steps at North Beach Car Park on their arrival for work at the closed café. Winter, the off season; time for redecoration and repairs.

The Victim lay on her back, partially clothed (shoes, tights, knickers, removed; knickers, tights, one black leather court shoe missing. Black leather 2 compartment purse/clutch handbag, and contents missing. (Clothing etc. – see statement of Ruth Draper V1/8.) No attempt had been made to conceal the body. (Photo files: Scene 1 & 2. Post Mortem: 3.)

Delicately invited, I looked at the photograph files. Files one and two were OK; not exactly a bundle of laughs. Views of the car park, views of the café, body (distant), body (close up). Head and neck (slight bruising); hands (scratches on backs); clothing (disturbed). Not too bad, but I do have these aesthetic objections to looking up the skirt of a corpse.

It was file number three I hated; I knew I would. I've hated post mortems ever since I was a sprog – Hey, look! There's a Baby Bobby; let's send him off to the mortuary to assist the pathologist. See if it makes him sick!

It did.

I do not enjoy PM photos, either; even now. Especially the one where they've clamped back the flesh of a strangled female neck to show the mild haematoma, and the delicate, fractured hyoid bone.

For the technically minded, Alice's trachea and the laryngeal cartilages were intact. There was evidence of an infiltration of blood at the site of the fracture and blood flecks in the lungs. The pictures of the minor bruises on the upper arms and right hip were pretty easy going after that. Nevertheless, it was a relief to get back to George's matter-of-fact words.

> The Victim enjoyed prior good health ... Signs of abortion undertaken within previous 3 months – confirmed GP and Easingholme Clinic, see statements. (V1/34–37.) (Records Easingholme Clinic: Pregnancy terminated Friday, 29 Sept. 89. Ten weeks.)
>
> Evidence of recent sexual intercourse. (Probably less than 12 hours.) Semen present and extracted for analysis.
>
> Conclusion: (Rape?) Manual strangulation; minimal force.

It was not until the last paragraph that I found evidence of George's black sense of humour, and his desire for revenge on his area Detective Superintendent. The prose was still dry, matter-of-fact, but his flat mention of the thirty-one suspects arrested, the nineteen who provided samples of blood for DNA analysis, the six eliminations provided by other means, and the six blank refusals on legal advice, followed by the laconic *'all subjects released'*, spoke volumes for the relationship between at least one Detective Sergeant and the enquiry boss.

I glanced quickly through the summary of the policy file and the instructions as to what was not to be released to the press. A cautious, straightforward decision; details of Alice Draper's missing underwear had been withheld, the contents of her handbag had not been released, nor the abortion evidence. The last sheet had been endorsed in longhand:

Follow policy instructions to the letter! Referred to Divisional detectives for enquiries, 1 April 1990.
                    R. Hacker, Detective Superintendent

Well, now I knew all about the prowess of the no-hope investigator; Detective Superintendent Hacker, alias Silver, George's friend.

I felt I was missing something, so read it through twice. As a briefing it was a bit like George, perhaps. Adequate, but hardly exciting. The refusal to give blood samples on the part of some of the suspects stuck out a mile. DNA analysis in crime enquiries was suspect, experimental, brand new then; the first-ever murder enquiry to use the technique had been to court that year.

Hacker, apparently, had neither the desire nor the resources to attempt tests on the entire male population of the town. Budget; policy decisions again. I could hardly blame him for that.

Then I looked at Appendix One: Suspects. A total of thirty-one arrests; victims of police harassment, no doubt; and no prizes. Quite apart from a secondary, two-page list of punters who'd been 'invited' to help. Hacker must have ended up the most popular man in town.

The usual paper chase, a going-through-the-motions grind designed to impress an Assistant Chief Constable (Crime), or one of Her Majesty's Inspectors of Constabulary glancing through the file on a wet afternoon.

Known sex offenders, former psychiatric patients . . . bike-without-lights and spitting-in-the-street bandits for all I cared. Everybody had been grist to Detective Superintendent Hacker's mill. Life must have been hell for males in Eddathorpe that winter. April Fool's Day 1990 must have come as quite a relief. A careful, thorough and competent enquiry it was not.

I arrived at the Links well before George, Joe trotting sedately beside. He liked pubs; noise, excitement, other people's crisps. He also liked a bit of respect. No clumsy feet; no uninvited guests in his personal space unless their owners came bearing gifts. Or blackmail: a way of life up there on the Cumbrian fells. Joe is your typical northern Tory; all for traditional values, backed by a strong set of teeth.

He didn't appreciate being slung out of the lounge by an uppity barmaid, either. No dogs where they're serving food: news to us both.

The landlord was in the bar. Three customers huddled around a table in one corner; two more played a desultory game of darts. I took it all in at a glance. The hub of the Eddathorpe social scene; the kagouled jet-setters, the raw excitement, the half-empty glasses of beer. It was almost too much for a provincial boy like me. Joe, ever sensitive to atmosphere, grunted, slid under a bar stool and slumped.

'Sorry about the lounge,' said the landlord, leaning across the bar to get a better look at the new hearth rug. 'The brewery say it's EC regulations or summat. Wouldn't be a bit surprised. Personally, I'd sooner put up a notice barring anything from Brussels, including their sodding sprouts.' He grunted briefly at his own joke.

Success made him bold; he pushed himself dangerously forward across the bar to stare at Joe. 'You're the new Inspector, arn'tcha? How's your police dog, then?'

Joe regarded him balefully from under his stool; bonhomie had its price. The cost of conciliation was grub.

I nodded. The jungle drums must have been throbbing all day. One thing about these townsfolk; they didn't miss much. Then again, from the general air of off-season droop, there probably wasn't all that much to miss.

'So you don't serve food in here?' I could have done with a snack, preferably hot. Save me cooking later.

'Whatever you like,' said our new friend expansively. 'Liberty Hall in the bar. Fourpence less on the beer, pork scratchings for the pooch and as many free germs as you like.'

Fourpence a pint next door for the sake of a sculpted carpet, leaded windows, and a view of something closely resembling a big Nissen hut seemed a trifle excessive. Mind you, I've known people who'd have paid a lot more to avoid a meeting with Joe.

I ordered a pint to go with a basket of chicken and chips. Joe crunched his way through a freebie pack of scratchings, snuffling disgustingly through the paper when he reached the end.

'Keith Baker,' said the landlord, sliding the beer across the bar, holding out one fist. 'You'll probably have heard of me, Inspector.' Just the merest touch of emphasis on the last word.

'Yes.' I shook the proffered hand. 'Likewise: news seems to travel fast. Bob Graham.'

'Know all about my troubles, do you?'

Sincerity: I hate getting the suspects' version of straight John Bull. It reminds me of that crack by some old-time movie mogul: be sincere; once you can fake that, you've got it made. But not necessarily with the CID.

'Nothing like the direct approach, is there?' I grinned.

'Well, let's put it this way; if somebody I could mention had been a bit more direct, and less of a devious bastard a few years ago, he might have got further. Geddit?' He looked around the bar at the assembled hedonists, and lowered his voice.

'You're talking about a certain Detective Superintendent, I take it?'

'You know him?'

'No.'

'Take my advice, son, and keep it that way. He ain't exactly a credit to the force.' He saw my expression, and smiled deprecatingly. 'No offence. I was in the job meself; ex-cadet. Then two years on the streets before I saw the light. Thirty-odd years ago.'

I waited. There's a lot of it about; ex-cops, and very ex-cops, if you know what I mean. What had happened to him – probationary constable, unlikely to make the grade? Or something worse?

He wasn't too bad at the game, wasn't Keith. Not a bad mind-reader, either. Burly, bald and into his fifties, he looked as if he could have done his thirty years, and retired a boozy, respected ex-member of the cloth.

'No; I wasn't given the push. I resigned without a stain on me whatsit.' He gave me a knowing, lascivious grin. 'D'you know what me wages was, in the sixties? Forty-four pounds a month, Inspector. *A month!* Pay peanuts, and you get monkeys, Hacker for example, so I left.'

His face grew heavy with disgust and his cheeks mottled. I didn't want to practise my first aid, so I never said a word about current police salaries, overtime or allowances; all in the midst of a recession, too.

I offered him a pint instead. He pulled the beer and sighed appreciatively. 'First today – and if you believe that you'd believe owt!'

'Tell me about Alice Draper,' I suggested. 'Not the statement; not what I can read.'

He snorted through the froth. 'You're different, I'll give you that. Beer and sympathy, huh? Better than Hacker, at any rate.'

'You don't have to confess, unless you want.' A joke and not a joke; he wasn't a bit rattled, but he jumped straight in.

'Confess! My God, you've hit the nail on the head, old son. D'you know about the club?'

'What club?'

'The Alice Draper Suspect Club – not a real one, of course, and nothing to joke about, poor little cow. But we're all members, Vic and Dicky Todd, young Buchanan – me. It's a small town, and they drink here. Not so much Alex, but he's here from time to time. And d'you know what happens?'

'No. What?'

'We all grin at each other and chat, and all of us thinking the same thing. All wondering if they're laughing and joking with the one who did it. Confess? We could do with some of that!'

'So you wouldn't mind helping to clear it up?'

He reached under the counter and produced a towel. Slowly, deliberately, he wiped up a spot or two of beer.

'Bob,' he said, uninvited, 'if that's a smart CID ploy, you can forget it. You're a new broom, and if you want to sweep it's fine by me.

'You couldn't do worse than Etches, the last DI they had. Surprised he ever got out of bed, that one. I'll talk to you – up to a point. But I've had my fill of Hacker, and I'm sticking to my legal advice. No bullshit from cops. Geddit; goddit; good!'

'OK. What about this Ian Richards character; isn't he in the club?'

'Little toe-rag. Needed his arse kicking when he was a kid. Too late now.'

'Unpopular?'

'Dead right. Doesn't come in here. Would bounce on the top step, and miss all the rest on the way down, if he did.'

'Why?'

'He's an unpleasant, foul-mouthed little git. Dad's got a bit of an electric shop in the town. In his twenties, now; spoiled rotten. Work-shy; not exactly washed. Have a look in your records; he's there.'

'Doesn't say much for Alice.'

He tossed the towel back under the bar.

'Alice. Description: stubborn, dizzy, daft about men. Some of us took advantage 'cos she wasn't adverse to dropping her drawers. Standing prick has got no conscience. You've heard?'

'Is that how you see yourself?'

Silence. Not offended. More than one kind of guilt; a man getting old, sad, wise. Confessions of a landlord, on the basis of a quarter of an hour of chat. Years later, girl dead, and it was still eating him up.

What was his problem? Once a cop, always a cop; niggled by an undetected crime? Guilty villain chewing over his past? A touch of sexual nostalgia; or what?

'Tell me,' I said, 'why did you fall?'

He shrugged. 'Wife in hospital, she was there; always good for a cuddle. Couple of leg-overs. Poor little Alice.'

'When was this?'

'Eight or nine months before she . . . died.'

'Thought she only started here in the September?'

'Saturday, Sunday lunchtimes, odd evenings. She'd been coming in casually for a couple of years.'

'Pay her for sex?'

'No. She wasn't like that.'

He flushed: Lothario, mottled. All at once he was late-middle-aged, bidding for old. Alice in her twenties; and she wasn't like that. I remembered the photograph – the one in the file, not the mortuary stuff. Those I could do without. Pretty, pretty girl. She must have been generous to a fault.

'Give her a present?'

He had no time to reply. The door swung open and George came in grinning, coat over his arm. The man who'd had his tea.

'C'mon, Keith,' I said quickly. 'Who did it? Where does the smart money go?'

46

'Nothing smart about it,' he replied bitterly. 'No odds; just one non-starter that never got to the gate. Believe it. Me.'

He retreated to his pumps and pulled for George, for himself, for me: three pints. A sorry, unhappy man.

6

The Drapers. Sitting on the edge of their seats in the interview room, cups of tea, untouched, on the table in front of them. Going through a ritual, an agony they must have enacted a dozen times before. Ruth Draper, in her best cloth coat trimmed with artificial fur, with her tight perm, her lightly powdered face and a touch of pinkish lipstick; trying, occasionally, to smile. Albert, seventy-one years old, in his best blue suit, a horizontal white handkerchief set, as if with a spirit level, in his top breast pocket; his wispy grey hair plastered down with water. Both of them semi-articulate, staring at me with dogged persistence as if I could work a miracle; conveying, at the same time, an air of weary suspicion. Another visit; another copper; did he care? Were they going to be fobbed off yet again?

'I know what they said at the time. But she was a good girl, Mr Graham; she were that happy and kind.'

The old man nodded vigorously in support of his wife.

'She were young, she liked a bit of life. Praps it was our fault: had her too late. I was too old; there's thirteen years between us, you know.' He glanced fearfully at his wife, then he turned his anxious, accusing brown

49

eyes back to me. A dog; a beaten dog coming back for more.

'No, Mr Draper. I'm sure it wasn't your fault: not hers, not yours. You've been dreadfully unlucky, that's all.'

I could hear myself; they'd sat around for years, blaming themselves for their daughter's way of life. I couldn't comfort; I couldn't help. My interest was in her death. And unless I found a line of enquiry, the official interest was going to remain pretty minimal anyway.

They always got clobbered, the people like this. They worked all their lives, they paid their taxes, and the best they could hope for was half an hour of my time and a few soothing words. And justice? Well, justice appeared to have lost itself in an eight-by-six cubbyhole, in a paper chase somewhere upstairs.

'What can I do for you, exactly?'

'Do? Why find him; make 'im suffer, just like our girl!'

'Yes. I'm sorry, I didn't put that very well. Have you thought of anything which might help? Any other enquiries we ought to make; anything new?'

'Do you know anything at all about our Alice, Mr Graham?' The woman's face was sharpening with disappointment. I was losing what little credibility I had. The run-around: I could see it in her expression.

'This is my second day here, Mrs Draper. But I've read the file.' An exaggeration, but it sounded better than a five-page brief.

It was a hell of a thing, that file. Big green boxes, full of things I didn't know. Were they relevant, anyway? Nothing worthwhile, perhaps, and the killer safely outside their confines, laughing. Days of useless reading; weeks of work. Asking silly questions when the equally stupid answers were already there.

'But surely, you know about her? It was in all

the papers. I mean, you're an Inspector. You must know.'

'I'm from a different police force, Mrs Draper. I've only just moved here.'

'Oh!'

'Just as well, maybe.' The old man introduced a note of false optimism into his voice. 'A new man. Them others weren't up to snuff.'

'I've seen what they did, Mr Draper, they worked very hard. Murder is a very special crime; they'll have wanted to solve it.'

'Pushing paper!' It was uncanny, how he'd followed my own thoughts. 'Rushing round with clipboards, until they disappeared up their own backsides. And that room they had with television screens and green lights. Incident Control, they called it; they showed us round. What good did it do, that's what I want to know? What good?'

He leaned back in the hard office chair, his face red, his breathing quick and shallow, while the woman turned anxiously in her seat, one hand reaching out to comfort, to restrain.

'Don't upset yourself, luv. Praps better if we hadn't come.'

'No!' Surely, I could do better than this. 'You've every right to come. Look, it's an old case; I can't promise to do anything better than anyone else. But if you want to tell me about it, and if there's anything I can follow up, I'll try.'

Oh God, I thought, listen to you. Your heart's ruling your head again and it never does any good. This police force has just acquired a certifiable idiot; another candidate for the vacant post of Lone Ranger.

'A watch; a gold watch, and a three-stone cross-over emerald ring. That's all her parents came up with.

They can't find 'em, and they think it's odd,' I said to George.

It was lunchtime, and I was back at the Links Hotel, that huge 1930s building with a green-tiled roof, boasting all of a dozen customers in a vast, cherry-carpeted, oak-settled lounge. We sat by a leaded, iron-framed window, looking out on to Eddathorpe's version of Shakespeare's blasted heath: the municipal links.

In the distance, the shuttered creosoted shed they called the clubhouse loomed like an abandoned Nissen hut at the edge of the fairway. Lavatories, lockers, changing rooms and a summer-tea spot for unwary tourists. The self-appointed 'members' used the lounge of the hotel. Instantly recognisable by their air of fish-eyed hauteur, they had a habit of staring fixedly at strangers. A happy band.

Illegal Joe, banned by the European Community, and oblivious to his latest social distinction, lay flat out under the table, twitching occasionally, chin on my right foot. Somebody had already bestowed a muttered welcome in passing; something to the effect that dogs weren't allowed. Neither of us had taken any notice; neither of us cared.

'Jewellery's already in the action file.' George took a long pull at his pint. 'They've been on about this before.'

'So, it's no go?'

He shrugged. 'I've read the completed actions; they're around, somewhere. The watch was a present from Dicky Todd; we interviewed him, and he admitted getting it for her. Come to think of it, we interviewed Dicky Todd about practically everything. That's why he's so sore.'

'So Todd was the prime suspect?'

'He was available, if you ask me. He was brought in or invited to co-operate, as Silver put it, four or five times. Until his solicitor put a stop to it.'

'No smoke without fire?'

'Precious little smoke, and no bloody evidence. Just a stubborn boss with a great hollow space between his ears!' Detective Sergeant Caunt, being more than indiscreet about Detective Superintendent Hacker; no love lost there, all right.

'Mr and Mrs Draper say they definitely remember her having her watch up to a few weeks before she was murdered. It's not in the house, and they haven't seen it since. They wonder whether she wore it the night she was killed.'

'No chance, according to Dicky. He says she had a row with him, and threw it at him months before.'

'And?'

'She stormed off, and he says he remembers picking it up; the glass was broken. Doesn't remember what he did with it.'

'He could be lying.'

'Why should he? We got him to admit giving it to her, and to the row. Anyway, one of the girls here at the Links remembers her wearing a watch, but not for weeks before she died.'

'What about the ring?'

'Young Alex Buchanan gave her that the previous Christmas. Wanted to marry her; she had other ideas. Again, nobody remembers her having it for two or three months before the murder.'

'A Gucci watch, right?'

'One of those things with a coloured rim? Yeah.'

'Statements?'

'Yep.'

'Did anybody tell the parents?'

'Well, I suppose so.' For the first time George looked uncertain. 'Malc did it.'

'Malcolm Cartright? Well, the ring's not at home,

53

either. They reckon it was valuable; four or five hundred quid.'

'Nothing to say she wore it the night she died; she was wearing a cheap zircon ring as I remember, when she was found. Oh, and one of them bracelets – bits fitted together; whatyacallem, boss?'

'Charm bracelets; chains?'

'No – no, a gate bracelet, that's it. It's listed. Nine-carat gold; only worth about seventy or eighty pounds, retail.'

'Did they look at robbery as a motive, in view of the missing bag?'

'Believe me, boss; Silver looked at everything he could think of. He'd have launched action files on UFOs and men from Mars, if he'd thought it would get him off the hook.'

'Thirty-one people nicked.' I tossed down a little corn; George pecked.

'He was buzzing around like a blue-arsed fly. The policy changed about twice a day; first concentrate on one thing, then another. The whole place was flooded with coppers, but nobody knew what was going on half the time. Ruddy chaos. The DI was doing his nut.'

'My predecessor?'

'Nope – the one before him, Paddy Butler, he's retired now.'

'Any good?'

'Yeah; good detective, decent guy. He'd had more than enough, though, by the time he went. Sick of the whole bag of mashings; that's what he said.'

'And Teddy Baring?'

'Kept his nose well out. Orders: because of his lad. He could have pulled things together, uniform or not, given the chance.'

'Tell me about the missing handbag.'

'Lipstick, comb, gold-coloured compact, other make-up, diary, purse, a few letters, a pound or two in cash, so far as we know. Mother gave us a list, but she can't be sure. Alice wasn't due to be paid until the end of the week, so she couldn't have had much. Parents reckon she was strapped for cash.'

'Part-time here at the Links, wasn't she?'

'Yep; left her other job in September. Personality clash, she told Keith Baker. That was about the time she had the abortion, but we never nailed the happy dad. Too many candidates in that direction.'

'What did her mum say to that?'

'The abortion? Neither of 'em knew. A few days' holiday, she told 'em. Afternoon appointment at the clinic, and a weekend somewhere in the country. That was her style: close-mouthed where it mattered.'

'But a good girl; happy and kind according to Mum.'

'Yeah.' He gave a long, expressive sigh. 'She probably was. Little Miss Round Heels, though. Men were her speciality: quantity not quality. Betcha we never caught up with all the men she had. Don't suppose it would stop her loving her mum and dad.'

'Philosophy, George?'

'Experience; being a parent, boss. I've a boy and two girls meself. D'you know the saying about dads?'

'Go on.'

'Fathers of boys worry; fathers of girls pray.' He finished his drink, rose, and swept up the two pint jars.

'Now then, Sergeant Caunt; I'll buy those!' *Sergeant Caunt*. More than a trace of irony there. A stocky man in his forties with receding ginger hair made his way between the empty tables, spirit glass in hand. He was smiling, staring directly into George's face. It was a challenge.

'Hello, Mr Todd.' George's voice was controlled, casually polite. 'I didn't see you at the bar.'

'Ah, that's because I was next door, squire; with the common people. Then I saw you in here. Thought I ought to introduce myself to the new local hero.' He grinned at me.

'Hero?' I was prepared to give him some rope for a start. I can grin too. And you catch more flies with honey than you do with vinegar, I find.

'Putting my dear ex-wife in pup – don't disappoint me, now. The story hasn't grown in the telling, has it? Not like certain other stories around here?'

'Detective Inspector Robert Graham,' murmured George gently, ignoring the second part of the crack, 'meet Mr Richard Todd; one of our local humorists, or so he thinks.'

7

What was I supposed to do? Bridle, look outraged, and claim that the incorruptible Inspector Knacker never let people buy him drinks? Especially if the prospective buyer had been ripped in for questioning on a murder enquiry, in days of yore?

So it was two pints of best bitter and another large Scotch for the gent in the Prince of Wales check, while we smiled at each other and wondered how far trust and mutual respect might reasonably be expected to extend. Not an inch, in my opinion.

Richard Todd; a small-town Tricky Dicky, if ever I saw one. He hadn't come over, giving his teeth an airing, just for the sake of my bonny blue eyes. I let him buy and waited for his marketing strategy to develop.

'Cheers.' He finished his original whisky, and picked up his new glass, swirling the liquid around as if he was wondering whether he'd received good measure. 'Only a joke: about the former lady wife. I like dogs, myself.'

I was pleased for him. A small, semi-quiescent object still lay comfortably within inches of his foot. Our guest was oblivious to the presence of Joe and I hoped his luck was going to hold out, for both our sakes. Joe's likes and even more spectacular dislikes remained a mystery, even to me.

I sighed ostentatiously. 'What a relief: thought I'd got another angry husband after me just then.'

'Haw! Nice one, a sense of humour at last; it's in short supply in the local cop shop, I can tell you.'

George smiled. It was the sort of smile you'd expect from a practical joker who had just been put in charge of the guillotine.

'Superintendent Baring', he said, 'is not a notably humorous man. Especially when defamatory remarks are made about a member of his family.'

It's true about redheads; they do colour easily. Richard Todd reddened, and slapped his glass down on the table. True about their volatile temper as well.

'Misunderstanding, that's all. OK, so I had a bit of a go about his lad. I admit he was no more to blame for Alice Draper's death than . . . than I was. We all know that. Didn't stop you lot making my life a misery, did it?'

'Mr Todd – Richard.' George leaned forward and spoke softly. 'It's all water under the bridge and nothing directly to do with me in any case; but you exercised your privilege to consult a solicitor about your troubles, and Mr Baring exercised his when he heard you had apparently been . . . indiscreet in your comments about his son; yes?'

'OK, I was winding you up. Out of order, especially after all this time. I don't suppose . . .' He turned to me ingratiatingly, '. . . that Mr Graham even knows what all this is about.'

'I've got an old, undetected murder on my patch, Richard. You'd expect me to know about that, wouldn't you?' I used his Christian name with all the pseudo-sincerity of a Detective Constable in the interview room looking for a cough.

'Yeah, yeah; we're getting into deep water. Sorry; wasn't what I came to talk about, anyway.'

'Right.'

'You don't mind me having a word?'

'Of course not; new Detective Inspector, a prominent local businessman. What do they call it? Networking. What could be more natural?'

My Detective Sergeant, mischief done, choked and hid his face in his beer. Dicky Todd wasn't stupid, either; but for the moment at least he was happy to take me at face value. He was after something all right.

'Mary,' he said unexpectedly. 'She isn't a bad old cow, y'know.'

'Another dog-lover,' I agreed unhelpfully.

He took a large swallow of his drink. 'What I mean is, well, we might have parted brass rags, and all that, but I wouldn't like to see her come to any real harm.'

'And you have some reason to think she might?'

'It's nothing very concrete; not yet.' He looked into his almost-empty glass; he might have been expressing a brooding concern for his ex-wife for all I knew. On the other hand, he could merely have been indicating that supplies were running out. I slipped George a tenner and touched my glass around the halfway mark. He nodded and made his way to the bar.

Joe, sensing a change in the order of battle, awoke with a start, and rumbled at the strange pair of legs. He took a couple of exploratory sniffs, and before I could stop him, he bounced at Richard Todd's knee, grinning. That dog has the most unaccountable tastes.

Idly, Todd fondled Joe's ears, and stared after my sergeant's retreating back. 'Thanks. George Caunt and me – we scrape up against each other a bit. D'you know an outfit called Superbarg, and a man named MacMillan?' Joe settled down again at the feet of his new friend.

'Major MacMillan, the military grocer?'

'Yeah, right.' For the first time Richard Todd appeared to relax, and he gave me a conspiratorial grin. 'You've got him in one. The military grocer.' Briefly, I wondered how far that remark might travel. Indiscretions can be fun – besides putting a down-payment on a disciplinary form for breach of confidence or discreditable conduct, if you go too far.

'Anyway, if it's just a bit of how's yer father, it's none of my business, right? After all, she's entitled. But she might be biting off more than she can chew.' He thought about his own remark for a second or two, flushed unexpectedly, and added, 'Nothing dirty intended!'

'You're walking round the problem, Richard. If something's bothering you, why not come straight out with it?'

'Look, we're divorced and I've married again. But, well, I don't mean her any harm, that's all. If she's having a fling, it's fine by me, but if she's investing in that Superbarg Cash and Carry thing, she might regret it.'

'How come?'

'Sounds totally stupid, but I know this salesman, OK? He travels in contraceptives.'

'I'm sorry,' I said. I must have been grinning like a Cheshire Cat. That silly old joke, the one about the man who travelled in ladies' underwear, had set me off.

'He cold-called MacMillan, and got an order. Fifteen hundred quid; no effort at all, just like that.' Todd snapped his fingers, making an effort to ignore the levity, intent on getting his message across.

'Then – and here's the crunch . . .' He looked at me sharply. '. . . they made a mistake processing the order at the other end. They added a zero to the value. He took delivery last week without a murmur. *Sign here, sir; and thank you very much.*' Fifteen grand in condoms on thirty days' credit and not a peep out of the bugger. What d'you make of that?'

George returned with the drinks and sat down heavily, pushing the glasses across the table. Two halves of bitter and another Scotch. He'd only caught the tail-end of the conversation, and he promptly crossed the wires.

'Fifteen grand in rubber johnnies?' He snorted lasciviously. 'Well, I'd say you've bought enough to allow the whole town to bonk itself daft!'

I grinned, but Todd barely managed to look pleasant. 'Not me, George; and not this town.'

'A good one-liner though, Richard,' I soothed him. '*Creditable*, even.'

Richard Todd leaned back in his chair and nodded in a self-satisfied way. Double entendres, conspiracies, intrigues, left hands not knowing what right hands were doing. That suited him fine and he thought he'd met a soulmate; third-division devious, like himself.

'Right. Just what I thought: delivery in November, no payment until the end of December. Credit,' he said.

I'd been right about him; Tricky Dicky, enjoying a bit of double-talk at George's expense. And the information could be worthwhile. I wasn't too fond of switching sides, even for a second to flatter him, but I was prepared to make a bit of a bet that I'd have some leeway now. A visit when I was ready; a few questions; a few answers. No solicitors. I was well prepared to gamble on that.

So, he was an informant of sorts. And a murder suspect; although I could perm any one from thirty-one – or even start a new forecast of my own so far as that particular lottery went.

One thing was sure; I wasn't going to be influenced in Richard Todd's favour by any four-legged fink either. Joe, careless of his reputation, was by this time sleeping comfortably, snoring lightly, with his treacherous chin resting on Tricky Dicky's highly polished shoe.

Dusk was falling when I paid my duty call. I felt stupid, to tell the truth. The cartoon cop: the one who visited the scene of the crime, heaven knows how many years after the event. It was, however, a great place for walking the dog.

North End Car Park is pretty bleak. In or out of season. The Grand Esplanade (ha, ha!) tapers away into a country lane, half submerged in sand, with a scattering of cedarwood bungalows on the landward side with names like *'Seagulls'* and *'Norahben'* for the intellectuals among us. The seaward side is fenced with cracked, grey wooden railings where the old chip papers and polystyrene coffee cups wallow at the base of the twenty- and thirty-foot dunes. A terrific view for the chalet wrinklies who've retired to be beside the sea.

The lane ends in a vast area of crumbled tarmac and puddles, netted and boarded around the seaward edges in a vain attempt to control the encroaching sand. There's a vandalised hut at the entrance (Parking 50p). The Dunes Café, long, clapboarded, painted white, with a bucket-and-spade emporium tacked to one side, huddles uncomfortably with its back to the razor-sharp grass and the mounds of sand.

Ignoring the acres of empty steppe, I parked next to a solitary Volkswagen Polo, and wandered over to the spot near the steep wooden walkway leading to the beach, where Alice Draper had been found. Right, I'd seen it. I was not inspired; I could only think of one reason why anybody would want to pay a late-night visit here. All right, two if you count what happened to Alice.

I peered through one of the gaps in the shutters of the Dune Café, and rattled the chain and padlock of the

62

place where they stored the iron tables, chairs, and a few lonely umbrellas they used outside in the summer. I could imagine it: the social whirl, the careless sophistication of the Eddathorpe season.

The place where Alice Margaret Draper had once worked, and close, remarkably close to where she'd probably died. Had she suggested the scene of her last, violent encounter? And why had she left her car behind – had she expected her killer to run her back to the hotel to pick it up? Friend, acquaintance, lover? Sexual partner, query rapist, for a cert.

I collected Joe from the car and let him run. A quickie: in twenty minutes it was going to be dark. He rushed up the ramp and disappeared over the brow of the dunes.

'Not you again!'

The voice, though distant, had lost none of its bell-like clarity, but I might have detected a note of amusement this time. I paused at the summit of the path and looked across the flat, darkening beach.

The scene, removed a mile and a half to the north, was very much the same as the previous Saturday: the sizable, elegant figure in the Burberry and the hat, the two dancing dots, the sea. There was one difference: this time she was laughing.

'Sorry,' I shouted. 'Joe!!'

'Don't bother! Days too late!'

I joined her, and we watched the dogs chasing each other in ever-widening circles.

'Seduction,' she said, 'not rape: it takes two to tango, I suppose.' It was the nearest thing I ever got to an apology.

'Romeo and Juliet?' I suggested.

'Well, if you don't fancy yourself as a Montague or Capulet senior, fifty per cent of the responsibility means finding homes for fifty per cent of any happy event, all right?'

'I hardly know anybody well enough, yet.' I could see it all: the latter-day Sherlock Holmes. Crimes solved, murders detected, homes found for unwanted mongrel pups.

'Not what I've heard. And talking of acquaintances, your presence on this beach is pure coincidence, I assume? You didn't follow me here?'

'Why should I do that?'

'Do the words "ex-husband" and "Links Hotel" hold any meaning for you, Inspector?'

'Yes, they do; but no, I didn't follow you. I was taking a look at the place where Alice Draper was killed.' Somehow, I felt I'd been pushed into uttering one sentence too many. 'How did you know?'

'Little bird: five foot eight, grey suit, glasses, small moustache. Ring any bells?'

'No. Must be a paradise for ornithologists here!'

'Name of Eric Goodwin?'

Another of Silver's victims, if only for a witness statement: what a town! I gave her a burst of the sinceres. 'Your ex-husband's garage manager? I've not set eyes on him, yet.'

'He was in the bar; he's set eyes on you. You appear to be well up on names. People you've never met.' She paused momentarily, then her expression changed. 'Oh, I see. You're not out to make friends, are you, Inspector?' She glanced at me suspiciously and jumped to a conclusion. 'Poor Eric.'

I ignored that, but I deducted ten good-conduct marks from my score: me and my big mouth. Still, poor Eric; and him not even on Silver's extensive hatchet-list. *Ho, hum*. But then again, five foot eight and glasses? He didn't sound a suitable choice.

'What was Eric carrying, an electronic bug?'

'Richard can never keep quiet. He confides: money, girlfriends, hobbies – same thing, really – and his thoughts about poor old Mary and her putative lovers. He thinks I'm in with a gigolo, doesn't he?'

'Toy boy, I think: the last gigolo must be pushing his Zimmer frame around Monte Carlo by now!'

She hooted with sudden, unrestrained laughter. 'Major MacMillan, my little toy soldier. How nice.'

'He worries about you.'

'Richard? Emotionally, financially – ah! Tell Dicky to bugger off. Only fools and their money are parted, Inspector. Dicky, of all people, should know that!'

'You are – er – thinking of going into business with the Major?'

'None of your business, but *he's* thinking about it. Quite a lot.'

'And do you regard it as a good bet?'

'It's getting dark,' she said. 'Time we were going home. Sophie!' she called. 'Sophie!' And for once the little bitch obeyed. Joe, disgruntled, returned to my side, and I fastened him to his lead.

She began to climb the ramp, Sophie at heel. Then she relented. Poised on the skyline, she turned. 'I don't see why either Dicky or you should delve into my affairs,' she said, 'but I'll tell you one thing I've learned by hard experience: never, never to bet. Neither on men, nor with money; and I'll tell you something else!'

'Yes?'

'If you're going to spend your time rooting into Alice Draper's murder, there'll be certain people in Eddathorpe who'll be seriously worrying about *you* rather than me, Inspector. Good night!'

8

By the time I rolled out of bed on Friday morning, beating Joe to the morning paper by the skin of his teeth, I was beginning to feel like an old Eddathorpe hand. For one thing, I was getting over the first cultural shock.

The bungalow, which on first sight resembled nothing so much as a largish garden shed stacked with a few battered domestic necessities, now seemed more like home. I'd pushed the furniture around a bit, shelved a few books, introduced a rented TV, bought two bottles of malt and filled the fridge with beer. The dawn of civilisation was at hand.

Joe thought so too; he'd abandoned his well-chewed basket for an armchair beside the fire, something he'd never been allowed to do in our pre-bachelor state. What the hell. Apart from my few odds and sods, the furniture ranged from twenties massive to sixties orange-box revival. Joe's depredations could go down as fair wear and tear, as per the lease.

Wednesday and Thursday had passed pleasantly enough. For me, anyway. I couldn't speak for the victims of the various burglaries, assaults occasioning actual bodily harm, criminal damage (shop window), or for the prisoners consuming microwaved gunge three times a day in our

67

cells. Nor for Detective Constable Malcolm Cartwright, of course.

Big Malc and I had fallen out. I'd read it in his tea leaves right from the start, although I'd been a bit reluctant to jump in straight away. Too much like creeping, when you've had the gipsy's warning about a bloke from the new Divisional boss.

As I drank my coffee and chewed my toast, I gave some thought to Malc. I promised myself a look at the work he'd done on the Alice Draper job, among other things. Past sins and current performance: both under review.

It had started a few minutes before knocking-off time the previous day. End of the month: examine pocket books, work logs, vehicle mileage, expenses and overtime returns. To be honest, it wasn't my favourite chore: it was usually scribble, scribble and away. But then, that was in the olden days when I'd had a long-established team. Guys and gals who'd earned a bit of trust.

I'd had the pile on my desk for half the afternoon while I'd been talking to Paula, putting her on to a couple of national credit reference agencies to check whether there'd been a sudden upsurge in business at Superbarg. Sorting out a set of microfilm records from Companies House. Preparing a Merry Christmas, Major MacMillan, from all us peasants at the local nick. If we were right.

Twenty to five, and I'd started on my quick bat through the overtime returns. The target was twelve hours' paid, per man, per month. Extra, and I had to seek approval from Teddy. We were slightly over the top, but the budget could live with that. Until I got to Malc: he was claiming twenty-two hours, and his pocket book showed he was out for the record. Fewer enquiries taking up more time than anyone else in the Division.

'George approved it,' he grumbled, when I hauled him in.

George, I was beginning to learn, did not like confrontation with his Detective Constables – keep the lads happy: a signature on a form was cheap at the price. Or so he thought.

'Sergeant Caunt obviously didn't know what you were up to,' I said. 'I've looked through your book. You've been playing second violin to Andy Spriggs all month. You've done one interview of your own, and you've spent most of your time at Todd's garage, out of hours. What's going on?'

'Somebody's pinching parts. He's been showing me the storekeeper's cards.'

'Who?'

'The manager.'

'And how much is missing?'

'Couple of thousand quid's worth, over the past three months.'

'You must be joking. What are you doing – clocking up enough overtime to pay him back?'

And he groused, and rumbled, and looked sullen until I gave him a burst of Get Your Finger Out, Jack, or else . . . And it wasn't as if I was keen on confrontation, either; not with my own side. I am even less keen on being taken for a mug.

The letter-box rattled, just as I was swallowing the last mouthful of coffee. I was up and away like an Olympic hopeful with his shorts on fire. This time Stalin was there first. He grabbed one of the two letters, and dived under the living-room table where he hoped to demolish his loot undisturbed.

Tug of war with paper is not my forte, so I nipped in after him and smacked him smartly on the nose. He dropped his latest rat-substitute and swore. My triumph lasted a matter of seconds: reversing out, I banged my head on the descending table leaf as I knocked the gate-leg prop away with a careless backside. The dog was ahead on points.

I opened the envelope; Stalin was right. I should have left him to it; I was the proud possessor of a psychic dog. I felt like giving the letter back, but he'd lost interest. It was the snap of the letter-box, the thrill of the fresh chase which interested him. He was bored by freely donated, captive stuff.

It was a Dear Bob, from my solicitor, no less. He'd graduated from Dear Mr Graham when the Angie news began to degenerate from bad to the financially disastrous. He gave me a couple of soothing paragraphs before he came down to the nitty-gritty. The woman appeared to want more than Fergie and the Princess of Wales combined. He said not to worry, early days, and enclosed a three-page questionnaire covering my financial position. Please reply ASAP.

I looked at my other correspondence: it was a mail-shot from a charity. Needless to say, its charter did not include aid to maritally entangled cops. Stalin, I decided, should be allowed to follow his instincts in future. Oh, it was Friday, bloody Friday all right.

The phone rang just after ten. Mrs Kelly presenting the Superintendent's compliments again, a pause, and a quiet warning. 'Detective Superintendent Hacker's with him.' There was a note of distaste in her voice.

'I'll be there in a couple of minutes, Mrs Kelly. Thanks.' I meant it: nice to have the Superintendent's secretary on your side.

'Hi ho, Silver, and awaaay!' said George with a grin as I made a smart exit. 'Them Apache drums have been beating at Headquarters, boss!'

Not a lot of help in the circumstances, but at least it proved he was old enough to have seen the Lone Ranger films as a kid.

Teddy Baring was on his feet, gazing out of the window, back to his visitor and shoulders hunched when I entered his office. His hands were thrust deep into his trouser pockets. He was struggling to appear at ease, but the hands were bulging through the cloth, knotted into fists. It was like walking in on one of those high-octane domestic disputes and wondering which partner was going to strike the match.

Baring turned as I entered, and gave me one of his brief down-turned smiles. Hacker, who'd been sitting precisely, ankles crossed, in one of the elegant office chairs, rose unexpectedly to his feet.

'Mr Graham? Nice to meet you; welcome to the force.' He held out his hand and we shook.

'Mr Hacker', said Teddy, 'is one of the six area Detective Superintendents, partially responsible for the work of the Divisional Criminal Investigation Departments and the investigation of major crime, of course.'

He made it sound as if Detective Superintendents held a fairly common and undistinguished rank with minimal responsibilities. And that last, unnecessary remark; was he putting me wise about the reason for Hacker's visit? I sat down.

Hacker was something of a surprise; I'd expected somebody bigger, thicker; blustering too, perhaps. Instead, this greying, smiling man, slim, with a clipped moustache, was neat, almost fastidious in appearance. He wore his expensive dark blue suit, white shirt, bird's-eye tie and matching silk handkerchief with a dandified air, and he gave the impression of being scraped, tubbed, brushed and aftershaved to the ultimate degree. A prosperous estate agent, I thought; or the stage version of a prospective Tory MP.

He leaned forward a little, and pursed his lips in a self-satisfied sort of way. 'As Mr Baring says, I'm responsible for major crime investigation. Not much of that in Eddathorpe, Mr Graham; pleasant town in the summer.'

'Yes, sir.'

Teddy Baring's eyes flickered for a moment; neither of us were giving anything away.

'There was, however, a murder here several years ago. I was the investigating officer, back in December 1989. Undetected, I'm sorry to say.'

'Yes, sir. I know.'

'You've reopened enquiries, I understand?'

'Not really, sir. The girl's parents came to see me. Told me about her missing watch and ring. But the information had already been actioned. There's nothing new.' Bags of humility; keep the bullshit rolling until I could add up the score.

'Ah.' He settled more comfortably into his chair. 'That would account for it, then. Of course . . .' He smiled, relaxed, staring at Teddy Baring. '. . . we've all got a bloody good idea who did it. Didn't take you long, either. Proof; well, that's something else again, eh?'

'I'm sure', said Baring, matching Silver with his own down-turned smile, 'that Mr Graham would bring anything relevant to your attention.' He gave me the ghost of a nod.

'Yes, sir.'

'You've read the file?'

'Only in part.'

'Yes; well, a blood test – intimate samples – and I could have had Mr Richard Todd. Him and his bastard shyster. Thought I'd mark your card, just in case anything worthwhile comes up!'

Suddenly, he seemed to lose interest. He was playing

a part: affable, the busy senior officer pushed for time, but making the effort to visit a junior member of the department out in the sticks. Keeping a supervisory eye. Two minutes' chat about nothing; it was obvious he wanted to be away.

And his real motive? To find out who'd been fishing in his pond? Whether some strange DI had hooked something, was likely to make him look a prat?

Once on his feet it was, No, no thanks; no time for coffee; you know how things are. Flying visit, but keep me posted, won't you? Always at the other end of a telephone line, if you want any advice.

Then he was gone, and Teddy Baring and I were left staring at each other across the width of his desk.

I was far from pleased.

'Sir,' I said, 'how did—'

'He know.' He finished the sentence for me. 'Is there a little bird, with a direct line to HQ? No, Mr Graham, set your mind at rest. You told him yourself.'

'No, sir!'

'Oh, but you did. You read your brief; you examined the actions, yes?'

'Yes.'

'And to do that, you interrogated the computer via the control room, didn't you?'

'Yes; I needed the reference numbers of everything relating to a watch or ring.'

He spread his hands. 'The audit log, Inspector. Every time you raise an enquiry on the system, you leave a trail. Time on; time off; what you asked. Mr Hacker appears to have the system flagged. Make an enquiry and a print-out goes to him. Quite legitimately, of course.'

'Of course.'

'Mr Graham.' Teddy stared coolly out from those

73

bleak, grey eyes, 'You've had your – er – card marked, shall we say.'

'Mr Hacker said—'

'No, never mind that. *About* Mr Hacker – Silver, perhaps? Far be it from me to criticise another senior officer, but . . .'

'Yes, sir.'

'Good. And your enquiries have not *quite* ended, I assume?'

He reached into his right-hand drawer and withdrew a bulky file. 'A full print-out of references, cross-references and codes of all the completed murder actions: alphabetical, numerical. You may find it . . . convenient . . . to use this, instead of going backwards and forwards to Control. It will enable you to go directly to the files without having to interrogate the computer.'

'It'll be very useful, sir.' *Thank you very much; you devious, devious man.*

'I have already said, you have my support.'

'Thank you.'

'And please, Mr Graham, remember one thing, despite what you've just heard; talk is one thing, evidence is quite another. We do *not* know who murdered that unfortunate young woman. I don't know if we ever will.' He was staring straight past me; that narrow face, those protuberant eyes, as grey and angry as the winter sea.

9

Nearly everybody's got one; practically every Divisional CID. The Friday-night breaker; the Saturday-night burglar; the borer; the transom window specialist; or some such thieving bloody pest. They do a series of similar jobs, and they soon get promoted from anonymous toe-rag to creature of myth. Flannelfoot, or some such stupid name. Trouble is, if it gets out they get a boost; it makes 'em proud of their contemptible little selves.

We had a Friday-nighter. Nothing spectacular, a serial breaker plying a steady, irritating trade in a dozen or so little streets near the railway station, tucked away behind the more impressive three-storey Victorian stuff on the Grand Esplanade.

It had been going on for months. The uniforms had kept observations and checked the late-night boozers, party-goers and the floating population of bed-and-breakfast pains living on Social Security in the DSS flops around the abandoned railway station. The CID had made enquiries, lifted a few bodies, convicted one or two thieves, but nobody wanted to cough to being our grubby local legend.

I arrived on my first Saturday morning to confront the long faces and the moans. Five more, and not one over two hundred quid, top whack. Entry, usually, through a cellar grating, or failing that, a ground-floor kitchen sash-window. Most of the terraces had central heating, or gas or electric fires, so cellar grates were no longer bunged up with coal.

Snip the chain, break the hook, and you were well into a relatively clean cellar, where, prior to the introduction of plastic cards, you had the possibility of a bonus – a money box, courtesy of the gas or electricity company. That, at least, has gone down the drain, thank heavens. Then upstairs to coats, jackets, wallets, change, and any portable nick-nacks lying around.

Golden rules: avoid dogs, bedrooms and bulky items. No TVs or videos, thanks. It looks odd, if anybody clocks you humping a stereo down the street in the middle of the night.

He just had to be local, damn him: a pedestrian, a candidate for our special lunch; microwaved lasagne and a plastic spoon.

Faced with similar situations, I've heard your old-style Detective Inspector – the one with the concrete noggin – inspiring his troops: *Get out there, and don't bother coming back until you get 'im; knock on doors; cultivate your snouts; find the fence; spread a few threats, a bit of cash in the pubs!* And, on one never-to-be-forgotten occasion, *saturate the area!* (There were two of us on duty at the time.)

Me? I had a moan myself and drank two of cups of tea. Then I borrowed a couple of uniform lads from the Duty Inspector, inspired the CID with the prospect of unlimited beer, and suggested the door-knocking bit, associated with a touch of crime prevention advice and assiduous sniffing around. Failing that; more observations, chaps, next Friday night, and the next – forever, or until we catch the bastard.

'But, boss, sod that for a comic song. Not a week on Friday? It's the Christmas do!'

'Bugger the Christmas do! Don't come back here, etc., etc. . . .' Which all goes to show: things haven't advanced much in the field of CID leadership during the past eighteen years.

And me, personally?

A rainy day; the ideal time to flush the peasantry out on to the streets and to curl up with a good book. It was high time I boned up on a little basic police law.

Police And Criminal Evidence Act, 1984.
Section Sixty-Two.
(Taking Intimate Samples – i.e. Bodily Fluids
For Forensic Examination.)

62 (1) An intimate sample may be taken from a person in police detention only –

(a) if a police officer of the rank of Superintendent authorises it to be taken; and

(b) if the appropriate consent is given.

Not exactly a wonderful start. Still, Hacker was a Superintendent, that much I knew. Problem: the Act was drafted and passed at the end of an era; at a time when 'intimate samples' – basically blood, saliva, urine and semen – could be grouped, but not pinned down to an individual. Then, within a matter of months, bingo! The beginnings of DNA analysis; a brand-new, highly reliable forensic tool. Within a year or two, it became available to the police. But the Act was already in force, and . . .

(2) An officer may only give authorisation if he has reasonable grounds –

(a) for suspecting the involvement of the person from

77

whom the sample is to be taken in a serious arrestable offence and

(b) for believing that the sample will tend to confirm or disprove his involvement.

Yeah, great. So far, so good, even if the investigators are constrained by the gobbledegook, right from the start. And before anybody starts tossing allegations about fascist police. I like having civil liberties, too; but what about . . .

10) Where the appropriate consent to the taking of an intimate sample from a person was refused without good cause, in any proceedings against that person for an offence –

(a) the court in determining

(i) whether to commit the person for trial; or

(ii) whether there is a case to answer; and

(b) the court or jury, in determining whether that person is guilty of an offence charged, may draw such inferences from the refusal as appear proper; and the refusal may, on the basis of such inferences, be treated as, or as capable of amounting to corroboration of any, evidence against the person in relation to which the refusal is material.

In other words, Silver, despite all the huffing and puffing and official authorisations, had to go to his suspects and say 'Pretty please' or something similar to get them to give a sample. Then, if they refused, he was stuck, and his sole consolation was to tell the court what naughty, unco-operative boys he'd been dealing with. The court could then take the refusal into account.

There is, however, this slight difficulty which seems to have escaped the attention of the finely honed legal brains at Westminster: if the conclusive evidence is contained in the 'intimate sample' and the suspect is refusing to give one, how, exactly, do the police get him before the court in the first place?

Of course, I was being slightly (but only slightly) unfair. Forcibly taking samples is a bit like bullying a man into incriminating himself. And in any case, nobody thought of bodily fluids as conclusive evidence when the Act was drafted.

One thing was obvious. Amidst the minefield of Section 62, Superintendent Hacker had tried to take blood samples and come unstuck. Either Tricky Dicky or his legal eagle had given Silver some vulgar advice on sex and travel. No blood sample, no evidence, no case, to Hacker's way of thinking, back in 1989.

I didn't realise it at the time, but both of us were missing out: a mixture of Murphy's Law and old police cliché number one: *there's usually more than one way of skinning a cat*.

I pulled the statement files and actions relating to Tricky Dicky Todd. First the witness statement: no problems. The statement had been taken within twenty-four hours of the murder.

He was the proprietor of the Dunes Café, among other things. He'd employed Alice Margaret Draper between 6 June and 30 September 1983, as a waitress.

He was also the proprietor of Todd's Garage and Car Show Rooms, Retton Road, Eddathorpe, and he had re-employed her as a receptionist between 1 February 1986 and 9 September 1989, on a part-time (job-share) basis. She had left of her own accord. He had not particularly wished her to leave; it was her decision. Her final salary was £86 per week.

At the time of her employment at the garage he was

a married man living with his wife, Mary Todd. He commenced an 'on-off' affair with Alice Draper some time around August 1986, and the affair terminated, following a row, early in July 1989. The affair was conducted on both sides as 'a bit of fun'. He knew Alice had other boyfriends, and he'd had other relationships with women. It was no secret; it was impossible to keep anything quiet in Eddathorpe.

His marriage had deteriorated, and by 1988 he and his wife were living separate lives under the same roof. They went to social events together from time to time.

On the evening of Tuesday, 12 December 1989, he'd attended the Eddathorpe Singers and Players' Buffet and Dance, merely a social duty. Neither he nor his wife were members; everybody went to everything in the off season in a small seaside town; it helped keep boredom at bay. Besides, as a local big-wig, Mary had been expected to turn up.

They had both arrived separately, he at about 8.30 p.m., and she a few minutes later, following a council meeting.

He had 'gone the social rounds' with his wife. He had danced with her twice; he had danced with other women, including Valerie Hill, a close friend. He had spent some time in the bar and had spoken to Alice a number of times. There was no animosity between them. They'd had a laugh and a joke. Other people, including his brother, Victor Todd, could vouch for that.

His wife had left the Links shortly before midnight. He had left about 12.15 a.m., after the bar closed. Alice Draper had been collecting glasses shortly before he left. That was the last he saw of her. He had driven straight home – alone, arriving shortly after 12.30 a.m.

A bit like wading through treacle, but nice and straight-forward so far as it went. Anyway, it was a detailed account of the evening of 12/13 December 1989, as enjoyed by Richard Todd.

He'd been wrong in one respect: if private lives were so openly discussed and displayed, and Eddathorpe secrets were so impossible to keep, why were we talking murder, undetected, still? And why had he, in his first statement, lied so blatantly through his teeth?

10

Picking over odd statements; chasing crumpled actions: not exactly fun. But it was, believe me, a damn sight better than ploughing through a couple of million words of verbiage in the files themselves.

Major enquiries rely on back-up. Lots of lads and lassies knocking on doors, checking and rechecking information, taking statements, filling in personal descriptions, questionnaires, and then filing the bloody stuff.

Not just filing it: kicking it into shape so it can be cross-referenced to the information the other investigators are churning out, so that discrepancies, parallels, sore thumbs, stick out. Once upon a time it was all done with filing cards and shoe-boxes; until it got out of hand.

Now we've got this computerised system – HOLMES. Somebody, somewhere in Whitehall, probably thought the thickos in blue serge could do with Sherlock, hence the humorous acronym: Home Office Large & Major Enquiry System.

The all-singing, all-dancing receiver, processor, cross-referencer and dissimilator of information. Do you want to know about a one-legged sailor with a parrot and a funny hat? If he's in there, the relevant statement, or the descriptive form, or the action enquiry will be up on the screen in the twinkling of an eye.

Which brings us to the snag, of course. Known in the trade as GIGO, another acronym: Garbage In, Garbage Out. The system is only as good as its operators; and it can be heavy on manpower too. Receivers of information, Readers and Processors, Action Allocators, Office Managers, typists and clerks. And that's before you find the manpower to go out there knocking on doors and feeling collars.

So now I'd been left to pick over the bones of a dead job. To find some meat, if I could. I couldn't use the computer; no high tech. Not unless I wanted Silver breathing down the back of my neck.

No kicks, no pressure, either. Nothing was cxpccted, except perhaps in Teddy Baring's office and by the occupants of a sad little bungalow down the road. Glad I was – almost – to be left with the copper's equivalent of an archaeological dig. It was just that I'd got a roomful of paper, instead of a pick and spade.

I went back to chasing up the circumstances surrounding the unfortunate oversight on the part of mendacious Richard Todd.

Action

67
Origin: Detective Sergeant 1093 Caunt, System Reader.
15.12.89.
Nature of Enquiry:
Inconsistency between statement of Richard Todd, over 21 years, Garage Owner, Highfields House, Grand Esplanade, Eddathorpe (copy attached) and Mary Todd (wife), over 21 years, District Councillor, same address (copy attached).

Not, I would have thought, the kind of inconsistency to endear him to the police. At best, it appeared that Richard had been playing silly games. At worst, he was a clumsy, lying killer.

I read the action and the accompanying copy statements carefully. According to Richard Todd, he'd left the bash at the Links at about 12.15 a.m. that morning, driven straight home, and arrived at the house some fifteen minutes later. No deviations on the way.

Mary claimed she'd left the dance before him, and he'd not arrived home until after two.

It didn't need an expensive computer to throw that one out; the linked action, numbered 108, was there, nevertheless.

Linked Action

Origin: Detective Sergeant 1023 Caunt, System Reader. 15.12.89.
Nature of Enquiry:
Inadequate Information — statement of Todd R.
Discover full details of relationship and nature of dispute between witness and deceased ...

Inadequate information! Silver must have been delighted; the beginning of the enquiry, and a suspect drops right into his lap. The curt, six-line result at the bottom of the forms echoed his frustration when it all went wrong.

He'd arrested Tricky Dicky all right; the reference to the interview file was there. So were the details of a second witness statement; liar or not, the suspect had slipped off the hook.

Denies Offence. Discrepancy at 67 due to allegedly wishing to protect reputation of Valerie Hill, Flat 2/24

Chandos Road, Eddathorpe. Visited approx. 12.40 a.m., 13.12.89, for sexual intercourse. Arriving home 2 a.m., plus. Denies involvement murder scene. Has not visited area – with or without a vehicle – since winter closure of café, October 1989.

The print-out ground remorselessly on; check, counter-check and reference, in a paper imitation of the mills of God. Say what you like about the police machine at times – lumbering, unimaginative, slow – it still conscientiously sets out to grind exceeding small.

Nobody, especially Silver, had wanted Tricky Dicky free. His car had been ripped apart (and reassembled) by Scenes of Crime. They'd bagged everything in sight and passed it on for forensic examination: grit, dust, the detritus of his glove compartment. Even a crumpled November poppy and a lost twenty-pence piece; all, as they so charmingly put it, with *Negative Results*.

The same with his clothing; I had this vision of them bundling up his wardrobe of hand-made shirts and made-to-measure suits, hoovering the insides of the pockets and generally creasing them up. Nothing but harmless, featureless fluff.

Another cross-reference; another linked action. A relatively long splurge about the 'intermittent' sexual relationship between him and Alice. Then the point: Alice keen on presents; she'd wanted a Gucci watch. Gold, with interchangeable coloured rims to match her frocks and fashion accessories. He'd apparently purchased one while on holiday in Jersey in the April of the year she'd died, and presented it to her.

Not that it had done him a lot of good: they'd apparently split up in July, after arguing about Dicky's mean, underhanded ways. That figured: the watch had turned out to be a cheap fake. Alice had apparently returned it; a swift overarm delivery which had smashed the glass.

Todd claimed to have picked it up, intending to have it repaired. He hadn't done so; they'd never got back together and he'd mislaid the watch. He hadn't even got the original purchase receipt. And he'd stuck to his story through the equivalent of thick and thin: Hacker's interview technique and a dose of the Eddathorpe cells.

Silver must have been a Boy Scout in his day: whistling and smiling in the face of all difficulties, including the insurmountable alibi provided by Valerie Hill. Not only had he sent the boys around for a witness statement to cover lover-boy and his whereabouts that night. He'd invited her down to the nick afterwards for a few friendly threats: accessory after the fact, offences akin to perjury and wasting police time.

She'd stuck to her version; Richard the wonderful lover, Dicky the innocent chap. Our dapper bully had retired hurt.

Nevertheless, Tricky had been a far from clever boy: telling silly porkies to the police. Even a thick killer tends to get his act together at times. Especially when the margin between the last live sighting and discovery is over six and a half hours and the corpse has been left in the open on a December night. Pathologists play with ground and body temperatures, rigor, material upon which the victim is lying, and the rest, but time-of-death estimates aren't exactly precise.

I treated myself to the amended version of his witness statement. His explanation for the lies: a chivalrous urge to protect the reputation of Mrs Valerie Hill. In version one he'd driven straight home; in version two he'd reluctantly decided to kiss and tell. Protecting his doxy's honour? Richard Todd, the epitome of the English gent? There had to be more to it than that.

*   *   *

87

The usual thunder of footsteps up the back stairs heralded a CID arrival, and George lumbered into the office shaking rain from his coat.

'Had enough of enquiries, then?' I called.

He poked his head round the door of the rabbit hutch, 'Sorry?'

'I assume you've left the commoners to tramp through the puddles!' Not that I blamed him; it was tipping it down outside. More like winter in Wales than the East Coast.

'A good copper', he said portentously, 'never gets wet. There's a couple of greasy-spoon caffs and no shortage of pubs round the old railway station. The working classes should do their enquirin' there, once it starts to pour. Common sense.'

'Yeah, OK. Can you give me any good reason why Richard Todd should lie in his original statement to protect the reputation of a woman called Valerie Hill?'

'Two,' he said promptly, 'Dicky would want to keep the looks the ladies love, and Valerie's husband of the year was a martial-arts freak. Enjoyed smashing people up.

'Second; Dicky fell for voluptuous Val in a big way. She's now the chatellaine of Castle Todd.'

'Poetic, that. So, he divorced the lady politician, and married the lass with the tits like chapel hat-pegs: post-murder and pre-vodka bottle, right?'

'More or less, boss. He remarried about three years ago. But Val used to lap it up, long before she married Dicky Todd. So did Alice, for that matter; over-proof women are just his style.'

'Not the night she died – I've been doing a bit of research. According to the pathologist, she had the equivalent of a couple of doubles inside her; no more.'

'Yeah; well, she was working.'

'True – but a barmaid, serving at a big Christmas bash; lots of people she knows?'

'Keeping her nose clean – conscientious lass.'

'And she wanted to nip off early; had a row with the landlord over it. A date, perhaps?'

I left it at that, but it was worth a thought. Liked a bit of life, a drink, a spot of knicker-dropping, did poor Miss Round Heels 1989.

Somebody she knew: so we had five apparent suspects, excluding the painters and decorators and Teddy's son. Matthew Baring had excluded himself by submitting to a blood test. Unless . . . Plus X for an extra who knew her and fell through Hacker's net. It wasn't a foolproof elimination technique, but five and a joker is better than thirty-one assorted nutters, to start.

George came over and looked at the computer copies, flicking through the pages, sighing heavily as he read what I'd got.

'I always get this feeling,' he said, 'every time I look.'

'What?'

'We're looking right at him. We've stuck it all in the magic box and if we keep on giving it a shake, we could come out with the right bit of paper, any time.'

'I like the idea – invest a few million quid, and the Home Office comes up with a superior tombola drum: stick your fist in to secure a prize!'

'Yeah.' He sounded abstracted all of a sudden. Separating two sheets of paper from the file, he straightened and flattened them in front of me on the desk.

'You're not playing fair, boss.'

I glanced at the actions; 338 and 373. The first was Ruth Draper's original information about her daughter's missing watch, and her three-stone, eighteen-carat, cross-over-style emerald ring. The latter recorded as a present from Alexander Buchanan, Christmas 1988.

The second action was another Hacker hopeful: Doreen Simpson, the former manageress of Richard Todd's café, claimed he'd been bedding Alice, probably using violence towards her in drink, some time way back when. If true, the story would have put the origin of the relationship back a couple of years.

The enquiry regarding the watch and ring had been unsuccessful: Mrs Simpson was a vindictive old bat. No supporting evidence. Just sore because, years ago, she'd got the sack.

'I don't get it; come on, George.'

He tried to look wise and cynical at the same time; the way coppers do when senior officers are winding them up. He pointed silently to the enquiry results:

Result: no evidence that deceased was wearing these items at time of death, or on any occasion immediately prior to the crime.

(ii) Reinterview witness Sandra Carter (X Ref. to married name Lawrence – friend/waitress Links Hotel). Watch definitely not worn since early Sept. 1989. Ditto emerald ring.

(iii) See interview notes Buchanan, nothing of further evidential value.

M. Cartwright, DC 1382.

So what? I turned to the second action; it was no more enlightening than the first.

Result: Todd warned to attend police station by Detective Constable Cartwright. Detained & interviewed Detective Superintendent Hacker – Negative: again refused to provide samples of blood for forensic examination. Claims police harassment; all future enquiries to be referred via solicitor, Charles Pringle. Released.

Then, an endorsement by Hacker:

Subject not to be further detained/interviewed without reference to Investigating Officer. Particular attention to be paid re number of hours already kept in custody. Origin Det. Superintendent.

'Well?' I was still baffled.

'Silver,' he said bitterly. 'You're following his line: dumping on Richard Todd.'

'No; I'm still chasing discrepancies, that's all.'

'Look,' he said bluntly, 'if you're not chasing Todd you're chasing Malc Cartwright's actions. You've had a run-in, so you don't trust the man. Don't screw him to the floor, boss. He's got his problems, has Malc.'

Richard Todd was big enough and ugly enough to look after himself. Not, I would have thought, a man to worry George.

But Malcolm Cartwright? Something to look out for there. Why was St George dashing about on his charger, protecting big, idle, overtime-fiddling Malc?

'Tell you what,' I said, tucking the domestic information safely into the back of my mind. 'First thing Monday, I'll give you another starter for ten. Come with me when I talk to Dicky Todd.'

11

I'd scarcely had a chance to go through the week-end crimes at Eddathorpe, followed by ten minutes of Monday-morning prayers with Teddy and Derek Paget, the uniform Chief Inspector, before she called. I'd just finished giving one or two pious assurances about our chances of catching our Friday-night nuisance when the Superintendent's phone rang.

He listened for a few moments, then with a brisk, 'Very well, Sergeant; I'll tell him,' he replaced the receiver and turned to me.

'Sergeant Baily,' he said. 'She's gone way beyond me. Something about a wholesale cash and carry at Retton; apparently you already know about it?'

'Yes, sir. A man called MacMillan, complete with what might be a dodgy military rank. Claims to have been in the Rhodesian Army.'

'Ah; I've heard. Something called Superbarg?'

'Yes.'

'Trading fraudulently?'

'We can't be sure, yet.'

He pulled a sour face. 'Tread carefully; no nasty rumours about a legitimate business. Better still, pass the poison chalice to the experts, if you can.'

'Sir?'

'The Fraud Squad, Mr Graham. Let them handle it.'

I took a deep breath; I could see a Headquarters squad traipsing across the county to a half-dead country town. It was the last place they'd expect to find a professional fraudsman. One week in the post and I was about to get the horse-laugh from the know-alls at HQ. That new idiot, they'd say, screaming for help; can't run his own patch.

Unexpectedly, it was Derek Paget who came to my rescue, feet first.

'Know the definition of an expert, Bob?' He looked expectant, head swivelling from Baring to me, and back.

'No,' I said, glad of the respite, 'no I don't.'

'Hah!' The sound was explosive, the pent-up resentment of years. 'An ex is a has-been – and a spurt is a drip under pressure!' His face turned puce, and he treated us to a self-satisfied guffaw. Not one of your academic cops, our CI.

I'm inclined to go along with the canteen comedians from time to time: the old 'uns are the best. Sadly, having seen his reaction, I don't think Teddy Baring was your man to agree. They were still at it hammer and tongs when I sneaked out, my opinion of a handover unuttered, and assurances about the lightness of my feet undelivered.

Not that it wasn't tricky, and, short of surrender and losing face, I wouldn't have minded a way off the hook.

Paula had the essence of the problem set out on three sheets of fax. The credit reference outfit had responded: a list of suppliers' enquiries over the past six months and a copy of their report.

'They don't like our Julian,' said Paula, handing it over, 'but they don't know enough about him to call him a crook. His bank says he's OK for a few thousand – but they're sitting on the fence. He's used a couple of recent suppliers as references: they say he's OK 'cos he paid 'em, so they would, wouldn't they?'

'How many new credit enquiries?'

'Forty-five in six months.'

'High; but not high enough to say for certain. A fraudulent business can raise a couple of hundred. He's a new man; he could just be expanding his lines. No references from bent wholesalers, anywhere else?'

'Nope.'

'So we're back where we started: we don't like his sweet little smile, and he's gotta lotta French letters on credit.'

'And twenty-six thousand quid's worth of crap Canadian whisky.'

'How do you know that?' Sharp, all right.

'I've tasted it.' She'd been dying to do that one; I got a full dose of the wide derisive grin.

'OK, so you've done the quality control test. Has he paid for it?'

'No, not yet anyway. He's sold two dozen cases to the local mini-market – Christmas stock. I've checked with the importers; payment in January.'

'You checked direct?'

'Yes.' Paula looked puzzled. So much for discretion, tact; not trampling around with big feet.

'Do you know any more of his new suppliers?'

'Six or seven: and the agency says he's had an artic-full of Bouncy Babe disposable nappies, and another order on the way. Enough to supply half a dozen maternity hospitals.'

'In case the condoms have holes?'

We indulged in a mutual yuk, yuk, but I was far from satisfied. Within an hour of Teddy Baring's warning, we'd inadvertently spread the happy word about Julian MacMillan's business. Which *might* be legit.

So, it was no more direct approaches: bolt the stable door, and see what the agencies could turn up. Quick.

One thing was certain: Christmas was coming, the season of goodwill, the time when unwary wine merchants, purveyors of spirits, tobacco, contraceptives, nappies, and anything else you care to mention, get taken to the cleaners by con artists and left flat on their backs in the New Year.

If we were right, we had two, maybe three weeks left to the opening of our very own pantomime: Robin Hood and the Selous Scouts. An expensive production with very few jokes.

Malcolm Cartwright was waiting when I got back, as lugubrious as ever.

'Boss,' he said, 'Eric Goodwin's been on the phone again; says his job's on the line, unless he can sort these stock leakages.'

'There's more?'

'Up to about three, three and a half thousand, now. He's worried sick; reckons he'll get the poke when the boss finds out.'

'Come on, then – but no more gash overtime claims!'

Why not? I quite fancied a meet, a chat with poor Eric; you never know what you might turn up. If he'd passed the whisper to Mary Todd, he might want to open his heart to me.

Todd's Garage: apart from a couple of back-street affairs and a petrol station, it was the only show in town. Accident repairs, coachwork, services, resprays, and, above all, new and second-hand sales. A forecourt jammed with highly polished tin and salesmen's smiles they could have used in a movie – *Jaws*.

Within a couple of minutes of meeting Eric Goodwin, it was pretty obvious why Mary Todd's sympathies had been engaged. The man was the antithesis of the former light of her life, for a start. He was definitely not the salesman type.

Her description had been accurate enough – five-eightish, glasses, and the moustache – but she hadn't prepared me for the nervous energy, the atmosphere of crisis he created at the slightest excuse.

His secretary, a young woman in her early twenties, smart rather than attractive, showed us in. His office was something like mine, a larger version of the glass-fronted rabbit hutch, which, in his case, looked out on to the showroom; sales desks, and a range of glistening new cars. Leather, chrome, white telephones and a flickering VDU, that was the style.

He was on the telephone as we entered, listening intently, and occasionally interrupting his caller with a mutter of 'No, no, no; I can't accept that.'

Momentarily, he removed the receiver from his mouth, smiled, waved us into seats, and went straight back to his conversation. Not so much the busy executive impressing the trogs: more your nervous cat, trying to cover too many mouse-holes at once.

Finally, with a plaintive 'Well, all right, tomorrow morning without fail; I really need the stuff *now*,' he replaced the receiver.

'I'm sorry,' he said, 'ruddy deliveries. They're always trying to make excuses. I'm glad you've come.' He half rose, reaching over the desk to shake hands.

'Detective Constable Cartwright tells me you've had a series of thefts: new parts.'

'It's been going on for months. We've tried everything; spot checks, traps, watching people going home. It's not as if it's bits and pieces either; it's boxes of stuff.'

'Any suspects?'

'Not really; I've spoken to the Service Manager, the

foreman's kept his eye on the mechanics; we've watched the storeman himself. Nothing.'

'What are you losing?'

'Well, they're leaving the engine blocks behind!' He grinned nervously. 'Mostly small stuff; headlamp kits, boxes of plugs, bulbs, oil and air filters, condensers; that sort of thing.'

'And you've clocked up three thousand, plus?'

'Yes.' He looked as if he was going to cry: the General Manager, a thirty-odd-year-old baby. Pedantic, conscientious, plugging away at the administration side, no doubt. The leakages didn't surprise me. I simply wondered how he prevented anybody, from the sales sharks to the junior sweeper-up, from walking away with everything, cars and all. He must have had hidden talents to have secured the job in the first place, I decided.

'Tell me about your ordering and delivery system.'

He did: at length. Nobody ever had such a foolproof system in the history of the motor trade, according to him. He could bore for Britain – for Europe – on the subject.

Raising orders, filing copies, checking authorisation; deliveries, checking deliveries, signing, receipt of statements, checking again, stock cards, job cards, and the payment system, all at his fingertips; delivered with the fervour of holy writ. Impressive in its way, but I wished I'd never opened my mouth.

'What do you think?' he finished.

I tried to sort it out a bit in my mind. He'd delivered great wedges of information, all suet and stodge; no jam. Then he expected us to leap up, clap the handcuffs on some overalled crook, and drag him down to the nick. Problem solved; Eric safe in his job. Happy days are here again.

Malc Cartwright stared stolidly to his front, wishing himself elsewhere; I could see why.

I asked one or two questions; the name of the delivery service; the frequency; bits and bobs about the driver; who actually signed for the stuff, and so on. Routine.

'Look,' I said. 'we haven't got any instant solutions; would you do me a sample file of documents covering your system? And I'd like to look around your stores: see where the stuff's received, kept and distributed. Chat with the storeman; OK?'

'Yes, of course. Anything.'

He stared at us with such a hang-dog, disappointed look that I felt guilty; sorry for him. All his swans had turned into hissing, unco-operative geese and he was only too obviously typecast as a perfectionist in a grossly imperfect world.

'We'll sort it out,' I said. 'Won't we, Malc?'

'Yeah; don't worry, Eric. Nobody's going to blame you and we'll get there in the end.'

A right pair of Job's comforters we were turning out to be. I did have an idea at the back of my mind, but I wanted to test it on Malcolm Cartwright first: bounce it around. Goodwin looked the type to jump at the slightest optimistic remark and cling like death. I hated to think what his attitude would be if I waded in with a dose of good news and then it turned out I was wrong.

'There's another matter, Mr Goodwin,' I said deprecatingly. 'You'll appreciate we get enquiries from time to time, even when a job's been undetected for years. You might be able to give me some background. Alice Draper; she worked here, didn't she?'

'Has – has that come up again? Terrible, terrible thing.' His voice dropped, and he shook his head, fiddling with a pile of blank forms he'd extracted from his desk drawer. 'Yes; she worked here. How can I help?'

'Can you give me some idea what she was like, for example?'

He stared hard at me for a moment, then he swallowed once, making up his mind. Then, 'It was a tragedy, of course; but she was a very foolish and promiscuous young woman. I'm sorry, but it's true.'

'Did you know her well?'

'She was already here when I came, in 1987. Had I been General Manager at the time she arrived, I don't know whether I would have wanted to employ her.'

'Although . . .' I let the word trail away.

'Although she was a close friend of Mr Todd? Yes, I'd have had to take account of that, but Mr Todd is not, you know, unwilling to take advice.'

He lifted himself in his chair, placed his elbows on the table, fingertips touching. He looked, for the first time, something more than a cipher, a superior clerk.

'Things were in something of a mess when I came, administratively speaking. The office systems were poor; VAT, for example . . . well, let's say there were problems with Customs and Excise; I won't bore you. Some people had to go.'

'But Alice Draper wasn't one of them,' I suggested gently.

'No, but she did represent – well, the old régime. People doing what they liked . . . to be fair, however, she could do her job. She could relate to people.'

'A good receptionist?'

'Yes; I have no complaints about that.'

'Did you have any other cause for complaint – using her position, perhaps: Mr Todd's friend?'

'Mistress. Between these four walls.' He pursed his lips disapprovingly; suddenly he was confident, telling it how it was. I waited.

'I have to say she did not abuse her position. She was

not a fool.' His voice had acquired just the slightest edge of frost. The memory of an uneasy relationship with an inferior: armed neutrality, at best.

'You say she was promiscuous?'

'It was no secret. Mr Todd was a married man, but there were problems. None of my business, naturally.' He shook his head dismissively; the loyal employee.

'She was . . . volatile. Rows, and so on. When that happened, she used to find other young men for a while. Even got engaged at one stage. I forget the name: Scottish, I think. Anyway, she flashed the ring around for a few weeks, then all of a sudden it was back to the old routine. Very inconstant.' He seemed pleased with the word.

'Did any of them work here?'

'I beg your pardon?'

'Her boyfriends?'

'No. That would have been going too far.'

'Who else did she go out with?'

He glanced at me nervously. 'You must know all this, Inspector. I don't wish to gossip.'

'If it was common knowledge . . .' I said.

'Yes. She made no secret of it – Mr Baring's son. A couple of years younger than her.'

'You know him?'

'Only as a customer; he had this old sports car at the time. Falling to bits.'

'Did the relationship last long?'

'I really couldn't say – weeks, perhaps. At the beginning of 1989.'

From what I'd heard, it must have been a busy year. 'Anybody else?'

'It was not something I followed with breathless interest, Inspector.'

'Of course not, but surely – in the circumstances?'

101

'Mr Todd's brother,' he said flatly. 'I don't know why you're asking. You know already: ancient history in any case, long before I arrived.'

'Another married man?'

'No, not in his case.' He genuinely didn't want to gossip. He sounded displeased.

'And the two brothers, Richard and Victor . . .'

'Don't get on. That's well known too. I'm employed here, Mr Graham. I'm not being rude, but I don't want to pick over old stories.'

'As I said, an old enquiry: an old murder, Mr Goodwin.'

He flushed, and his voice became very precise, 'If I had any real information, Mr Graham, I would pass it to the police.'

'I'm sure you would. Tell me, do you remember Alice's wristwatch?'

'Oh, yes. Something else she flashed around. She thought it was real.'

'Real?'

'Richard – Mr Todd gave it to her. A present; she'd always wanted one. Then it turned out to be a copy. She raised a hell of a fuss. Told everybody.'

'When was that?'

He shrugged, 'I really couldn't say. A few months before . . . you know.'

'Before she was murdered?'

'Yes. I don't know when. I can't be expected to keep an eye on—'

'No, of course not. I just wondered if it was something you'd noticed, that's all. And when she stopped wearing the ring . . . you know, the engagement ring?'

'I've no idea: it's women who notice that sort of thing, Inspector.'

'Just one more thing: why did she leave her job?'

He lifted his shoulders fractionally, 'Why did she do anything? Whim?'

'She wasn't sacked?'

'No.'

'There was some mention of a personality clash.'

'She was very angry about the watch, I suppose. It was the last of a long line of rows she'd had with Mr Todd.'

'What about you?'

'No. Under no circumstances would I have entered into . . .'

'You misunderstand me, Mr Goodwin: did you clash with her – as a manager?'

'I kept a distance between us. If you call that a clash, so be it.'

'So she left in September 1989.'

'Yes.'

'No other reason?'

'None that I know of, Mr Graham. Again, I don't want to be rude, and I don't want to appear selfish, but to be honest you're raking over dead ashes, whereas I've got an ongoing situation here that could have serious consequences for me, personally.' He must have been on a course to talk like that. Or scanning *Reader's Digest*, perhaps.

The telephone rang, and he leaned forward to answer it; then he placed one hand over the mouthpiece, 'My wife; I wonder if . . .'

Nothing new: time to smile and walk away.

As we passed through the showroom, *en route* to the stores, Malcolm Cartwright nodded in the direction of the plumpish young woman behind the desk.

'The receptionist,' he said, 'Mrs Sandra Lawrence; Sandra Carter, as was.'

'Yes?'

'Worked at the Links Hotel, boss; still does, part time.

103

You know; my enquiry about the watch. A woman as notices things.'

Detective Constable Cartwright getting a bit of his own back; a touch of sardonic humour in his voice.

12

It was lashing it down. The rain bucketed off the roof of Eddathorpe nick and streamed down the snap room windows. We watched with a kind of gloomy satisfaction while one of the uniformed PCs made a dash across the yard, collar turned up, cap streaming, car keys clutched in one sweaty little hand.

'Sooner him than me,' said George.

'A good policeman,' I said pompously, pausing for effect, 'repeats himself every time it rains!'

George gave it the hollow laugh. It wasn't two-pints-and-a-pie weather, that was for sure. Nobody fancied a good soaking on the way to the pub. A big pot of tea from the kitchen and pasties hot from the oven instead. Only a raving alcoholic would want to go out in that. Naturally, deprived of my fix, I was spitting feathers; I could practically taste the beer in my mouth. It took an age for the kettle to boil.

Malcolm Cartwright sat at one end of the dining table unwrapping his sandwiches, a pile of Todd's Garage paper-work beside him. Andy Spriggs leaned over his shoulder and leafed through the specimen forms and cards.

'Why didn't you take the completed records?' he said, 'Instead of this junk.'

'Boss,' grunted Big Malc, *sotto voce*. 'Specimens only, he said.'

'Didn't say much to the storeman, either.' I embarked on a clumsy wind-up. It was that kind of day. 'Just looked at a few delivery notes, ruffled through his cards, and looked dumb. Right, Malc?' I watched his reaction.

Something that might have passed for a smile flickered briefly over Big Malc's face.

'That's right.'

'Us thick country bobbies don't understand all them complicated forms, do we?'

'Nah; we had to ask clever Mr Rankin, the storeman, to explain, didn't we, boss?' He was definitely coming round.

'And did he?' George had a wary half-grin on his face, expecting a punchline, not knowing when it was going to come.

Malc shook his head, 'Confused us a bit, he did: he knows we're not very bright.'

'Means you'll have to go back tomorrow – a couple of hours after Expressapart make their delivery, eh?' I said. We were laying it on a bit.

'Yeah; and get him to explain why some of the new parts recorded on the delivery notes and entered on the stock cards in his very own handwriting aren't there.'

'And in the meantime,' I said, dropping the heavy humour, 'Andy and one of the other lads can arrest the Expressapart driver as soon as he leaves Todd's, and lock him up until we're ready to interview.'

'So,' said George, catching on, 'a conjuring trick – the stuff never gets delivered in the first place. Dropped off somewhere else.'

'That's what we think. Eric Goodwin's perfect system. Just one thing wrong: the storeman. He checks the stock; he does the reordering. It's rubber-stamped, it goes to

Expressapart, they deliver. The storeman signs, he racks the parts, he makes up the stock cards, he issues the gear, he amends the records . . . Basically, they let one man run the entire shebang, on about a hundred and fifty quid a week.'

'Generous-hearted bastards!'

'And the Expressapart driver: newish, been coming for about three months.'

'About right, then.'

'Just one problem,' I grinned. 'I'm going to look an utter prat if it doesn't work out. Civil liberties destroyed in Eddathorpe – Gestapo rides again!'

Might as well get the horse-laugh over in advance. It was good logic, but was it going to work out? Or was I kidding myself; playing an older, cruder game? When in doubt, stick some poor bastard downstairs for a bit; see what turns up. And then, unbidden, it came: wasn't that how Silver thought?

Back to Alice Draper. Back to Detective Superintendent Hacker and his obsession with Tricky Dicky, come to that. The gospel according to Silver – he must have done it; the man who wouldn't give blood.

According to the records, he hadn't been the only one: Keith Baker, the landlord at the Links, he'd refused; so had two of her old boyfriends, Richards and Buchanan – and Victor Todd. Matthew Baring was the only suspect to oblige, so that left a single refusenik from the ruck, one additional refuser from the outside chances; from among the group of sexual adventurers and nutters. I supposed I'd check him out too, whoever he was. A thought whizzed into one brain cell and out the next. I'd missed a trick. The refusal question had deserved a few more milliseconds of my valuable time.

Funny; why should anybody refuse? Apart from the killer, that is. Something in the Eddathorpe air? Proud citizens of a bloody-minded town? We had five local refuseniks, all sitting in the front row, and a single unco-operative stranger. Why put yourself on offer as a suspect, when you could walk away smiling with a small sticking-plaster on one arm? Conspiracy, cock-up, a wind-up-Hacker day; or what?

Sex within twelve hours of the discovery of Alice's body: perfect DNA evidence, once we caught our rabbit. Some police forces, I knew, had involved a cast of thousands in similar circumstances – blood-testing everything in sight. But only volunteers: eliminate the innocent, take a closer look at anybody who refused.

An expensive trawl of an entire population. And in this particular instance Hacker, with one eye on a shrinking budget, had baulked, so it wasn't going to do me any good. Always assuming . . . and we *were* assuming the man who'd had sex had also killed. Just supposing the assumption was unwarranted. Suppose the intercourse was unconnected with her death . . . Forensic evidence down the pan. A big zilch. Abso-bloody-lutely perfect, that!

I only half noticed when Malc Cartwright struggled to his feet, collected his sandwiches, and left the room. He reappeared a few minutes later with the teapot in one hand, and a plate containing a couple of pasties in the other. He poured the tea without comment and slouched back to his seat.

Somebody switched on the radio for the one o'clock news, and conversation became general: sport; what they'd like to do to certain members of the Cabinet; who'd nicked who, what for, and when. The pasties were good.

I finished my tea, got up and went into the kitchen to dump my dirty pots. George followed me and nudged the door with his elbow, swinging it almost shut. He put his own crockery down on the draining board and opened the pedal bin with a grunt of disgust. Exhibition time.

'Look,' he said, 'she's at it again.'

'What?'

I stared uncomprehendingly from George to the open bin. It was empty apart from a disintegrating pile of semi-wrapped sandwiches.

He took my dirty knife from the sink and delicately parted two pieces of bread. It was a first. Each neatly made, meticulously buttered sandwich contained a single rectangle of newspaper. To Malcolm, from Wifie, no love.

You can't let things slide, allow people to idle their time away, walk all over you. It was part of my job to make Big Malc toe the line. His private life: I wasn't being asked to interfere. Not my affair. Irrationally, I felt about six inches tall.

I wasted five seconds on the usual management whirl: fatherly advice, counselling, the welfare officer, the usual senior officer's crap. Doing him no favours at all.

'The man has his troubles,' George Caunt had said. Understatement of the hour: not a problem I was going to solve.

I stared almost superstitiously at the evidence of Malc's domestic troubles, and took a trawl through my own. Newspaper sandwiches! Women! Angie, at least, had never been there, had never done that.

No exact parallels with my recent leanings, either; but somehow I took it as a warning. Keep to your good resolutions, pal: hands off the female staff, and don't play too close to home.

Especially games involving murder suspects' former wives.

13

It was one of those improbable colour-washed mornings; November the last, with a chill-blue sky merging into a flat calm sea, and a sun climbing rapidly out of the water, shivering a bit, reluctant to surrender an iota of warmth.

It was a day for walking dogs and throwing sticks on the beach; followed by bacon, eggs, sausages and black pud, not forgetting the heavily buttered toast and coffee afterwards, beside a blazing fire. It was not the moment to brood over estranged wives, or to work out the possible permutations of Murphy's Law as it applied to a delivery man and an ingenious, but unoriginal storeroom thief. Nothing to worry about there. Push it to one side, take the day as it comes.

Nevertheless, Angie lurked at the back of my mind while I exercised the dog. Stupid, really; the less I saw of her the more she loomed. Trouble with a capital T, she was, I kept telling myself: a perfectly normal woman whom I'd loved, married, lived with, and somehow mislaid along the way; and now we were getting a divorce. Tens of thousands doing it; no big deal at all.

Nine years of marriage; no kids. Part, a substantial part, of the trouble. A more than attractive woman of thirty-five with the old clock ticking away. Both of us capable; neither of us super-fertile, either. And me; not over-anxious to bugger about in clinics, you might say. But that didn't bloody excuse her, did it? What about being fair to me? I hadn't spent my time yowling on the rooftops like next door's tom.

I'd been out there grafting: she knew the score when she married into the CID. After all, her father had been a cop. The hours, the shop-talk; home in the middle of the night, smelling of booze. *I'll take you out tomorrow, love*. The broken promises. Yep, I remembered those too. Not all one-sided; I was prepared to admit that.

But Clive Jones, Brain of Britain 1348? With his frank, boyish smile and his well-publicised degree. Not forgetting his seats on the force working parties, the study groups, the everlasting committees. His bags packed ready to sod off to the other end of the country for the sake of another pip on his shoulder, or the elusive laurel wreath of an ACC?

Too busy moving from force to force, collecting kudos, to collect a wife of his own. Half the lads thought he was queer until he'd seized on Angie. And then most of the bastards had known . . . the bit that really rankled. Robert Graham, the big detective and about the last to know.

And now? It was down to the lawyers: could she really have her cake and eat it? All the fun of adultery and take an idiot husband to the financial cleaners as well? But was she like that anyway, the woman I'd married: was I creating my own monster on the basis of a run with Super-sodding-intendent Jones, a pile of legal documents and the latest solicitor's questionnaire?

A stroll, a think, a nice mull-over of current wrongs. Nothing like it to start the day. And what had I really got to grouse about, anyway? Neither of us had inhabited Malc's little hell on earth with its suicidal depressions, steady climbs through normality to manic highs, and back down again to unimaginable gloom. Its hatreds; the squares of newspaper for Hubby's lunch. And still they were together. One taking the pills, the other sending the kid to some sort of boarding school to keep her out of the way, dragging out the overtime to pay for it; fighting every inch of the way. Poor, crazy woman; poor old Malc.

So, walkies were over: pack up your troubles. Call Joe, post the letter to your professionally qualified liar, and off to work to smile nicely – or something – at villains. Ensure that they get more troubles than you've got, mate!

Brinkmanship. Frank Rankin, prisoner, and Charles Pringle, solicitor of this parish, and the prisoner was the least of it. Eyeball to eyeball stuff.

The arrests had gone all right and the Expressapart driver, Barry Mason, one previous conviction – theft of twenty-six cases of frozen chickens, would you believe – had coughed the lot.

Yeah, he'd received the gear at Expressapart. Yes, he'd made short drops and made a few quid on the side. OK, he'd shared it with his mate, Frankie. Three thousand plus? You have to be joking . . . couldn't possibly be that much; a thousand, fifteen hundred, maybe . . . Well, you lose track, don't you?

Who bought the stuff? Can't go around grassing . . . yeah, all right; you coppers seem to know everything about Carson's Garage and the By-Pass Service Station at Retton, anyway. Yeah, yeah, it was them.

Rankin was different; totally bloody-minded, right from the start. Evidence; what evidence? He'd been set up, hadn't he? Somebody must have stolen the remaining stock last night; that would account for his updated stock sheets being wrong this morning, wouldn't it?

No? Not enough new stock, and old batch numbers on some of the stuff in the stores? Well, honest Frank knows nothing about that. You're all out to get him; on the side of the management, the lot of you. Fit-up, that's what it is. Mason's confessed? Rubbish; doesn't believe a word you say. Wants a brief: Charlie Pringle – soon sort you lot out.

Frankie-baby; not a previous conviction in sight and spouting the televised version of thieves' slang like something out of *The Bill*. GCSE in persistent stupidity and proud of it.

Malc and George conducted the interview and they soon got fed up to the point of being almost pleased when he made his bid for a legal rep. But not for long. They were expecting sweet reason to prevail in the end, but Charlie turned up instead.

It wasn't that they'd expected any favours, according to George. The wife's cousin maybe, but they weren't exactly buddies. Just a bit of straightforward common sense would have been enough.

Twenty minutes of private legal advice along the lines of see all, hear all, and say nowt is about par for the course. They were used to that, but cousin Charles had taken the bit firmly between his teeth.

First, he'd complained that he hadn't been brought in at the kick-off; then he hinted, according to George, that the uniform sergeant's custody record might not be accurate. His client might not have declined legal representation when he was originally brought in. After that it was all downhill.

Once the interview began he started answering on Frank's behalf: 'No comment', 'No reply', 'My client does not have to answer that', and even 'I'm not having questions like that put to my client!'

I'd not intended to tie up the whole department as

witnesses, especially me, but George took the stairs up to my office two at a time, with tidings of Portia, Ironside and threats of the Police Complaints Authority I just had to hear. The interview tape was apparently all Charlie Pringle: the suspect couldn't get a word in edgeways, even if he'd been so inclined. That solicitor was downright obstructive, and he wouldn't shut up.

I went for a listen, and I thought he must be defending Al Capone. Not that Charlie was much to look at, sat in the interview room in his unbuttoned, dandruffed black overcoat over a worn blue suit. He was small and slim with sandy, prematurely receding hair, a smooth pale face, and gold-rimmed glasses. He seemed to be permanently irritated about something. Little or nothing to do with his client: anti the filth, scoring points in his own private game.

George restarted the tape and introduced me. Rankin, middle-aged, still wearing his brown dust-coat over a beige pullover and open-necked blue shirt, stared at me uneasily for a moment, and looked down at the scattering of stock cards and papers on the table.

Charles Pringle went straight into the attack.

'Inspector; my client has now been here for nearly three hours, for two of which, despite the custody record, he may have been denied legal representation. I have made his position clear; he is not answering police questions. I insist on you charging him or letting him go.'

'The custody record is correct, Mr Pringle, and I'm not going to argue with you. My officers are conducting a proper enquiry; they're entitled to ask questions, and I'm here to oversee what's happening.' I enjoyed these conversations; the enemy seldom caught on. The quack-quack technique.

'I insist—'

'You are entitled to give your client advice privately.

115

You are also entitled to be present at the interview, but not to continually obstruct. Now, please be quiet; if your client has anything to say we'd like to hear him, not you.'

Twin spots of colour glowed high on his cheekbones and the voice rose. 'I won't be bullied. I warn you, Inspector, against oppressive conduct. I will represent my client's interests in any way I wish!'

'You will behave reasonably, Mr Pringle, or you'll leave.'

I knew this game. I'd played variants on it before. Even temper; a bit pompous; keep the voice formal, precise. The tape was gobbling it all up.

Familiarity bred contempt with some people; smart-arse solicitors, I mean. They tend to forget the machine records both sides of a conversation, not just their civil liberties, indignation stuff. Only one problem: I couldn't chuck him out. That was down to Teddy, or failing him, an independent uniform Inspector.

'Detective Sergeant Caunt and DC Spriggs will ask their questions; Mr Rankin'll make his own mind up on his replies. Can we get on?'

'What's the point of this? I've told you, my client will say nothing.'

'That's up to him. When we've asked the questions, nobody will be able to claim he didn't know the nature of the evidence, didn't get a chance to explain, will they?'

I grinned at him in a way that made me glad we weren't on video. He choked, and, as a purely temporary measure, he shut up.

The Custody Sergeant looked at the charge sheets with a certain wary respect. Four prisoners; a stack of paper looking something like the manuscript of *War and Peace*.

'No thefts for Rankin?'

'A bit iffy: the stuff was never in his possession. Fourteen charges of false accounting, one for every stock sheet, for now.'

'What's this other one: executing a valuable security?'

'Mr Rankin . . .' I gave it a bit of emphasis, '. . . signed the delivery note this morning; an acknowledgement for the transfer of goods he never received. We say that's a valuable security; he did it with a view to gain for himself, or to cause loss to his employer, and deceived 'em; therefore he's on the sheet.'

Rankin looked stunned; Charlie Pringle wasn't liking this one bit.

'I want this noting: the number of charges is oppressive.' Oppressive: one of his favourite words.

'Covers the criminality,' I said smoothly. 'Up to the Crown Prosecutor to decide on numbers and joint theft charges, in the end.'

I was uneasy about leaving out a few joint thefts; maybe I should have run them straight away. Never mind, the Crown Prosecutor could spew out enough in the way of additional charges to destroy a rainforest.

'And the others?' The sergeant scowled professionally at not-a-bit-of-trouble Mason, and the two overalled garage men. Carson looked stolidly ahead, but the man from the By-Pass looked as if he was going to need one, any minute now.

'Thefts for Mason, and handling stolen goods for the others.'

'Those men are nothing to do with us! We'll elect separate trials from them!'

Charlie was definitely losing his rag. The royal we, or the editorial, I wondered; but, all circumstances considered, I kept that particular provocation firmly behind my teeth.

Still, I couldn't work out what was eating cousin Charlie; the job is just the job, not the Third Crusade.

'OK,' I said amiably, 'but we haven't got to that stage yet. Anyway, the Crown Prosecutor will probably want separate hearings. Mr Mason,' I said helpfully, 'will be appearing as a witness against your client, once he's been dealt with at court, and there may be other charges, once I've consulted the CPS.'

'What other charges?'

'Conspiracy to steal, maybe.'

Looks could definitely have killed.

Malc recited the contents of the sheets, cautioned the victims of our bow and spear and they lined up to sign for their bail. A civilian custody officer opened the charge-room door and they all trooped out, Charles Pringle Esquire, Solicitor of the Supreme Court, bringing up the rear.

'Well,' said the Custody Sergeant, 'what was all that about? Your cousin's an awkward sod, George, but I've never seen him wound up like that before.'

George was silent. He stared, almost accusingly, at me. The sergeant, sensing a canteen legend in the making, smiled.

'Doesn't he like you, sir?'

I shrugged in a non-committal sort of way. Win a few, lose a few; make an enemy here and there. And once you've made him, keep him, cherish him if you can.

'Funny bugger,' muttered George, coming to life, getting flip. 'Maybe he woke up this morning, found out his goldfish died.'

That could have accounted for it. Me too.

14

— ◆ —

'Lapsang Souchong, Earl Grey, or would you prefer Assam?' She beamed at us over the chapel hat-pegs. 'You might as well have something while you wait. He won't be long.'

Overdoing it a bit: three sorts of tea, an expensive perfume that made its point from halfway across the room and a beige wool dress into which she had been poured rather than zipped. The second Mrs Todd; busty, bright, and friendly; overstated in a way that said it all.

Our Valerie; could have gone a long way, a model, Miss UK . . . but she married *him* instead. Well above his class. Then she married the other one; money there, of course. But credit where credit's due; she keeps a lovely home.

'Assam,' I said firmly.

George nodded, and spread himself comfortably in his armchair. 'Lovely, thanks,' he said.

'I'll just tell Brigid.' The smile stayed well in place; we hadn't failed any tests by choosing Indian tea. Lavish, I decided, rather than snob. Chuffed about having the au pair, too. My opinion of Tricky Dicky rose a notch, but where did the vodka bottle fit in?

She clattered out, and I took a look at the room.

Not what I had expected. Expensively furnished, yes. A square of oriental carpet; a couple of rugs with names I could look up on a well-polished floor. The chintzy suite, well-filled bookcases on either side of the big old-fashioned fireplace, good-quality reproduction furniture; a table and writing desk among it, both genuine antiques. One or two carefully positioned pieces of Worcester. Heavy, dark blue drapes, an open fire, as well as the radiator tucked into the window bay. Confident, comfortable, established; we're not as vulgar as you thought, said the room.

So, a bit of a contradiction, Richard Todd: what about the car sales image, the seaside entrepreneur, the fairground touch? And what was that word I was looking for? Stereotype: perhaps I'd misled myself.

George watched me carefully; I got the impression he wasn't altogether sorry to see that the boss had been fooled. He too looked around the room with a complacent, almost proprietorial air.

'Great-Grandpa Todd', he offered, 'was a builder; did most of the houses on the Grand Esplanade. Moved into this: Grandpa continued the business, but the grandsons didn't fancy the building trade. Sold out.

'Richard is the garage, the café, and half a dozen of these houses. Victor is gift shops, amusements, and you can say that again. Amuses himself all over, he does. Lives in a house like this at the other end of the Esp. Jealous of big brother: thinks he should have inherited Castle Todd.' He blew out his cheeks and laughed.

'You're well into it. Dynasty stuff,' I said.

'Wife.'

'Oh, yes. Women talk.'

'Nah. Thought I'd told you; wife was a Needham. She's descended from one of Great-Gramp's daughters.'

'I thought your wicked relation was Charlie Pringle, not the Todds?'

'Yep. Him too: his mother was one of Grandpa's brood. Makes 'em second cousins, or once removed or something. Tell y' what, though; they'll be churning out village idiots from a production line if they intermarry for much longer round here.'

'So what was all the "Mr Todd" when we were talking to Richard?'

'Well, he's not that close, is he? Anyway, I couldn't care a monkey's meself, but none of the money travelled in the female line, so the wife isn't keen. Besides, all coppers are . . . y' know the rest!'

'*Dynasty*,' I muttered incautiously. 'More like the Mafia.'

'Well, I'm not in business to kiss Don Riccardo's ring!' That was George being vulgar: cross.

'Sorry!' Nevertheless, the conspiracy theory of everything had just raised its ugly head. Murder: Todds sticking together. Just suppose.

'George,' I said, 'there's no easy way to say this: are there any more of your Todd relations lying around? Buchanans, for example, or that Ian Richards kid?'

'Bloody hell, boss; haven't you got enough of 'em with Richard and Vic? Alice Draper wasn't the clan bike, if that's what you're asking.'

'The other suspect, Keith Baker?'

'Incomer; had a pub Leicester way. He's been here seven or eight years. Copper for a bit. Did he say?'

'Oh, yes he did.' Fine to fly a kite; but that one just crashed.

I was beginning to feel a bit fed up. Old man Draper and his whipped-dog eyes. How far had I got? A scan through a few actions, statements, and a bit of gossip here and there. Tales of an emerald ring, and a Gucci watch. A fake Gucci watch, the gift of Richard Todd Esquire, cheapskate and married man.

Buggered up in a row months before the murder, according to him. Confirm his story; see the old folks; kick it into touch: don't get obsessive. Murder, undetected, ancient history; let it lie. No; not just like that: you owe it to yourself. Put your boot behind it now and again, whenever you get the chance.

Valerie Todd returned carrying the tea tray herself, placed it on a low table in front of us, poured, and sat down in the armchair directly opposite me. Brigid stayed firmly out of sight.

Graceful, nice legs, skirt well tucked in. I stared, perhaps, for an instant too long. Your typical sex-starved male: I was becoming a voyeur on the brink of middle age. Perhaps I had a whole new career in front of me as a dirty old man.

'There you are,' she said. 'Maybe I ought to have offered you a real drink?'

'Tea will be fine.'

'Well, if you're sure. Anyway, it's in all the books, isn't it?'

'Sorry?'

'Detective stories: they always say, "Not while I'm on duty, madam!" You know.'

'They do, don't they? Not very realistic.' I grinned at her; wished she'd offered us a large one before she went for the tea.

'Still, you didn't refuse a drink with Dicky the other day; when he told you about Mary and that man, did you?'

'He told you then – that he's concerned about—'

'Her losing her money, yes. Reckon we know why you're really here, though. Why you're taking an interest.'

'Oh, yes.'

'Tick tock, tick tock!' She pointed to her wrist; the beam was losing definition; a bit lopsided, and for the first time I realised she'd probably had her large one already, or even two. 'No point, the watch. Nothing to do with anything, Dicky says.'

'Eric Goodwin, spreader of glad tidings,' I said.

'And Keith – but he's just stirring it: trying to put the wind up people. New sheriff in town; top gun.' She giggled. 'Anyway, he's got a surprise for you.'

'Keith Baker?'

'Nooo – Dicky. He didn't do it, you know; he *was* with me that night.'

'The night of—'

'The night of the Song and Strut Ball – the Singers and Players, to you. Yes; he came straight round to my place. Got there before a quarter to one.'

'And he, er, didn't want to get you into trouble, so he didn't tell the truth?'

She laughed abruptly, without much humour. 'He didn't want to get *himself* in trouble, either. Brian – that's my ex – was a muscle-bound bastard, if you'll pardon my French. Wish I'd known that *before*, instead of *afterwards*. Know what I mean?'

'He was a violent man?'

'Still is. The only thing he was good at, y' know? The *only* thing. We went through hell when I finally left him. Had to get a High Court injunction: arrested in the end, before he got the message.'

'You took a risk.'

'That night? No; he was at the other end of the country, being the big, bad trucker. "Hello, Rubber Duck; two smokies on your trail!" That sort of thing.'

'Stereotype,' I said. Rude, but on past performance I owed it to myself.

'What?'

'Body-builder, lorry driver, martial arts, and a CB radio. Not too good at . . . sex. Tattoos as well, Mrs Todd?'

'Now you're being a cynic, Inspector.' Her eyes snapped into focus like twin headlights. 'Self-stereotyping, perhaps. That was his image: that's Brian. I'm not trying to sell you anything; no need.'

That voice, the well-modulated tone, the perceptible crackle of annoyance, the occasional East of England slip. Elocution lessons, I was prepared to bet.

I tried to look innocent, disarming. 'Just trying to get the real picture, y' know. I'm a stranger here. Tell me, this Eddathorpe Singers and Players thing, are you a member?'

'No; there's probably a couple of dozen of 'em at most; but practically everybody goes to everything at the seaside out of season, especially at Christmas. Nothing else to do.'

''Cept go away on holiday,' said George helpfully. 'Seaside landladies – go to Lanzarote and shout at waiters. That sort of thing.'

It was George's contribution towards a relaxed social occasion; a civilised oiling of the wheels. Afternoon tea, murder enquiries, the occasional irrelevant joke. Memo to self: ignore George.

'Did you have a partner, that evening?'

'Went with a girlfriend. I knew I'd see Dicky; Mary didn't care, you know; not by then.'

'What about Alice Draper; did she care?'

'Alice? I shouldn't think so. I mean, she was yesterday's news, so far as Dicky was concerned, and she wasn't exactly exclusive. No, sorry; that's catty. She liked a good time, and never pretended otherwise; full stop.'

The front door opened and closed; Valerie Todd stood up.

'Here he is!'

She left the room at the trot, and we heard a low murmur of voices in the hall, followed by a short male laugh. Dicky Todd entered the room alone, grinned, and with a perfunctory 'Hello, you made it, then?', he nodded us back into our seats, walked over to the sideboard and poured himself a stiff drink.

'Tea', he said, his glance going from his glass of whisky to the tray in front of us, 'rots your guts. Ugh!'

He nodded hospitably towards the drinks tray.

'Thanks very much.'

What the hell; I could visualise it, though. Counsel for the defence with his lip curled for the benefit of the jury, putting it to that wicked, cringing plod. Swilling whisky with his client, promoting a false sense of security, and then locking him up. It was wonderful whisky too; the twenty-year-old Macallan, enough to make any barrister jealous. And none of your dirty glasses either; no piffling singles; a good, solid slug.

'Well, here's to crime. Cheers!'

'No police redundancies!' I agreed. He raised his eyebrows, and George laughed. It's always as well to have an appreciative sergeant around, but I must admit I've got one or two replies to that particular toast worked out in advance.

'OK,' he said, 'fire away.'

'Well, there's one or two things really, Mr Todd.'

'Three, I should think.'

'Yes: three things. You're perfectly right; first, Julian MacMillan and Superbarg. I've spoken to your ex-wife; she isn't about to invest in his business, so far as I can gather.'

'Just mindless sex, then?' he said, taking a run at the sardonic humour bit. Not a great success.

'Not part of my enquiry; I wouldn't even guess. But she asked me to pass a message – "tell Dicky to bugger off," she said. Exact words.'

'Sounds authentic. Took your time letting me know, didn't you? Putting my mind at rest.' His lips twisted sardonically.

'Meant to come yesterday, but we were busy at your garage.'

'Ah, yes: item number two. But surely, first things first: you're still going to do something about MacMillan?'

'I'm still interested.'

'And you're in the business of gathering information; not passing on juicy gossip. OK, but we're still on the same side. MacMillan is bad news.'

'Yes?'

'Stop playing policeman. I'm in the motor trade, remember? *Hire Purchase Information*; credit protection; I'm a ruddy subscriber, Bob. I've got access to the same information as you. Or at least . . . you have got access, haven't you?'

'Yes; it's being assembled now.'

'Thank Christ for that! For a minute there I was beginning to think you were deaf, dumb and blind!'

Asserting himself, was he? *Two can play, mate; and my gang's bigger than yours.*

'Look,' I said, 'I'm already getting where he buys, what he buys, and whether he pays his bills, Mr Todd. I need to know about Julian MacMillan himself, and his staff. Who he is, where he came from, if he is Julian Mac, or Theodore Popodoplis, or what. Local employees we can ignore. I want to know if he brought any sidekicks with him; book-keeper, shelf-stacker, even a bloke pushing a broom. Right?'

'All right; I'm just trying to help. I'll do my best.'

'Item two,' I said.

'Item two: shall I give incompetent Eric the push?' Turning the tables again.

'Because of Rankin? I wouldn't like to be in your shoes at the industrial tribunal if you did.'

'Eric is employed to prevent leaks, among other things. He devised the system and some little oik in the stores drove a coach and horses through it. What about that?'

'Your decision; not mine. But if Eric has a go for compensation, he'll very likely put some of the responsibility your way. After all, you're the boss.'

'And Eric is your prosecution witness; OK, I'll kick his backside and tell him to do better in future. Besides, he whispers things into my ear – as well as yours.'

'Good citizen.'

'So am I: the good citizen who had a bit on the side for two or three years; nice lass. Had a problem; she didn't know what she wanted – who she wanted – from one month's end to the next, so she was never going to be British and Commonwealth fidelity champion. Right? I met somebody else, it drifted for a month or two; then we had a final bust-up, and parted. End of story.'

'Not quite.'

'She was murdered in the North End Car Park, next to my café, yes. Not by me!'

'You gave her a watch.'

'Oh yeah, the famous watch. See here now: I'm sorry for her; I'm sorry for her mum and dad. But this watch business is complete crap. C-R-A-P: understand? She always wanted one of those Italian things; what do you call 'em?'

'Gucci.'

'Yeah; a Gucci watch, with different-coloured discs to go with each change of clothes. I went to Jersey that spring; saw a similar watch – a copy; it cost about seventy-five quid. I bought it, I gave it to her. Never pretended it was the real thing, but when we had our final bust-up she chucked it at me. Told me I was a mean bastard, and a womaniser. Pretty rich, coming from her!'

'And when did she chuck the watch?'

'Some time in the summer; early July when we had the row. Months before she died; right? So what connection can it have?'

'There's a discrepancy; evidence she had the watch still, in September.'

'Not possible.'

'And what about her leaving the garage; September again. Personality conflict, she said.'

'We finished in July. She got over it pretty rapidly, believe me. No hard feelings, right?'

'Why did she leave?'

'Ask bloody Eric; he never liked her. Puritanical little creep!'

'Eric manoeuvred her out. Eric the echo, who'd like to keep his job?'

He simply stared at me, an angry man.

'September again; an abortion. Was it yours?'

'No.' He spat the word, then, fists clenched, he brought himself down by a sheer effort of will. 'No, it wasn't mine; you wouldn't appreciate the irony of that.'

On the edge, the very edge. Accepting his booze, failing to caution a suspect, winding him up. George was beginning to wriggle; could see Complaints and Discipline looming, could George. Nevertheless, he sipped his drink like a good 'un; didn't try to interrupt.

Me, I had other problems: was Tricky Dicky a genuine suspect, alibied by the current lady wife? And the watch; no evidence it was ever with the body. Just Mum and

Dad's senile obsession, and not worth a tinker's cuss, perhaps?

'Just a minute: I've got a present for you.'

He bounced up, face set, and strode out of the room, leaving the door open. We could hear him clumping bad-temperedly up the stairs. There were muted sounds from above, a door slammed, and he came down. He re-entered the room; calm again, almost smug.

'Years of domestic chaos, and divorce', he said, 'but I found it months ago.'

He held the object in the palm of his hand: smug maybe, but he looked rueful, sad, as well. Then he tossed it over to me, and I caught it in one hand.

'Souvenir; July 1989: five months before she died. I was going to have it repaired; give it to her; wish I had, but I never got around to it. Picked it up, bunged it in a drawer instead. And if you're going to ask why I didn't make any effort to find it for that bastard Hacker, you're out of your mind!'

A gold-plated watch, rigid bracelet, white face, removable lavender-coloured rim. A suspect, for God's sake, and they hadn't taken the trouble to search his house thoroughly at the time. And now he was a volunteer: match-point, you could call it, advantage him.

I looked at the splintered glass, at the tiny letters on the dial; Gocci, it said, Swizz Made. Misspelt, or a Hong Kong joke?

Somebody hadn't been doing their job. I pocketed the watch; and no, I didn't wrap it in a handkerchief, or drop it in a plastic bag. I felt silly enough; the proud if tardy possessor of somebody else's greedy, commercial scam.

15

Not a carpeting; I was seated comfortably in one of
Hacker's office chairs and he was baring his teeth in
an avuncular, hail-fellow-well-met sort of way. Popular,
however, I was not. Summoned to Headquarters for a
grilling as soon as I'd reported recovering Tricky Dicky's
little gift.

I knew he wanted to retire and he'd got eight months'
service left. He knew that I knew, and he was sending
smoke signals. The eleventh commandment: thou shalt
not rock the boat. The broken watch glittered menacingly
on his blotting pad, directly under his fluorescent light.

'I'd love to get that bastard Todd,' he said, 'break his
alibi, stick a cracker up the backside of that snivelling
little brief!'

'I believe he telephoned you, sir?'

'Too bloody right he did; Mr Charles snotty-nose
Pringle. Claims we had an agreement not to interview
his client except in his presence. Told him to sod off!'

I wasn't entirely convinced: soothing ruffled feathers,
watching his back, a bit of judicious creeping, that was
more Hacker's style. Confining his bullying to those
who couldn't bully back. *And Teddy Baring's son? —
a mistake; a real mistake.* Besides, I remembered the

contents of Tricky Dicky's action form; there had been some sort of agreement, but it didn't include me.

'Of course . . .' He stared malevolently at the watch. '. . . you're in a bit of a quandary here, aren't you?'

Who, me? Yes, definitely: entirely on my own and by myself. It was well worth watching him do it: an art-form in itself. Detective Superintendent Hacker shovelling the brown stuff out of his yard and into mine.

'Richard Todd was interviewed as a witness; then arrested as a suspect. Now you've seen him again. You failed to caution him, and you've gone and seized this.' He poked one distasteful finger at the watch.

'Don't see the problem, sir.' (*Didn't I just!*) 'He volunteered the information; and the watch. Part of a discussion during an entirely separate enquiry. No reasonable grounds to suspect him: said he'd had it since July 1989.'

'Yes; yes, not bad. I can see you getting away with that.'

So could I.

Hacker reaching for his parachute; bailing out. Or a very substantial rat, deserting the sinking rowing boat. Personally, I hoped the cords were tangled; that the tide was out. Prayed he'd land on something spiky, or up to the proverbials in stinking mud.

'Tricky,' I said, shaking my head sorrowfully. 'Not enough to arrest him, and now, if he's got his solicitor to complain . . .'

'No, it's not quite as bad as that.' Hacker cheered up. 'Todd hasn't consulted Pringle, apparently. He rang me off his own bat. Acting in the best interests of his client, he says.'

'Prat,' I said. 'The National Council for Civil Liberties rides again. Had his nose put out of joint, that's all.'

Hacker seemed fascinated by the watch; he poked it

again. 'Just called Liberty these days,' he said absently. 'They've changed the name. Doesn't take you any further by itself, does it, the watch?'

'No, sir.'

'Shame they didn't find it earlier; when they searched his house. Still, no point in stirring up a hornet's nest over that, eh?'

'No, sir.'

'Got any more enquiries to make?'

'Well, there's still the emerald ring. And the discrepancy in dates. Todd says the row was in July, and this girl, Sandra Lawrence, claims she saw Alice Draper wearing the watch as late as September.'

'Lawrence? Never heard of her.'

'She used to be Sandra Carter, the waitress; married a guy named Lawrence.'

'Oh.' He waved one dismissive hand. 'Not really evidence, though, is it? Nothing to say Alice was wearing this stuff when she died?'

'No, sir. The parents, thought . . .'

'Yes. Satisfy the old couple, if you can. Quite. But nothing . . . contentious. Routine enquiries, naturally. I'm not suggesting that anybody can dictate to the police.'

Of course not.

'Take each day as it comes?' I offered. When in doubt, give 'em a cliché, relevant or not.

'Er . . . that sort of idea, yes. I think we understand one another: keep attacking, Bob!'

The interview was over. I understood my bit, all right; I'd got my own way. Whatever Hacker thought he understood was down to him. Treasure trove, or an in-tray full of blood and manure, it was going to be all mine. Or so I hoped.

*   *   *

'Look,' he said, 'I don't care what they say; she was a lovely kid.'

Alex Buchanan, leaning across the table, late twenties, fresh-faced, earnest; trying to tell it how it was.

'The Christmas before she died: you got engaged?'

'Not really; it was a bit vague on her side, I suppose. I wanted to marry her, but she – well, she didn't want to be tied down.' He took a sip of his beer.

It was not the ideal place for an interview, but it was all I was going to get. A corner of the bar in the Links Hotel, with Keith Baker hovering just out of earshot polishing glasses, staring speculatively across the room. I stared back, daring him to encroach, but he seemed happy enough for the moment. He'd effected the introduction: it was good enough for him.

Early evening again, and eight or nine people in the bar, all ostentatiously minding their own business. Or was I getting paranoid perhaps? It didn't seem to bother Alex Buchanan much.

'Wouldn't you rather we had our chat somewhere else?'

'At the police station? No: I almost lost my job, last time. No reason for it; nothing to connect me and that Hooker man hauls me in.'

'Hacker,' I said absently. 'Hooker was an American Civil War general – believed in brothels for the troops.' *Come to think of it* . . .

Reluctantly, I returned to the point. 'It's not the best place in town to have our talk.'

'They'll gossip anyway. Better to sit and have a beer together; the police don't go boozing with their victims.' He looked and sounded entirely serious.

It was victims already, was it? And as for the boozing; tell that one to Richard Todd.

Archetypical schoolmaster, too, in his tweed suit; a

generation behind the times. Slim, educated English accent, highly polished shoes, lurid tartan tie. I'd be able to identify a Buchanan in future – at two hundred yards. I was inclined to be smug: Graham is a quieter sett, mostly green and black. Not that I'm over-fond of the tartan tea-cosy stuff; I'm two generations removed.

'OK: cards on the table, Mr Buchanan. I've been approached by Mr and Mrs Draper, and they're—'

'Still worried about Alice's ring. It isn't the first time, you know. They've been on about it before. I've no idea what she did with it.'

'How did you come to give it to her in the first place?'

'I met Alice in the long vacation; summer 1987. I was still at college. I liked her; I went out with her. I finished my course the following year; got my first job at Eddathorpe Comp. and we started going out again. I was more serious than she was; I bought her a ring: Christmas present, engagement ring – you tell me! A couple of months later, we split up. She kept the ring; end of story.'

'That's a bit stark.'

'What do you want me to say? That I knew she was putting it about a bit before she met me? OK, yes, I knew. But this isn't fairyland, Inspector, or haven't you heard? No unicorns left; and nobody cares, anyway.'

'Eh?'

'Unicorns – whenever they found a virgin, they'd come and lay their heads in her lap.'

'Really?' I took a long pull at my pint. You learn something useless every day. Mythology; and there was I, just for a moment, thinking he was cracked.

'Was she – er – putting it about a bit while she was going out with you?'

'I don't know.'

'Educated guess?'

'Probably.' The voice strove to be neutral; succeeded in being bitter. Walking wounded, so many years on.

'Richard Todd?'

'Very likely, yes. This is hindsight – twenty-twenty vision, you know. Funny, isn't it – a woman's magazine story; the receptionist and the boss.'

He looked at me sideways, turning up one corner of his mouth; anything but funny. Expecting, almost wanting to be mocked.

'And the others?' I nodded across the room; Baker, assiduously polishing glasses, still just out of range. 'Him?'

'That was before, I think.'

'And she was still a lovely kid?'

'All right: supposing I'd said she was a little cow? She's dead; what does that make me, and what good does it do? She was still fantastic; face, body, everything. Fun to be with – she lit everything up, wherever she went. Always wanted to be on the go. Laughing.'

Whatever the disease, he'd had it – had probably still got it – bad. Could this be him? If so, for an intelligent man, he'd pushed himself way out on to thin ice. That; or he thought he could handle a plod. Or he was sincere, or it was a double bluff, or . . .

'So you gave her a ring – Christmas, engagement or whatever – now you tell me!'

'Engagement ring, but that's my version. Looking back, she was always a bit elusive, somehow. She never quite believed in it.'

'You don't get much more positive than emeralds, surely. What was it – three hundred, four hundred quid? On a new schoolteacher's salary – not a family heirloom by any chance?'

'No, definitely not!'

He pressed his lips together, then he shrugged. 'She had me down as a bit of a – a young fogey, I think. Give her a ring, and it was sort of OK for me . . .'

'To have sex?' I finished the sentence for him.

'Yes. I think that's why she took it; she fancied me. A bit of fun; nothing long-term. Give me a boost, accept the ring.'

'When did you pack her up?'

'In the spring – March time. And she, er, *packed* me, not the other way round.'

He was an absolute whiz for language; no slang, no split infinitives, I was prepared to bet.

'And you didn't object when she kept the ring?'

He shook his head.

'Maybe you thought you'd get back together?'

'No; she made that perfectly clear. She said she wasn't my sort. Couldn't see herself as a schoolmaster's wife.'

'How did you feel?'

He stared miserably at the table in front of him. I knew exactly how he felt. Very much the same as me and I wasn't happy to ask. Coppers are not necessarily bastards, but they're bloody useless if they can't put over the act.

'You saw her again?'

'Just to say hello: around town; here in the bar.'

'And was she wearing the ring?'

'Sometimes.'

'Did she stop wearing it?'

'I don't know.'

'When did you last see it?'

'I've no idea.'

'What about the baby; was it yours?'

'No! Surely, even policemen can count? We parted in March '89, remember?'

'Did you kill her, Alex?'

'Christ!' The word was an explosion; one hand smashed

137

down on the table, and the glasses jumped, drawing every pair of eyes in the room.

'No, I didn't. What are you trying to do to me, in a place like this?'

'I'm trying to find out who killed her; thought you knew that. I did offer to do this somewhere else.'

'Well, Mr Detective . . .' His voice sank to a venomous hiss. '. . . your sadistic little playtime is over. I hope you're satisfied; I'm off.'

'All right, Alex; needed to ask. Just one more thing?'

'Yes?' He stared at me with a kind of fascinated loathing. Anxious to be away, yet unwilling to disengage; a man deliberately running his tongue into a bad tooth.

'Why did you refuse to give a sample of blood?'

Slowly, he stood up. Then he placed both hands flat on the table, bent forward with his arms straight, his face close to mine, and spoke very deliberately.

'Tell me, Inspector; about the DNA technique – what does it stand for?'

'Well – it's genetic fingerprinting: everybody has a unique genetic code, inherited from their parents. We can match—'

'You're waffling: glib. DNA – you can't even tell me what the letters mean. And you and your pals expect me to submit to your crackpot test? And what about at the time they asked me? They'd only just started using it then; I don't suppose you even know that. That daft Superintendent of yours – he thought it was black magic!

'Even now, with half the experts arguing, giving different odds; courts in America throwing the so-called evidence out? You must be joking!'

He straightened up, squared his shoulders, distributed his scowl impartially among the meagre ranks of the assembled drinkers, and walked out. He did not slam the door.

DNA. What did it stand for, anyway? I'd been told in CID lectures, more than once. Probably after a heavy lunch; putting up a few zizzes at the back of the class.

Shame-facedly, I made a promise to myself: I'd definitely look it up.

He hadn't answered the question, though; not properly.

16

———————

The following morning I decided not to leave Joe in the car; he wasn't doing the upholstery, let alone the rear seat belts, any good, so I sneaked him up the back stairs. Basket in the corner of my cubbyhole, bowl of water, and a rubber bone. What more could a dog want?

The morning shift, Messrs Robey and Lamb, looked pleased; they'd got something, however minor, on the new DI. Bending the rules: give a little, take a little; it might work out to their advantage, they hoped.

'Maybe', said John Robey, 'we could teach him to sniff out illegal substances, boss.'

'Like guest-house kippers, or landladies' porridge,' said Roy Lamb.

'Thanks, fellers. I knew I could rely on the loyalty of my staff!'

They reached out, tentatively, and let Joe sniff their fingers; then they scratched his ears. Stalin rolled over, and grinned. Knew when his bread was buttered all right.

'Thought he was hell on wheels?' Robey sounded disappointed.

'He has his likes and dislikes,' I said.

'We could provide him with a list.' Robey was grinning. 'Like Charlie Pringle, for example.'

'Not again!'

'He's along the corridor now; with Mr Baring. Two other crackers with 'im – one named Todd.'

'Richard Todd?'

'Nope; the younger one with the big beer belly; Vic.'

That was OK, I hadn't been oppressing any fatties lately; no doubt they'd come to moan about some other poor slob. I was wrong, of course.

The phone rang about ten minutes later; a bad sign, no Mrs Kelly, Teddy Baring direct. An invitation to visit; cool, very formal. Precise.

They were ranged in a semi-circle round Teddy's desk. Charlie Pringle, flaunting his unbrushed, dandruff-speckled coat like some disreputable academic gown, had the usual bad smell under his nose. Victor Todd, a younger, grosser version of his brother in a blue pinstripe suit and multi-coloured silk tie, looked uneasy from the start, while the military grocer sat bolt upright in his chair, slightly flushed about the gills, the epitome of the injured citizen making his complaint. Or a bandit carrying out an unexpected raid into enemy territory.

'Do sit down, Mr Graham.' Teddy waved me into a seat, carefully positioned close to the window, beside, rather than in front of, his desk. An unsubtle if comforting arrangement: both of us facing the same way.

'Now, gentlemen; I think you all know Detective Inspector Graham?' He looked calmly round our merry little group. I nodded and gave each of them a dose of my puzzled smile.

'No,' said Victor Todd, 'we haven't met. G'morning to you.' He nodded quickly, his eyes resting on me for a second or two, before his glance slid anxiously across to Pringle. He was giving all the signs of having been pushed into this, whatever it was.

Teddy Baring turned to me, his face expressionless,

'Mr MacMillan is a director of Kagabow Ltd, which trades as Superbarg Cash and Carry,' he said. 'Mr Pringle is representing him this morning, and Mr Todd is here in his capacity as a new shareholder. This is not a formal complaint, but they've got some – ah – concerns they wish to discuss with you.'

There was an almost imperceptible down-turning of that rat-trap mouth. Was Teddy Baring amused, or was he cursing his luck? Landed with a reckless CID man: arrogant, looking for a block to fit a swollen head and an overstretched neck?

I turned my attention to Kagabow Ltd: another product of the dream factory, probably bought off the shelf from a company formation outfit and a few shares issued for cash. Poor old Victor; not as bright as his ex-sister-in-law, obviously. His new investment was already blowing in the wind. MacMillan had brought the local patsie along to add a bit of substance to his tale.

Charlie Pringle jumped into the mire straight away. 'Superintendent; my client is in fact complaining about—'

'No.' Baring's hand slapped down on his desk. 'If this is any kind of complaint, Mr Pringle, this interview will terminate immediately. I've already told you; complaints will be recorded, and passed on for investigation at Headquarters. Which is it to be?'

MacMillan intervened. 'It's not a complaint, as such. Not at this stage, anyway.' He looked at me to see how I took it; the implied threat. 'This may be a misunderstanding, the result of some malicious piece of gossip, perhaps. I think, Mr Pringle, that I can straighten this out.'

Smooth all right; bidding for his gold medal in public speaking. I sat back to listen, to suck it all up like a sponge. Problem: if he was what I thought he was, he was more than capable of giving me a run for the

143

punters' money. He was just as likely as me to know the score.

He started with his background; his rank, his military exploits, his travels. He claimed to have extensive business experience and to have made his money in Hong Kong. Nothing too specific; I could try, but it was going to be difficult, practically impossible, to check.

Then he went on to his purchase of Superbarg, the limited company he'd set up now his wanderings were over: the middle-aged bachelor in the little country town. The exile's dream of home; I could practically hear the sob of the violin.

That Paula Baily: somehow, she'd got hold of the wrong end of the stick. Inexperience, perhaps: it was, after all, a small town with smallish crimes. Too much attention to gossip, couldn't expect her to appreciate the subtleties of men's business . . . the knife went in.

Anyway, it had come to his attention: the police were asking questions about the company's purchases and its debts. Damaging: did we appreciate how very damaging, and on the verge of being defamatory, her conduct might be?

'Nevertheless, Major . . .' I didn't intend to let him gallop away with the whole scene. Vinegar and oil in equal measure looked about right. '. . . one or two of your suppliers may not have received—'

'Payment; quite!' He snatched the words from my mouth. 'And do you know why? They've let me down. Short deliveries, broken promises, poor-quality goods.'

'That's why Major MacMillan wants me here,' Charlie Pringle again. 'I have been instructed to institute proceedings against three companies for breach of contract!'

Unwisely, he slapped down a slim bundle of unpaid invoices and letterheaded statements on Teddy Baring's desk. We both took a speedy gleg at the names and did a swift burst of mental arithmetic: twenty-seven thousand quid. MacMillan treated Pringle to a very hard look. Not information he'd been over-happy to give.

I looked carefully, enquiringly, at MacMillan. It was a try-on; I could feel it in my bones. A quick spoiling tactic to keep the wolves at bay a bit longer. An attempt to scare us off. He was risking it for the sake of a few more deliveries: we hadn't got much time.

But how did Baring see it? He'd never done any big-city Crime Squad stuff. I'd ignored his suggestion – his order, almost – to get rid. Now trouble was coming to meet him halfway. An honest citizen with his lawyer down at the nick. Explanations; sweet reason; High Court writs; hints of future bother for the cops if they didn't lay off.

'We wouldn't want to harm your business, Major.' Sweet reason versus structured hypocrisy, and why not? 'Nor would I wish to get involved in a civil dispute, but by placing the orders you do represent yourself – your company – as being willing and able to meet the liabilities, don't you?'

'Who says I can't?' The words came out in a rush, and his face darkened with rage. A short fuse, too.

'You've missed my point, sir. It's you, by your conduct, who says you can.'

'Of course I – my company can pay. But you're not snooping into our affairs, I can tell you that!'

'Just your assurance, Major – Kagabow can meet its liabilities at the cash and carry, as and when they fall due. Yes?'

'Bloody cheek!'

Keep smiling politely; maintain the expectant look, and . . .

'Yes; yes we can.'

Gottim! As witnessed by one Superintendent, one

Detective Inspector, his own solicitor, and the investor who'd soon be crying out for his cash; all witnesses to the dirty deed. A straight-up, nailable lie once the balloon went up.

If it went up. If that reckless CID upstart was right. Otherwise, it was going to be last requests, followed shortly thereafter by the chop. Somehow, I didn't see the Chief taking kindly to the new boy ruining a respectable cash and carry, the property of a retired military gent.

'You've received Major MacMillan's assurance, Inspector.' Charlie was on the air again.

'Yes.'

'I take it, then, there will be no further harassment from either yourself or your subordinate? No more unjustified enquiries?'

'We would, of course, act on a specific complaint.' My voice trailed away apologetically: conceding victory to the forces of light.

'But not in relation to disputed deliveries and civil debts? Very well, we are prepared to leave it at that, for the time being.'

Depending on how you define harassment, unjustified enquiries, disputes and civil debts, old chap.

Smile some more and let him think what he liked. I wasn't going to nail my colours to the mast.

He nodded loftily to MacMillan, picked up his briefcase, and rose to his feet; over-impressed with himself, Charlie-boy. MacMillan opened his mouth to speak, then he changed his mind. The interview had not, I suspected, gone entirely according to plan. He and Charlie Pringle had somehow crossed their wires on this. Objectives had been confused. Not surprising; he could hardly bare his heart to his legal eagle, not when he was running a fraud.

Ignoring me, Pringle and MacMillan made ready to

depart amid the usual expressions of mutual esteem: keep the senior officer happy, once you've slapped the peasants down.

Victor Todd kept quiet. He trailed behind his companions as they left the room.

He paused at the door, half closing it behind his associates, and turned. 'Y've been done, Inspector Graham; done brown by that brother o' mine. He's the one who's been opening his mouth, right?'

I grunted non-committally. I half knew it; another Tricky Dicky; it must be in the blood. A punchline was about to wing its way.

'Thought so. Didn't tell you about his own little scheme, then?'

I waited while he grinned in a self-congratulatory sort of way. 'Thought not. Ask him about the Cloverleaf Consortium – better still, ask our Mary. She's on the Council, she'll tell you. She's about the only one who's not in his pocket. Ask her about the planning permission to build a cash and carry, out Retton way. Just like I say; you've been done!'

I sighed; big towns, little towns, they're all the same when it comes to local political games. From ring roads to supermarkets, whenever a contentious planning application goes in, the opposition starts singing the old, old song. Corruption; chicanery; bent.

It's all too easy – have a go at the in-group, cheer things up by slinging a bit of mud. Vic Todd had the air of a man who was trying to convince himself. Nevertheless, Eddathorpe being Eddathorpe, it was worth bearing in mind. Probably sour grapes, but he could, just possibly, be right.

Teddy Baring and I exchanged a single, wholly cynical glance: Florence under the Medicis; Eddathorpe under the Todds.

17

Back in the office, Joe in his basket snoring, I sat down for a serious think. No use feeling sore: Teddy Baring was being over-cautious, but he had a point. He hadn't put the blocks on things entirely, but it was all going to be very low-profile from now on. Until we had something called evidence, apparently.

Call Paula, go through what we had, think philosophical thoughts. Teddy's responsibility, he gives the orders . . . Suppliers' money on the line, not ours . . . We'd get him in the long run . . . Everything comes to he who waits . . . A stitch in time saves the bacon . . .

To hell with all that. Try another old police proverb: there are no second prizes, mate. You win or you lose, and only idiots fall face down in the manure in front of bogus bloody majors from foreign parts. He was a crook; nothing else mattered. Not even if Tricky Dicky and his pals were seeking planning permission for a nuclear dump on Eddathorpe Prom.

A leak-proof enquiry; that was the ticket. Complaint-proof sources of information: the military grocer would never know.

Royal Military Police records, for example – overseas army; no good. Home Office Immigration, Lunar House

149

– worth a whirl, if the bastard really was a Zimbabwe national: more than doubtful. Royal Hong Kong Police – possible, but how long would it take?

Besides, the lying bugger's real name could well be Smith, his adventures confined to the Boy, not the Selous, Scouts, and he'd probably never travelled further than Southend.

Fraud Squad Index, New Scotland Yard: now we were cooking with gas. Names Index; Modus Operandi Index – all the conmen's little lies and quirks – fun and games with the Rhodesian Special Forces; and my mind clicked over. There it was, literally staring me in the face. In Teddy Baring's office.

Around 1980, 1981; the newest suit in the Divisional CID. Boring, routine paper-pushing, and somebody's got to do it. Every morning, as soon as the post arrives, sort out *Police Reports* and the *Police Gazette*.

Murder enquiries, bodies found, missing persons, persons wanted and suspected of crime. Get your pen and scour through the lot, young man. Go back to the old editions and draw a line through the cancelled entries and cross-reference 'em in the right-hand margin. Keep you quiet for an hour.

And I'd read about him, or a similar villain, fourteen, maybe fifteen years ago. Stacking up thousands in fraudulent credit; running a long firm fraud, and explaining away his lack of business background to the punters. *Just returned from Rhodesia, old boy; used to be in the Selous Scouts*.

The depression lifted: stuff philosophy, console yourself with that when you've lost. My ageing murder enquiries collapsed and my villains brought their solicitors along to mock. In some quarters opinion might be hardening against me: couldn't detect a fart in a colander, they'd say. But never mind, all would yet be well. In

Teddy's office, in his well-polished bookcase, in one of those impressively bound volumes of the *Police Gazette*, a previous incarnation of Julian the smoothie MacMillan lurked. Perhaps.

Then the phone rang.

'It's your wife, sir,' babbled a female voice on the switchboard. 'Shall I put her through?'

Why, why was it that God didn't like me today?

The whole art of management; delegate. In other words, let the poor bloody infantry do all the work. The woman with the iffy credit card – George; a couple of DSS-type multiple shoplifters – the dog fanciers could cope. As for Teddy Baring, I conveyed a smidgen of good news; Paula and one of her Detective Constables were going to spoil the symmetry of his bookcase for a few hours. Could I have the afternoon off?

Naturally, if it was as important as all that.

I could have left Angie to simmer for a few days, but in my view at least, things had dragged on for long enough. She'd seemed anxious to meet, to discuss, she said, the future. No lawyers; see if we could wrap things up.

Not, I noticed, sort them out. Wrap as in parcel; tie up with string: leave it, bulky, misshapen, menacing even, in some unvisited corner of your mind. Then go away, or on, or start again, or whatever phrase suits the activity in which you've engaged. Getting out of the mincer, probably: and it's no consolation to know that you sharpened a good proportion of the blades and helped to switch on the motor yourself.

We met in a fake black and white café where the road from the Midlands divides; turn left for the north, according to the big green and white notice, to Grimsby, Hull; straight on for the East Coast. With a fresh daily experience of the one, and a lively recollection of working visits to the others, I could hardly imagine anybody willingly travelling in either direction. But no option; there was no going back with her.

I parked the car and wound the window down a couple of inches for Joe. He was already eyeing the buckles of the seat belts at the back. Nothing sissy like biting through the webbing for him. There were already Lakeland dents in solid metal from jaws designed to deal with foxes, ten times stronger than those of a man. I distributed one or two threats and tempted him with his official bone. He turned his nose up: he didn't care.

December now, and the place was practically empty, apart from a middle-aged couple by the window and a pair of wrinklies sipping tea. Retired; off to the coast for a Spartan weekend at their caravan or chalet, I guessed. Idly, I wondered if they visited their little piece of heaven every week throughout the winter. The envy of the neighbours; Thursday till Sunday, returning in triumph to some centrally heated suburban bungalow, blue with cold. Perhaps me and Angie could have ended up like that: Darby and Joan. Angela was late.

I was trying not to think about her too much. The steps from Angie to adultery, to money and back again, were sharp flints on raw bare feet. But I could grow calluses as well as the next man, given time.

Genuinely, I hadn't seen it coming. I thought we'd been trotting along like everybody else. Both of us working, seeing one another in the evenings, at weekends: watching television; making love a couple of times a week; going out. But it hadn't been quite like that.

First and foremost there had been the job: I wasn't at home every evening, and I was getting two weekends in five. When I dug in my heels and took 'em, that is. Was that a cause or a symptom of the trouble? More excitement at work than there was at home?

And Angie: full-time schoolteacher, bringing stuff home, sitting at the table marking work, preparing lessons, telling me about the funny things they said. Other people's kids; I could not have cared less. Did I go around boring *her* about police work – *a funny thing happened on the way to the Crown Court today*?

She'd taken to running an evening class; twentieth-century fiction, twice a week. We hardly needed the money, but it gave her time with adults, stretched her mind, she said. It had stretched Clive Jones's too, apparently.

And now? I was damned if he was going to get the woman and a dowry at my expense! I knew it was stupid, and childish, and unfair; that there was another point of view. It didn't make me feel any better, being able to see one or two things from the other side.

Somewhere in the background, deep in there among all the resentments, a little niggle of conscience stirred. She'd worked at it too; her money had gone into the mortgage, the living, the home, as well as mine. And that had been the least of it. Precisely what was I trying to achieve?

I watched her arrive, park her silver Metro on an acre of almost empty car park well away from the estate. She spotted me immediately. She came in and crossed the room unhurriedly, threading her way between the tables, her face serious, giving nothing away.

She was exactly as I remembered her – a little fuller in the face, perhaps. Blooming, I thought. Then: pack it up. No need for the irony, if that's what it was.

Angela; not exactly beautiful; striking, attractive, instead. Blonde, soft-skinned; that smooth oval face, full mouth, and candid blue-grey eyes. She was wearing a short, bright red winter coat over a black skirt and black patent high-heeled shoes. She placed the matching patent leather bag on the table, and slid into the seat opposite me.

'Hello, Rob.'

Rob: I was Bob everywhere else.

'Hello, Angie, how are you?' I signalled to the waitress, who was leaning, elbows up behind her, against the counter. The girl came over, licking her pencil, indifferent to significant moments in other people's emotional lives. We both ordered coffee, cream, jam and scones. I was glad of something to do; unwilling to make the first move, reluctant to kick this one off.

She looked at me thoughtfully, neither embarrassed nor ill-at-ease. I wished I could have looked the same. It's OK, you're the injured party, said the little devil inside. Not a lot of mileage in that.

While we waited for the coffee we gave the state of traffic, the weather, the roads a quick trot. She even asked me about work; I forget what I said. I certainly didn't let on about my stunning successes, so far.

The girl returned with the coffee; cups, saucers and plates, all in anaemic green to set off the dense, formidable-looking scones and the dollop of dead straw-berries in the jam.

She poured while I watched the coffee slobbering from the chipped pot spout. A wonderful, wonderful place.

'Can we talk about it sensibly,' she said, 'without going over the top?'

'We can try.'

'OK, it's like this: I want to – I need to sort things out financially. Especially the house.'

I waited for more.

'Is this your idea of trying? Aren't you going to say anything at all?'

'I was giving you a chance to say what you wanted to say, first.'

'You won't make things easier, will you?'

This was nothing like what I'd intended. I wasn't trying to score any points. Cross-purposes, straight away. Maybe she saw it on my face. She left it at that.

'Right.' Her voice was hurried. 'We both know that, roughly speaking, courts put the income of both spouses together and divide by two. Then the person with the largest income – usually the husband – pays maintenance to equalise income. Yes?'

'Yep; more or less.'

'And a division is made as far as assets are concerned – assuming there aren't any children to provide for?'

I nodded: there were no children to provide for. My attention wandered; I didn't want to have this conversation. She'd triggered better subjects to talk about. Some time in the past.

'I want to sort this out with you, Rob. Let me have the house; pay off the mortgage, and we'll call it quits!'

I came back with a thud.

'That's quits?'

My Scots grandpa would have been proud of me. Of the mental arithmetic, at least: a forty-five-thousand-pound purchase in 1984. Valued at around a hundred and ten, despite the recession, today. Less an endowment mortgage of twenty-five thousand. As things stood, she was living in eighty-five thousand pounds' worth of equity; and she wanted the lot. Game, set and match: nice one, Mr Jones.

'I helped with the deposit; I contributed too, in lots of other ways, Rob. I need that house.'

'Your boyfriend seems to want a lot of compensation for one smack in the mouth!'

Her face flamed: any moment now. The old, bad-tempered Angie, brewing up another dose of her full and frank opinion of her wandering boy. She could call me as big a bastard as she liked. I was not playing the quiescent gravy train opposite her starring role; the suburban Zsa Zsa Gabor. *Goodbye, dahling! – and thanks for the hundred and ten K!*

'Rob; you care a damn sight more about your pride than you ever did about me, don't you?'

She got that one home all right: the trying hadn't lasted long. Then I pulled myself up short: more in this than met the eye.

Angie had been pushing for money lately. Now she was raising the odds for a pay-off. But however many snide remarks I'd made to myself, she'd never been a greedy woman.

'Come on, Angie; I'm sorry. Tell me the rest.'

Her eyes filled with tears and for once I can give myself a bit of credit. I never gave it a passing thought: feminine wiles, technique.

'I'm pregnant, Rob.'

Knockout in the third round. That bloody animal! That lucky, lucky bastard! I looked down at my plate, at that horrible purple jam. A cheap crack: jam for Clive! An easy omen there all right.

'I'm not going to marry him; it's finished. I'm going to have my baby, then I'm going back to work.'

I started to formulate the question and suppressed it straight away. I hadn't got any right to ask. Who did the breaking; her or him? How, when and why?

But satisfying my prurient curiosity was out; so was anything other than a very subdued, very mean, totally private gloat. Afterwards: if at all. Thought for today, however: *he was out, out, out!*

'How are you going to manage?'

'I'll have about eleven hundred pounds a month, after tax. Pretty good; and my mother says she'll look after her, during the day. You'll be free, Rob: clean slate.'

A female ba – baby. A her; definitely not a him. She was saying something there, aside from the pleading. I looked across at my wife; just the same as ever: almost.

Angie and her little girl: for once I was on the wrong side of the interview table. Don't we all make a bloody mess? I jumped in with both feet. The Robert Graham formula; instant revenge.

'You can take him to the cleaners, for a start. The Child Support Agency. You'll have money to—'

She almost laughed. 'There you go, running another of your blood feuds. It's my baby, Rob. I don't want her to be anything to do with him.'

I could have said something to that, but I didn't. Her baby, my money, and Super-duper Jones walks away. But I wasn't in the mood to make debating points, or to fight. Confused; no particular objective in mind.

'Does he even know?'

She shook her head, 'We haven't been in touch.' There was a note of something, not quite humour, in there somewhere. 'And you? Nothing about him on the grape vine; no throbbing of jungle drums?'

The rumours, the gossip, the innuendo; the whole inward-looking, self-regarding world. Something else she didn't like about Britain's modern police.

'What?'

'He's got a new job: Staff Officer to an Inspector of Constabulary down south.'

I could see it all . . . Staff Officer, followed by the Senior Command Course . . . Assistant Chief Constable . . . Onwards and upwards. A lot of kudos. And my personal claim to fame: I'd probably belted a future Commissioner of the Met.

'The rat-race is over,' I muttered ungraciously. 'The rodents have won!'

'God, you and your ego: that's it, then!' She pushed back her chair and stood up. Before I could say anything she was away across the room. The waitress came to life: somebody making off without payment. She advanced.

Clumsily, I pushed the table forward, got to my feet.

'How much?'

'Six pounds forty.'

It was daylight robbery: liquid brown paint-stripper and scone mix they could have used to manufacture a batch of garden gnomes. Toxicologists would have drooled over the cream and the strawberry jam.

'Here!'

I did my Rockefeller: a ten-pound note and out into the car park, double quick. Somewhere behind me the sour, suspicious bitch was holding my banknote up to the light.

Just in time.

'Look . . .' I took Angie by one elbow while she was fumbling in her handbag for keys, right at the door of her car. 'This isn't easy for me – for either of us. OK? Give me a chance to think.'

'There's n-nothing to say.'

'Yes there is. Just give me a day or two; give me a chance to think it out.'

She was almost back to the tears. Then Joe decided to take a hand, jumping up and down in the back of my car; yipping like an idiot. Attracting the notice of a long-lost friend. She took one look at the frenetic, bouncing figure with the ridiculous moustache, bowed her head forward and absolutely howled.

'Come on,' I said. 'Come and sit down.'

I tried to urge her towards my vehicle. Probably the worst thing I could have done. Absolutely no chance of her mixing it with Joe.

'No.'

She fumbled with her keys, managed to open the driver's door, manoeuvred sideways into the driver's seat and sat down. It was my turn to panic.

'For God's sake, you can't drive off like this. Calm down; think of the traffic!'

'Just go. Look, I'll be all right. Go; give me a ring when you're ready. But please, get that dog out of here!'

I didn't move.

'All right; look.' She placed the keys on the seat beside her. 'I won't move until I've sorted myself out; now please . . .'

'OK; I'll be in touch, I promise.'

I walked over to the estate and joined Joe; he was half mad with excitement. I had to be quick to field him as I opened the door. He jumped into the back as the engine started and I swung away with him scrabbling at the glass.

I could see the Metro in my rear-view mirror, the driver's door still open, her head and shoulders clearly visible above the steering wheel; the face was a blur.

No chance of clocking her expression. I suppose she was simply watching Joe perform. That stupid, gyrating dog, accompanied by his ridiculous, Pavlovian man.

18

The Fisherman was not exactly jolly; unbearably noisy, maybe. It was yet another out-of-season watering hole; another place for the gathering of cliques and Eddathorpe clans. No lounge, no bar; just one long, tarted-up room with a couple of dozen tables on a bright red, brass-edged carpet, and a broad quarry-tiled area in front of the counter where they hoped the punters were going to stand ten-deep at the height of the season.

Horse brasses, warming pans and plastic beams. Piped music, too; something sixtyish was apparently blowing in the wind amidst a roar of voices calculated to convince their owners they were having a marvellous time. A few women; a lot of landladies' husbands at play.

We watched Big Malc managing three pints between his hands as he wove his way back from the bar. There were five empty glasses on the table; Andy and Ron had left already, amidst a certain amount of nodding and winking about an anonymous snout. Malc, jealous, I suspected, at being abandoned by his usual partner, hoped sourly that Andy's new informant had big tits.

'Definitely,' said Andy, helpfully, 'and the Battle of Trafalgar tattooed on her—'

He stopped, noting the interest in his revelations being

161

taken by a party of women, fortyish, raising fifty-five, thickly enamelled and empty glasses well to the fore, who infested an adjoining table. Our friends and colleagues exited promptly with a snigger, leaving us to take care of the significant nods, winks and smiles emanating from the grab-a-granny club. No thanks.

A member of a loud, middle-aged group at the bar called after Malc as he sat down, something about never finding one when they were wanted, but the boozers always being packed out at taxpayers' expense. The comedian's pals treated us to a raucous hoot.

'Don't forget to enjoy yourselves,' Malc bawled his rejoinder. 'It's Thursday, chaps: cash-a-giro day!!'

The hoot died away, to be replaced with something of a sullen growl and sideways glances across the room.

What with the disappointed harridans dying of thirst on the next table and a native uprising being plotted at the bar, it looked like being a lively night.

Malc emptied his pockets of packets of crisps and offered a couple of cheese and onion to Joe, slumped on the floor beside me. We were becoming something of a conversation piece around town, but what could I do? I wasn't leaving him to his own wicked devices, back at the ranch all day. Besides, he was a sociable soul: within strictly defined limits, that is.

'I knew a police dog, once,' said Malcolm mournfully, 'hated this uniform Chief Inspector. Used to sneak up beside him whenever he got the chance and piss up his leg.'

We all took a long, contemplative pull at the beer. There were times when we could've all done with a dog like that.

'Police Federationist, then?' asked George, deadpan.

'Eh?'

'You know: a strong trade unionist at heart.'

'Anarchist, more like,' said Malc, and huffed crumbs happily across the table. 'They should've knighted that dog.'

I could see it coming; one of those times. Funny stories. Shop. Not that I had anything against a pint and a saunter down memory lane, but my mind kept drifting back to Angie.

The sheer effrontery of the woman! Once out of sight, she mentally reassembled herself in her demonic role. I was supposed to make her a gift of a house, sans mortgage, to make her and her rising bump happy. Not my bump, either; the putative papa didn't even know; was not going to be called upon to contribute, 'cos Angie wanted her little bundle all to herself. I should definitely cocoa.

I contributed a couple of nods and grins to Big Malc's story about a disastrous night crime patrol, and went back to my brood.

She was entitled, morally, to fifty per cent; OK. That meant fifty per cent of the endowment assurance, too. Cashed, that would probably fetch around fourteen grand altogether. Then there were our life policies: I'd proposed and paid for the ones on Angie's life, but so what? Count them as hers: encashed, another twelve or fourteen grand; maybe more. Enough to clear the house.

I'd still have my own policies to pay or pop, depending whether I wanted to buy afresh. What was I getting? With all the bits and pieces, something over thirty thousand a year. I could, as she said, walk away. Clear conscience; clean slate. There I went again, crackers; thinking of handing it all over on a plate.

And then there was Angela with a baby; Angie, unlost . . . Totally bloody impossible. Certifiably, irredeemably mad. All living happily ever after: her, me, and the cute, nappied souvenir of smart-arse Jones. The kid would be better off in the Foreign Legion than living with me, would he – she – not?

Think of all those coppers laughing their heads off from Land's End to – to Eddathorpe on Sea. I could just picture it, a great night out in the pub, a terrific combat story. *Did ya hear the one about the guy who was soft in the head: our cuckolded DI?*

Besides, she was away already; couldn't stand me, she'd said, or the CID. Hours, people, attitudes, gossip; the whole damn job.

Obviously untrue; think again: she'd jumped bail with a Superintendent of police – of sorts. So it wasn't policemen as a whole she'd found so absolutely resistible; merely me.

All that on a couple of pints of beer.

'Yer the one, are yeh?'

The voice was unmistakably Scots, but a long time from home. I looked up at a fleshy, balding man in his sixties, dressed in a hound's-tooth sports jacket and grey trousers, his tie in that virulent clan tartan seriously awry. An ageing Buchanan for a certainty, hot from the Glasgow glens, and he didn't look pleased. He didn't look sober either; his complexion was more puce than pink and he was holding the back of a vacant chair for support.

'Sorry?'

'Leave my lad alone, yeh nasty man; that's alla got to say tae you. Ifya want t' talk murder, talk tae the bastard Todds. Talk about the planning permissions an' the backhanders too, if ye've got the guts.'

'If you want to talk, come and see me at the office, Mr Buchanan.'

'Stuff you!'

'C'mon, Ian.' George got up and tried to steer him away. 'Inspector Graham's right; this is no place to talk like that. If you've got a grouse, come and see him tomorrow.'

'Graham? He's got the name, but he's no Scot; just a mannie little Englishman. Todd-lover, like his boss. An' you're no better!'

He wrenched himself free of George's helping hand, and stumbled back to the bar amid a mutter of approval from his friends. They'd probably stirred him up in the first place; a stage-managed drunk.

George resumed his seat.

'Ian Buchanan,' he said unnecessarily, 'Alexander's dad; he's not usually like that.'

'Another professional Caledonian,' I murmured. 'My round, I think.'

Whatever charm the Jolly Fisherman had possessed, it had just lost it so far as I was concerned. But not a time to drink up and leave if I wanted to stay on the winning team.

Smile, chat, drink ale I didn't especially want and face 'em down. Smile some more, and give them the occasional hard-eyed stare. If anybody was going to feel uncomfortable, it wasn't going to be me.

Worth looking them over, too. A tight little bunch of five local businessmen. Part, at least, of the anti-Todd faction: interesting, in more ways than one. Helped bugger up one of the unlikelier murder possibilities, too: some pleasure in that. Unless, of course, Buchanan senior was a better actor than he appeared, a conspiracy between Todds and twits to frustrate police enquiries had just flushed itself down the pan.

When it came to cock-up versus conspiracy theory, however, I'd prefer to vote for a cock-up, any time. Which left a separate problem; I was no great fan of a five-handed coincidence, either. Five bloody-minded individuals on the trot? Not credible. Five spontaneous

Hacker-haters? Tempting, but unlikely, and probably unfair.

Supposing, just supposing, there was no shared self-interest: why then would the suspects have refused to give blood? Or, looking at it another way, what made Matthew Baring different, apart from the profession of his dad? I addressed my pint; not that I was going to find the secret of lateral thinking at the bottom of a glass.

Silly really, but George and Malc were just as determined to sit it out. Another pint, and George resurrected the tale of an ancient police feud. Another, and Malc treated us to the legend of the sergeant, the whore and the orange plastic beacons: a good laugh twenty-odd years ago; today the sergeant would be well in line for the sack.

The noise and laughter at the bar redoubled. Five fat bottoms on five bar stools. They'd no intention of moving, either. It was getting on for closing time; nothing else for it, another one apiece, and we could all go home. Call it a draw.

I went over to the bar once again, glasses in hand. Close enough to our laughing boys to show 'em, far enough away not to provoke. A young brunette on a bar stool smiled at me; smart, plumpish, short-haired. Perhaps my luck had changed?

'Hello, Inspector Graham.' She was vaguely familiar. 'This is me husband, Roger.' A beefy, good-natured face surmounted by a shock of blond hair grinned at me. Luck had deserted this particular pub.

'Hello,' he said. Not the voluble type.

'You know me,' smiled the girl. 'Garage reception: *Links Hotel*. Busgirl's holiday tonight.'

Yes, I remembered; Sandra Lawrence, née something or other. Alice Draper's friend.

'Hello,' I said, 'nice to see a friendly face.'

'Oh, them.' She sniffed, with a chuck of the chin towards the group at the end of the bar. 'Load of old women; talk through their b-t-m's most of the time!'

'You and Roger,' I said expansively. 'Have a drink.'

'Love one, ta; wouldn't we, Roger? Gin and orange and a pint of best for him.'

I bought the round; Roger was still grinning. It was obvious who did the communicating in that household. And who chose the sides.

She lowered her voice. 'That old man's really sore,' she said, meaning Buchanan. 'Moaning on to his pals about you having a few words with his precious boy. Says Alice were a tart and all. Did decent people a favour when she got the chop.'

'Not the general opinion,' I said softly, including muscle-bound Roger in the conversation. 'Fun-loving is the term, but not a lot of harm.'

'That's right. Daft, but you couldn't help liking her. Y'know that watch you've been on about, well—'

'Hey, Rodge! Watch it, lad, or she'll be well away there, with the big Dick!'

One of the over-upholstered mob was weaving a bit on his stool, red-faced and leering. Roger, slow on the uptake, began to turn.

'You hear me, Rodge? Strange Dicks should leave young girls alone!'

The voice, louder this time; vulgar, high-octave stuff, split across the rest of the noise in the room; its owner making his second bid for fame. There was a supportive whoop from the claque.

Roger levered himself off his stool: message received and understood. A big lad; not the sort you'd want to upset as a rule, especially if you were conceding a beer belly and a good fifteen years to the fray like the potential coronary overflowing his stool; a man who had to be depending on his mates.

Fortunately, Roger was slow. I was past him before he'd cleared his seat. If a gang of ageing kids wanted to play, it was more than OK by me.

'All right! That's enough; no dirty talk in here!' The landlord, pale, shirt-sleeved and nervous, tried to intervene. Not on my side especially, but thinking about his chances at the February Brewster Sessions. Thou shalt not upset the filth: not if you want to remain a landlord, that is.

'We don't need strangers telling . . .'

Big Mouth was on the air again. Fat and fortyish, in a zip-up jacket; pushing his luck too far.

'Time to leave, gents.' I moved directly in front of Buchanan. 'Take your megaphone home!'

'Can't talk t' me like that – what right have you tae—'

'Let's put it this way; friendly advice. Home, or I can take him in for insulting behaviour: breach of the peace. The lady's husband's in a knuckle-sandwich mood!' George and Malcolm were on their way; Roger loomed at my back.

Two of them were already sliding off their stools; drinking up, not the heroic type. Uneasy, too; the lower-middle-class embarrassment factor was climbing through the roof. Not done. A couple of shopkeepers, an estate agent; small hoteliers in a rumble with the police!

'Hey, Dick! Well, y'are a Dick, arn'cha? All ah said was . . .'

But he didn't finish. A tiny snarling object insinuated itself between legs that were suddenly anxious to provide plenty of room and set itself before the bar. A few pints, a bag of crisps and a punch-up to round things off: what more could a moss trooping border bandit want?

Definitely Stalin; no trace of mischievous little Joe. Eighteen pounds of fury, and you'd better believe it, pal. Fur bristling at the shoulders, lips peeled back to display a perfect set, and noises reminiscent of a faulty circular saw: he was taking nothing from nobody, tonight.

'Christ!' The landlord was impressed.

'Come on.' Somebody hauled the comedian off his stool, and the group started their strategic withdrawal, followed every inch of the way by a pair of beady black eyes and the sound of a steady, whining scream.

'Dangerous dog; ah'll report it. See if I don't.' Buchanan was getting the last word at the door.

'Rubbish!' Casually, I picked Stalin up. He was trembling, almost rigid; every muscle quivering with rage. A bomb waiting to go off. I kept a firm hold, stroking him until he began to subside and that vicious racket died away.

'Wouldn't hurt a soul. A bit of an actor; just doesn't like drunks!'

I tried to smile convincingly at the silent bar-flies, at the landlord, at Roger and Sandra Lawrence. It was witness time: an alibi for one. Loyally, George and Malc nodded in support of my terrorist, in confirmation of the boss. Liar, bold liar that I am.

19

They were queuing up the next morning; Teddy, George, Paula and Andy Spriggs, set out in rank, not alphabetical order. Flattering, to be in such great demand.

George was doing his ironic grin and Andy had the joyous expression of a man on the short end of a hillbilly feud. It looked like a departmental huff, so I decided to leave that one until last. The Superintendent's note was of the come-up-and-see-me-some-time variety, so it was ladies first.

Paula, short-skirted in a turquoise suit, looked more than decorative, as usual. She sat down opposite my desk and crossed her legs, tilting the office chair back on its pillar to display a good six inches of thigh. She could have been trying to push out a touch of compensation for the bad news.

'We went through the *Gazettes*, boss,' she said. 'Two full years: not a smell. No MacMillan; no Selous Scouts.'

'The whole of '80, and '81; are you sure?'

'Yep; and you can meet the new expert on Rhodesia, Rhodesia-Zimbabwe and Zimbabwe, in every boring detail.'

'How come?'

She shrugged and gave me a wry smile. 'Serves me

right for being too clever,' she said. 'I rang an old Chief Inspector at Headquarters; been holding up other people's promotion for years. He went out with a contingent of British police to see fair play at the Rhodesian independence elections. Highlight of his career, and they gave him a medal too.'

'Fascinating.' I hadn't really meant that; it just slipped out.

'That's what I thought, after the first twenty minutes of getting my ear bent.' She gave me a look to curdle milk. Hours of searching through old records; chewing the fat with a guy that could have bored for Britain: irony was something she could do without. Probably felt entitled to a word of thanks from the boss.

'Sorry – you were saying?'

'Nothing much, really. He told me the whole story – the negotiations; then Rhodesia-Zimbabwe for a bit in 1979; elections in '80, et cetera, and the marvellous time he'd had. Now there's a man who'd never been further than Blackpool before!'

'In other words you checked the *Police Gazettes* for '79, as well?'

'Yes: we did the lot. Then we swapped over and cross-checked each other. Nothing.'

'It must be later,' I muttered. 'I could have sworn . . .'

'Probably a bit later,' she said soothingly. 'Scotland Yard haven't found it either, so the notice must have been cancelled. Not to worry, though.'

'Is this a bad news/good news story?' Suddenly I was suspicious; she could flash as much leg as she liked, I refused to be impressed. She'd been leading me up the garden path.

'Sort of medium news. Good news to come; I hope.'

'Go on,' I said with mock severity. 'You've succeeded in winding me up. This had better be good.'

172

'I spoke to their Fraud Squad Index: they said it was bloody typical of provincial forces, not checking with them straight away.'

She saw the look on my face and continued hastily, 'Anyhow; I fed 'em everything we knew – what I'd learned about the Rhodesian Army, the Selous Scouts, the Light Infantry, even the British South Africa Police – that's what they called it, way back when. Result: eleven possible names. Conmen who've told fairy stories about Rhodesia, South Africa, or being mercenaries. Stuff like that.'

'Eleven of 'em,' I said ungratefully. 'Nothing succeeds like a popular lie.'

Paula looked wise. 'Adds a bit of convincing colour to an otherwise boring existence. Lying little scruffs who can pretend they're financiers and ex-officers and things.'

'When do we get the stuff?'

'They'll fax the descriptive forms, photos and convictions as soon as they can. Today, all being well. Some of it's a bit ancient, though. A couple haven't been heard of for years.'

'And the others?'

'There's three or four still active; two currently wanted; one in Cheshire, one by the West Mids. Similar sort of thing; running up credit in some crummy business and clearing off.'

'How do we stand, otherwise?'

Paula smirked. 'Nice little list of creditors,' she said, 'around ninety thou' and rising, but very little overdue. More deliveries on the way – beginning of December, and he's still taking lorryloads of stuff.'

'Unlikely to sell it by Christmas?'

'Not legitimately: not round here. And there's his driving licence, boss.'

'Go on.'

'Checked him with DVLC: he applied for a provisional in May, took his test and got a full licence here in July. Gives his date of birth as 23 June 1939. A businessman of that age without a driver's licence? Rubbish!'

'He's lived abroad.'

'He got himself a false identity, more like. I'm trying to trace his national insurance and credit cards now; but it's a long job.'

'How's the warehouse?'

'Still pretty full; but not for long. Let's arrest him now, boss, before he gets rid of the lot.'

I had a swift, not entirely pleasurable vision of Teddy Baring's face. An innocent ex-major banged up in the bogey hole; the excitement, the interviews, the disciplinary hearings . . .

'What do you want to arrest him for, exactly?'

'Fraudulent trading, obtaining goods by deception – theft?'

She shone with enthusiasm; goodies in charge, baddies about to bite the dust. Have the gunfight, roll the credits, and ride away into some triumphant Western sunset leaving MacMillan in the jug. In Eddathorpe, in December, on a depressing Friday morning at about twenty past nine.

I began to feel middle-aged; the old fuddy-duddy who spoiled other people's fun. Then I pulled myself up short: no need to order the wheelchair yet, she was only five or six years younger than me. And it was my job to stop us all becoming instantly unemployed.

'I'd like a bit more evidence first,' I said sadly.

'He'll flog the lot and go. Probably sold some below cost already. A few lorries, gear off to the smoke, and us left holding the baby. We'll look like the Keystone Kops!'

'Evidence,' I said firmly. 'Identify him; show there's

no possibility of him paying up; find out who's pulling his strings, if we can; then lock him up.'

'He's not fronting this for somebody else; he *is* the boss, and we're going to lose him if we don't rip him in: now!'

Paula wasn't making this easy; she was using the same arguments I'd used on Teddy Baring the day before. I could hide behind him, of course . . . Superintendent Baring says . . . and I'd sound like little Sir Echo; a right prat.

It didn't improve my temper one bit, remembering how I'd felt about over-cautious Teddy. Now it was my turn to look feeble; the whingeing old woman. I thought I could read it on her face, and I managed to contain my resentment. Just.

'Think about it, Paula: he might be a bad businessman, he might have ordered too much stock, too late for the Christmas trade. He might be getting into debt, but none of it amounts to evidence of crime – yet.'

She took the legs off the menu and swung gracefully to her feet, ready to exit, determined to have the last word.

'We'll lose him, boss, if we aren't prepared to take a risk!'

She surged out, treating me to the rear view of a stiff, indignant back and the elegant turquoise suit. She looked considerably starchier, brighter than I felt, all circumstances considered. Still, look on the bright side: ninety thou' in unpaid bills looked a lot better than the twenty-seven K MacMillan had passed on to his solicitor in duff complaints. The military grocer, twisting a rope with his mouth; we'd hang him yet.

The latest outbreak of internecine warfare didn't help me much. Something else to chew over as I made my way to Teddy Baring's office. It had, as George pointed out, been nothing but a crossed wire, a slight communications problem; no harm done. Not, as Andy Spriggs thought, a deliberate attempt to wind him up. To induce hypothermia among members of the junior staff.

While I was speeding Angiewards on Thursday afternoon, George had captured one Anita Smith, alias Geraldine Donnally, and half a dozen other improbable names. A credit card specialist living in one room, down on her luck. The careless cow had flourished an elderly piece of stolen plastic in the wrong place – a grocer-cum-newsagent within a couple of hundred yards of her grotty DSS hotel.

Now she was admitting offences all over the shop: Luton, Ipswich, Great Yarmouth, Hunstanton, King's Lynn . . . quite the East Anglian odyssey, and always travelling north until she'd run out of steam in Eddathorpe. Thank you very much, m'dear, and clang! One up to George.

Unfortunately, Andy had been courting the lady as a snout – donating a few quid to her version of the black economy. He'd described in heart-rending detail how he and his fellow DC had left us enjoying ourselves in the pub while they'd gone off to do their public duty. In an Esplanade shelter of all places, sought out by a fierce east wind: impatient, beerless, freezing cold.

They'd waited ages for their informant . . . And waited . . . And all the time, thanks to their uncommunicative sergeant, credit-card-toting Anita had been counting bricks downstairs in our centrally heated cells.

Not beyond redemption, I thought. Anita might like to show her goodwill towards the police and more particularly the Bench by playing the copper's nark. Get a remand in custody; go down and talk to her afterwards.

Sorry about the frostbite, Andy, old son!

*　　*　　*

Friday, a red-letter day after all. Teddy Baring was looking happy; well, moderately satisfied for once.

'How are you fixed for your burglar tonight?' he asked.

'I've got a briefing prepared for nine o'clock. I'm using everybody from Eddathorpe CID, plus Paula and two of her three Detective Constables. The Duty Inspector says he can spare a couple of uniformed men.'

'We can do better than that.' He looked positively pleased. 'Chief Inspector Paget has scraped the barrel for you, Bob. Stripped the morning shift, cut down on the afternoon. A sergeant and five PCs in plain clothes until two a.m. A dog van; maybe a bit of casual help from our neighbours. How does that sound?'

'Fine, sir, thanks.' He sounded as if he was giving me the Golden Hoard to play with. He probably was, so far as our thriving metropolis was concerned.

Christian names too; things were certainly looking up. I'd apparently been doing something right. I reviewed the highlights of my recent career. I was puzzled; no outstanding triumphs, so far.

We went through the details together, the usual routine. Numbers of staff, deployment, checking of late-night pedestrians, vehicle checks, searches, handling of suspects. A straightforward message: do it, do it thoroughly, but try not to upset the public. Do not exceed your powers.

I could imagine the reaction in some of the places I'd been. *Stupid old bugger, thirty years behind the times. Ought to get out and feel some collars! No way to catch thieves, pussyfooting around. Why doesn't he sod off and join the Band of Hope?*

All those big, bold city ways. To do him justice, I wondered how well they'd go down in a small seaside town. The one God probably created at five minutes to midnight on the Saturday night.

'Matthew will be home for Christmas.'

The words, so unexpected, so totally irrelevant to the matter in hand, brought me and my speculations up short.

'Sir?'

'Matthew; my son. Christmas leave.' He looked at me steadily; obviously a reaction was called for. He'd never said one word about his personal involvement with the Draper case until now. Just those oblique remarks about his objectivity, independence, and my right to a clear run when we first met.

He waited, and when the hoped-for reply didn't come he smiled his down-turned smile.

'I kept quiet', he said, 'because I was determined to let you make up your own mind. No prejudice, no bias. You started with a clean slate. Yes?'

'Yes, sir, I understand.' Well, sort of; suspending judgment on the motive for the time being.

'Well, now you've had a chance to settle in. What do you think?'

'I don't think I've got much to ask your son, for one thing. Not if the man who had intercourse with Alice also killed her.'

'That does seem probable,' he said dryly. He was still waiting.

'I haven't got very far,' I admitted finally, 'and I don't have any real idea who did it. Thought there was a bit of a pattern – five out of six refusing a blood test like that.'

'And what was your hypothesis?'

'Mud in the water; getting together, doing a favour for somebody – one of the Todds, perhaps. Even thought they might all be related at one stage. Pretty far-fetched.'

'And now?'

'Well, they'd be pretty diverse conspirators, wouldn't they? Baker doesn't seem to have an axe to grind, Richard and Victor aren't exactly bosom pals, and the Buchanans think the Todds're poison.'

'And Richards?'

'Haven't come across him yet,' I said, 'but there doesn't appear to be a connection. His dad's in business, certainly; but he's not part of the Todd faction. Sonny boy's just a local yob.'

'And that puts paid to your conspiracy, does it? No other connection?'

'Never liked conspiracy theories in the first place, sir. Not unless they're all Freemasons or something,' I added flippantly.

The cold grey eyes glinted for a moment. 'Something else you've heard, Mr Graham? You're right; I don't care for Masonry in the police.'

'No, sir.' Personally, I didn't care if they had chapters of Dancing Dervishes on every division, so long as they left me alone. In any case, what had happened to the first-name stuff?

'Of course,' he said sweetly, 'they're all Papists. Apart from young Richards; I don't suppose he professes any religion at all.'

'What?' I was stunned. Catholics and Huguenots were not on my agenda; not at this late stage. As for Papists, I hadn't thought of encountering the word at all this side of the Shankill Road.

'Forgive me, Mr Graham – it never occurred to me that you might be – er – Roman Catholic. No offence.'

'I'm not – Catholic, I mean. Surprised, that's all.'

'We all tend to use the words of our youth from time to time. I grew up with that one, I'm afraid. I was merely divorcing the Todd family from Freemasonry. Catholics, you know . . .' The precise, almost pedantic voice faded away and he looked at me with some embarrassment.

'Yes, sir. I know; Catholicism and Masonry don't

179

mix. Talking of divorce, surely Richard Todd can hardly—'

'He apparently preferred the registry office, both times.
Another bone of contention with his brother.'

'I see.' I absorbed that lesson too: do not be flippant
with Teddy. The man with the literal mind.

Another piece of useless information: the Todds, the
Buchanans and Baker all kicked with the left foot;
so, presumably, did George. And Teddy Baring was
a Calvinist or something. Maybe I could do a survey,
write a book – *Religious Observances on the East Coast.*
Make a change from not detecting crime.

'I hear', he said, his voice carefully neutral, 'that you
terrorised Buchanan senior last night. Set your dog on
him, so I'm told.'

'No, sir; nothing like that.'

'Ah . . .' He smiled thinly. 'Another disappointment. I
was rather looking forward to the story.' Was *that* why he
was in a good mood? Boot-a-Buchanan day? If he wanted
a story, a story he should have.

'Buchanan had too much to drink in the Jolly Fisherman,' I explained, 'a bit offensive. Then he encouraged
some of his middle-aged pals to have a go. One of 'em
went too far and insulted Sandra Lawrence – used to be
Sandra Carter, a friend of Alice Draper.'

'Yes, I remember; go on.'

'Well, Mrs Lawrence's husband, Roger, is a big lad.
A bit slow on the uptake, fortunately. By the time
he'd decided to go over and punch his lights out, I'd
managed to persuade Buchanan to take his pal out of
harm's way.'

'That, I assume, is the official version of events?'
His voice contained an open tinge of irony, but he was
definitely on our side.

'My terrier doesn't like noisy drunks,' I said simply.

'He growled at them a bit, quite spontaneously. He's not dangerous and they got a bit over-excited, that's all.'

'My informant admired the size and whiteness of Joe's teeth. Did he bite?'

'Certainly not.'

'Excellent. Mr Buchanan cannot expect me to invoke the police disciplinary code against a small dog.' He considered his words for a few moments, and added, 'A small, and probably playful dog?'

He was going a bit far: there'd been too many people present, all with a lively recollection of Joe at play, to push my luck.

'Couldn't really say, sir; but he enjoys a game.'

'Thank you, Bob. I appreciate you being so frank. You may leave Buchanan with me.' He sat back with an air of quiet satisfaction; another Eddathorpe game in progress. I'd been right about Teddy Baring, a man with a memory for insults. Keep your size nines off his corns.

I was pleased to have got my version home prior to the enemy attack. All the same, as I left the office I was chewing over the question of Eddathorpe and its anonymous flock of birds, each with its sharp little beak and its nasty half-truthful little song to sing.

Not tuneful thrushes, not even seaside gulls: a sky full of bloody great vultures, more like.

20

Hurry up and wait; it was one of those days. George and Andy reforged their alliance and went down to interview Anita Smith. Three days' police custody for further enquiries, said the Bench, and there she was expecting immunity from prosecution as Andy's favourite grass. She didn't get it, so she shut up like a clam and turned sour. Silly cow, but I think I've said something like that before.

That's the trouble with informants; they think you owe 'em the earth. *Let me out and I'll drop me mates in the mire*, on the one side, doesn't measure up against twenty fags and a look at the weekend telly, which is all we had to offer. We didn't want her to admit offences; she'd done that already. If she wanted to do an exposé of Eddathorpe's multi-million cesspit of organised crime, the going rate was twenty smokes and a kind word to the judge in due course.

Fair? Nobody ever told the CID they ought to be building a land fit for fraudsters, folks. Besides, time is a great healer: Andy was confident she'd come round to his point of view – some time in the next sixty-nine hours.

I spent another couple of hours with the Alice

Draper file, not that I learned anything very exciting. I couldn't decide who, whom perhaps, I liked the least; Charlie Pringle or his bloody-minded clients. Charlie was obnoxious, deeply unlovable, although George told me he'd got a pretty wife at home, totally devoted to the little creep. Four years of married bliss, according to George, whose wife had dragged him along to the wedding. Collecting some sort of expensive tableware, he grumbled, so the nuptials cost George a twenty-one-piece breakfast set; wholesale, of course.

A stupid conversation which brought me down with a bump. Weddings; marriage; Angie: I'd told her I'd be in touch in a couple of days. I felt like a big lunchtime drink. George came along for the ride.

As usual, it was the bar at the Links Hotel for us and Joe was a welcome guest. None of us recognised Keith Baker's rendition of '*See the Conquering Hero*', although Joe cocked his ears. So far as George and I were concerned it was just a tuneless whistle, but it's the thought that counts.

Once we got the ha-ha's over, and the compliment to terriers sorted out, Sandra Lawrence stretched herself across the bar. She was almost wearing this purple sweater with a deep V neck; definitely my day for glimpses of unattainable female flesh. Or maybe I was becoming some sort of ageing satyr: time to don the greasy raincoat, very soon.

'Sorry about last night: they upset Roger a bit. I'd like a quiet word,' she said.

'Buchanan's pals? Don't worry, they asked for it.'

George weaved his way between the empty tables and sat down. The bar was never popular, although I could hear bursts of laughter and the clink of glasses coming from the upwardly mobile next door. I bought Sandra her gin and tonic and we joined him, leaving Keith Baker to another session of unsatisfied curiosity. Unfortunate, in the circumstances, with bar staff costing all of three pounds twenty an hour.

'Move in, if y' like,' he muttered, disappointed. 'Don't mind me; start a cop shop in the corner over there.' Missed his vocation in Eddathorpe, had Keith. He'd have been happier doing the top society gossip column for the *News of the World*.

We settled around the table and I dealt out the drinks. George treated her to his big grin. I was reminded of one of his sayings: *Don't mean there's no fire in the chimney, just 'cos there's snow on me thatch!*

An obvious member of the George Caunt Appreciation Society, she gave him a tiny quiver of the shoulders and a sexy look.

'Ah,' he said, with exaggerated regret, 'if only I wasn't spoken for, love!'

'Excuses, always excuses.' She shook her short-cropped hair and treated us to another quiver. A better Eddathorpe game than usual, and they both seemed to be enjoying the fun.

Why not? Let them get on with it; ten minutes of aimless, harmless chat. Far better than her unfinished business of the previous night.

If there was one conversation I could do without, it was the one about unsolved murders and redundant Gucci watches. I was not looking forward to my inevitable visit to the Draper home: *Sorry, very sorry, but I haven't found anything worth a light*. I could see the elderly, downtrodden faces, taste their disappointment. Cowardly, but it was something to push aside.

'Not working for the boyfriend today?' asked George.

'Eric the Viking? Nah, job-share at the garage; eighteen

hours a week, and lucky to get it. Three evenings and the odd lunchtime here.'

'Eric the Viking,' I said idly. 'Why's that?'

''Cos he isn't. It's a joke.'

I looked blank.

She giggled. 'You know, a Viking – raping and looting and stuff. Eric couldn't impress our cat. He just sits there with his sweaty little face, lifting your skirt with his eyes.'

'I don't think I'll come to you for a reference.'

She gave me a slow, semi-comic appraisal. 'Oh, dunno about that,' she said, 'once I've sorted out my old mate George.'

'What will Roger say?'

'Oh yeah, Roger; I almost forgot. Better cancel our date, George. Could make you feel proper poorly, my Roger.'

George shook his head sadly. 'Never mind,' he sighed, 'but twenty years ago—'

'You could've taken me for a walk in me pram!' She leaned back in her chair to hoot, then a look of childish consternation came over her face. 'Oh God, me and my big mouth. It wasn't meant as a put-down, honest!'

'Tut,' said George severely, 'lying about your age, again. Bet I could've given you a push on your trike!'

We both gave him a dutiful yuk, yuk, and I glanced across at him with a trace of envy. It was nothing special; *The Wit and Wisdom of George Caunt* was unlikely to hit the bestseller list, but at least he could trot out the lines. My perfectly formed ripostes usually surfaced about ten minutes after the event.

Somewhere behind me there was a series of irritated clatters and bangs. She half turned in her chair and gave me a cynical grin. 'Keith's decided to chat with us in Morse code. Anyway, best get on: I was going to tell you about Alice's watch. The one you've been enquiring about.'

'Her mum and dad spoke to me,' I said, 'but I think it's sorted now.'

'You've found out where she sold it?'

'What?'

'I've been putting two and two together. That big detective – Malcolm, is it? Well, he came to see me, ages ago. I told him what I knew about it, which wasn't much. I mean, she used to flash it around something rotten. She'd always wanted one.'

'Yes,' I said, 'I know; and when she found Dicky Todd had landed her with a fake, she threw it at him. But that must have been two or three months before she walked out of her job.'

'Not that watch; she told Toddy his fortune over that, I can tell you. Called it a crappy load of tin when she found out. The real watch.'

'What real watch?' I began to experience what they call a conflict of emotions: a touch of elation mixed with a score of a hundred on the cock-up meter somewhere in the pit of my stomach. Court martial stuff; someone had blundered.

'Hell's bells.' George was already doing his calculations. If it came to bungee jumping without the elastic rope, who was going to win – Hacker or poor, incompetent Malc? Hacker had botched the whole enquiry, Malc had failed to push the question over the watch; no comparison, but, as I might have pointed out before, rank has its privileges. Good old RHIP!

'You never told the big detective there were two watches.'

'He never asked.' Her eyes became huge, innocent circles. 'You didn't know there were two? Toddy's and

187

the other? Well now, you have been getting your knickers in a twist!'

'All right.' George made an effort. 'You can have my job; Detective Sergeant, OK?'

For once I was in there with him, dropping the smart remark.

'With guaranteed promotion', I said, 'to Detective Superintendent within a couple of weeks.'

'Please God,' said George.

'No thanks; I'll settle for another gin and ton. Keeps Fatso sweet when the money rolls into his till.'

I got the round, bought Keith a big one and told him how much we appreciated the loan of his staff. Told him how vital it was all turning out to be. Deadly secret, though: sure he would understand.

'OK,' said Sandra, putting back half the contents of the glass in one go, 'she'd always wanted one of those dinky little watches with the coloured discs, right? And she was over the moon with the one left over from Toddy's Christmas cracker, until she found out. Made her look silly, she said.'

'How did she find out?'

'Looked at the name on the dial with a magnifying glass; crikey, she was mad! That was the end of Richard Todd. Fancy a man with money pulling a trick like that!'

'And then?'

'Well, she had this other string to her bow, didn't she? Another boyfriend on the side. He gave it to her. She was so pleased, I bet she wore it in bed – especially in bed, if you see what I mean.'

'With her track record,' muttered George, 'we see exactly what you mean. Does this boyfriend have a name?'

'Sorry, no. She'd never let on, if they were married men. Except Toddy; he couldn't have cared less.'

'And this other boyfriend; he was definitely married?'

'I should think so, otherwise she'd have said.'

'And then?'

'And then, nothing. She had the watch a few weeks, and it disappeared. I'm as daft as a brush, I never put two and two together. Mind you, I was never sure she was in the pudding club, was I?'

'Best friends, and she never told you?' I asked sceptically.

'Little oyster was Alice at times. But I can guess why she had to sell it.'

I was ahead of her for once. 'So now you think she sold the watch to pay for the abortion.'

'That's right.'

'Any idea where?'

'No; I can't be sure about the reason, anyway. Just putting two and two together, right?'

I remembered George's briefing notes; ambiguous. *Evidence of abortion not to be released to the press.* So the pregnancy itself hadn't become common knowledge. Hence the belated putting together of two and two. And Alice, Miss Round Heels 1989; but close-mouthed when it suited her. Married men; abortions; being landed with a bogus trinket: pride?

'Who told you about the pregnancy, Sandra?'

'One of Fatso's little secrets; he only let on the other day, after you came in and stirred him up.' She turned to George. 'That Superintendent you don't like had Keith down for Daddy at one time.'

Of course, everybody gossiped about everything in this town. George and his idle chat across the bar: *my Detective Superintendent is a prat.* True enough, but it was his neck on the line.

'Could Keith have been . . . Daddy?'

She spluttered into her drink. 'No chance; Fatso was a

charity bonk ages before. He talked himself into trouble, boasting afterwards. Couldn't keep his mouth shut, the silly old sod.'

'Not the Gucci type?'

'Tight as a gnat's whatsit, more like.'

'So, what exactly did you say to the detective?'

She shrugged. 'Dunno, really. Think I might have confused him, come to think.'

'Which watch were *you* talking about?'

'Both, really; although he was harping on Toddy a bit.'

'And you told him about the row in July?'

'He asked me about the last time I saw her wearing the Gucci, not the fake.'

'Yes?'

'So I told him – September.'

George groaned.

She smiled at him pityingly and finished her drink. Sandra the dentist's daughter, the child of one of Alice's early employers, according to George's notes. Hence the friendship with our murder victim.

Not what you'd expect from the offspring of a suburban professional type; then again, she'd got this taste for gin and a muscular version of the Speaking Clock for spouse. Intellectual giants, the both of them; a perfect match.

Sandra and Alice, both pretty, vulgar; another two of a kind. Sandra would have to be pushing it, though, to compete with Eddathorpe's Alice; the small-town sexual successor to Catherine the Great.

'Sandra,' I said with difficulty, 'you've been a great help. If she did sell her watch, now, maybe she sold the emerald ring. Remember that?'

'Yeah, but she didn't wear it often. Trophy from Alex Buchanan, but I don't think she was too proud of that.'

'When did you last see her with it?'

'Can't really say. Alex was serious, you know, and Alice – well Alice just couldn't stop herself, somehow. That's it.' She stood up. 'Better get back to the chain gang. Otherwise he'll have a fit.'

'Just one thing, love: who's your candidate?'

The muscles of her face went rigid, and her mouth spat hate. 'I don't know,' she said, 'I really don't know; but some really mean bastard. Some dirty pig who welshed on her, let her scrape up the money for the abortion. Maybe he killed her because she was going to tell!'

She leaned against the table for a few seconds, white-knuckled, breathing hard, then, hips swinging, she tapped her way decisively in the direction of the avid face at the bar. Keith Baker was awaiting her arrival with open ears. Witness chats with low-grade suspect: oh well.

George stared after her admiringly. 'A goer; definitely a goer, there. But two and two make twenty-two, with that little lass.'

'Detective Constable Malcolm Cartwright,' I said coldly, changing the subject, staring hard. 'Let's talk about people who leave jobs half done. Decide what we ought to do about our supersleuth, instead.'

He winced.

21

———➤———

Dark, almost pitch dark. Like whitewash, darkness covers a multitude of sins. We stood, uncomfortably close, down an alley, with our eyes on the gardens of the crumbling tunnel-back houses between Cromwell Avenue and Albemarle Road and our thoughts, mutually disparaging, on each other.

It was true enough; Malc had done what he'd been told. He'd obeyed his instructions to the letter, neither more nor less. Gucci watches were on the agenda early in 1990, so he'd gone along to dizzy Sandra Carter and asked a couple of questions about a stupid Gucci watch, and she'd credited him with a knowledge he didn't possess.

Watch, singular, elicited a straightforward reply; no fancy explanations from Sandra, a girl with a literal mind. No significant insights, either, on the part of stolid, unimaginative Malc. Todd questions had elicited Todd replies; Gucci questions must refer to the genuine article. Simple, really.

Last seen Septemberish, Officer, 1989. A spot of bosom-thrusting in the general direction of the big, strong policeman: then it was bye-bye, do call again some time! And that was it. Absolutely nobody, from captain to cabin boy, had picked it up, the discrepancy between Tricky Dicky's story and the gospel according to our Sandra. And computers, as I may have mentioned in passing, store what you tell 'em; they do not think.

Right now, Big Malc was so full of resentment I could practically hear him tick. Poor feller: bollocked for a bit of a slip-up he'd made all those years ago. Not as if it'd been important at the time. There he'd been, doing some footling enquiry, landed with some inconsequential crap, as usual. Just his luck. So he'd done the minimum, got the minimum in reply, and gone on his way rejoicing. Until now. Now he was standing at the entrance to a dark alley, in company with a bloody-minded Detective Inspector, getting frozen, feeling sore, hating Robert Graham's guts.

He'd absolutely no idea how carefully, and with what weasel-words, I'd padded the information I'd put into the computer. Buckets of whitewash: let Hacker make of it what he would.

The generous DI? Not exactly, no. Bloody-minded was probably closer to the mark. I wasn't going to solve the Malcolm Cartwright problem by getting him posted: shoving him off on the first stage of a journey round the force. And I wasn't about to institute disciplinary proceedings against the silly sod, pulling Hacker's chestnuts out of the fire.

Besides, I'd seen it all before. The problems, the misfits bouncing from one posting to the next until they retired. Or, very occasionally, until some genius dumped on the rest of us from a very great height by getting an unsuspecting Chief to promote the problem out of his division.

Well, the square wheel had served in so many places, had acquired so much experience of policing by that time, he deserved promotion, didn't he?

I had this theory, tried and tested on the battlefield,

if you like. About the tendency to promote coppers one step above their level of competence. That probably left Malc a civilian. Fair enough: but where was it going to leave me?

Perfection: it started to rain. My personal radio hissed smugly, enjoying the joke. All these idiots on the street getting wet, while the criminals sat at home watching late-night cops and robbers on the box. No fights, no incidents, no name-checks. Our part of Eddathorpe was dead.

It's an old cliché, but it's true. Search as much as you like; you can never find one when you want one. Villains, I mean. Beside me, curly and hairy, my personal excuse for wandering the streets so late at night stared without enthusiasm at the rain.

Across the back gardens, half seen, criss-crossed with deadly, throat-high washing lines, a bedroom light went on; Malcolm stirred. He needn't have bothered, she was about a million years old, and she drew the curtains carefully, anyway. It was so quiet you could hear the scrape of brass curtain-rings against wire.

'There was this tottie,' muttered Malcolm, staring at the light, 'years ago.' An olive branch was being offered.

'Yeah?'

'Really fit; blonde, big knockers, the lot. She used to perform downstairs, in the front room of this little terraced house. Fanlight over the door.'

Oh God, I thought, a uniformed Peeping Tom: a shiking copper tale.

'Anyway,' said Malc, 'we had this old-time bobby, Walter Rutt. Six foot five or six and as thin as a lath. He could see over the top of the door.'

'I can imagine,' I said, a trifle sourly.

'No, boss, that's not the point.' Malc was in charge. 'Practical-joking bastard, was Walt.'

'Oh.'

'He was passing one night, just as this young probationary constable came round the corner on his bike, so he waved the lad over to take a look. She was giving this navvy a real good time.'

'Uh-huh.'

'Well, the lad was a bit of a short-arse, see? Couldn't see over the fanlight. So Walt got him to prop his bicycle up against the door and stand on the pedals to take a look at what was going on.' He choked with suppressed emotion. 'As soon as the youngster stood up with his weight on the pedals, Walter whipped open the door and ran away.' He paused impressively for it to sink in. 'Big bastard, that navvy.'

'Cross?' I offered.

'Just a bit!'

We spluttered and heaved. Crude, uncaring, sordid buggers, cops. This left-wing critic has been telling the public about it for ages: damaged personalities to a man.

The distant click of a gate reduced us to silence: somebody was moving through the walled footpaths between the gardens and alleys linking us with any one of half a dozen entries on to Albemarle Road. The whole district was a rabbit-warren of arched entries, footpaths behind houses, greenhouses, sheds, outside lavatories and jealously maintained boundaries between a few square yards of black, exhausted earth. A breaker's paradise: a choice of targets and plenty of places to hide.

I could feel Joe quivering beside me. So far as he was concerned it was just a late-night game, but if we wanted to play hunt the idiot it was all right with him. The top half of a human figure broke the symmetry of the boundary wall and Malc grunted in an anticipatory sort of way.

'Ebenezer Cartwright,' moaned a hollow, doom-laden

voice, 'I am the ghost of Christmas past! Oh Christ! Sorry, boss.'

'Bugger up my observations and you will be, Andy,' I promised. 'Where have you been?'

'Having a bit of a scout round,' he said apologetically. 'It's the original urban jungle around here. Lucky to spot anybody in this.'

'OK,' I said, 'but keep together now; you're supposed to be a team.'

I slid down the alley and into Cromwell Street, Joe at my heels. It was well after midnight and, apart from the occasional flicker of a television set behind drawn curtains or the odd first-storey light, there were few signs of life. One call on the radio in twenty minutes: name-check. A couple of teenagers making their way home.

I visited the static observation points, cracked a couple of jokes in the fug of the area cars, exchanged banter with the lurking dog van, whose driver suggested that Joe should be fitted with a string, a platform and a set of wheels. I stood listening in the shadows while a middle-aged drunk pleaded with an obdurate female to stop pissing about, unlock the door and let him in. They kept their voices down, but she had a very nasty tongue, that woman.

George and a uniform PC had seized a temporary command post. Henderson's Bakery, the back door left open all night and mashing tackle thoughtfully displayed for the convenience of beat-men on one floury bench. An old-fashioned tea spot. I'd almost forgotten them, the night and very-early-morning people who look after dripping, lonely cops.

The teams began to drift in for a snack and a warm; it was easier than going back to the factory for a brew. An air – not depression, exactly, but an attitude of *here we go again* – began to spread among the troops. Joe went around begging bits of ham sandwich, and defaming the absent baker by pretending to hunt for mice in corners.

By two o'clock everybody had either taken their turn and prised themselves back out on to the street, or were busy unfreezing their fingers and pouring tea. The six–two uniformed shift vanished and one of the area cars deserted us; a brick through a shop window half a mile away. Boring; heigh-ho!

I was reminded of the preface to my ancient edition of *Moriarty's Police Law*, the training school Bible, in which some long-dead chief constable suggested that the perfect policeman ought to lack imagination. He extolled the virtues of the stolid plodder, grinding round, shaking hands with door-knobs, doing his job. No flights of fancy, nothing to distract him, no bright ideas. I knew exactly what he meant: the trouble is, too many of his ideal bobbies have become senior officers over the years – never Chief Constables, of course.

Not exactly glorious, but at twenty past three we scored. The static points were no longer exactly static; the remnants of my teams were moving around a bit, occasionally gossiping, huddling into groups. It nearly always happens: a touch of the sod-it factor, once life turns dull. Paula, George and I had a bit of a problem, chivvying the reluctant, keeping a grip. Not that we were perfect plods ourselves.

We'd gathered outside a factory, under a covered loading dock at the bottom of Albemarle Road: a conference, we called it. A bit of a disgruntled gas. George was all for winding it down by this time; send one of our CID teams and one of Paula's off duty, leaving a token force. Somebody had to be at work at 9 a.m. today.

Paula was giving us her full and frank opinion of the Met. They hadn't faxed the descriptive forms of the MacMillan suspects.

'Poet's day, Friday,' she moaned, 'especially in the Met. They hold boozy parties on Friday afternoons; then they clear off home and leave us in the lurch.'

'Poet's day?'

'Poddle off early, today's Friday – and that's the ladylike version!' She said.

We swapped disparaging, how-do-they-get-away-with-it sagas of the Metropolitan CID: the sight of plastic carrier bags, the deafening clank of bottles in police station foyers on Friday afternoons. How they gave the impression of effortless superiority: thought the colonies began about a mile above the North Circular Road. Myth, legend, rank green-eyed jealousy: it did us no end of good.

'Seventeen twenty-four to DC Cartwright.' The personal radio burst into life: one of the uniform teams.

'Cartwright: pass your message.'

'Movement in the gardens; coming your way.'

'Received.'

Silence for two or three minutes while the supervisors, itching for glory, sorted themselves out.

'Spotted 'im: doing a ground-floor window, rear of Cromwell Street, the bastard! Moving in.' Strict attention to radio procedures – my eye.

It was the dog man who started the rot; chirping up for a location, eager – too eager – to let Fido loose. To be fair, most people obeyed their instructions; they covered the exits, the alleys leading into the streets, but they all wanted to babble, to have a share.

'Bloody well shut up!!' isn't accepted radio procedure either, but it works.

George made for Cromwell Street, while Paula and I shot on to a walled footpath leading into the maze. Joe bounced along beside me, full of the joys of spring.

'He's away! He's running – watch it, Albemarle!' Andy's breathless voice.

Somewhere up ahead the darkness solidified into a slight, rapidly moving figure. Detective Inspector makes capture: he was coming our way. Then, almost at the last moment, this huge, wolf-like shadow took the lateral wall halfway between us and our fugitive and cut him off. With a yell of terror, the suspect turned and started to run back, the Alsatian hot on his trail. Joe, grasping the rules of this new and exciting diversion, launched himself, yapping madly, in pursuit. I just knew it. Tears before bedtime: not an official dog.

It was chaos; the burglar bawled as he ran, cops cursed and stumbled through cabbage patches and entangled themselves in underslips and knickers hanging from carefully positioned anti-police washing lines. Lights flashed in houses; voices were raised, but not in prayer, from end to end of the street.

An eternity passed in doubt; I lost all vestiges of control. We began to run. My only consolation was a glimpse of that leaping, dedicated wolf. Then, thankfully, I heard a crunch, a snarl, a groan; all the sounds of canine success.

I had no chance to gloat, or recover my breath. In the act of turning to Paula for a spot of mutual congratulation, I was stopped dead in my tracks. The whole neighbourhood reverberated with an unearthly scream compounded of agony and rage.

The cursing, the complaints, the demands for explanations suffered instantaneous death. Verbal power cut: a horrified silence fell. Sordid visions of police brutality and South American death squads invaded countless neighbourhood minds. The Police Complaints Authority would soon be drooling over this.

But our critics were wrong: Stalin, over-excited by the

chase, deprived of his chosen victim and consumed with jealous rage, had nipped underneath for a mouthful of wedding tackle, the hitherto exclusive property of an unwary constabulary mutt.

22

—— ▬ ——

'It's easy!' Andy Spriggs was having a go at Roy Lamb, the junior DC. 'All you do is catch your thief, take him out in the CID car, and every time you pass a burgled house you slam your foot on the brake.'

'So?' Roy wasn't getting the joke.

'He jerks forward, Dumbo. He nods: then you chalk up another detected crime.'

The sheer immorality of the suggestion had its appeal. It sounded better than the abolition of the right to silence. Perhaps some right-winger ought to get it included in the Queen's Speech next year.

'Maybe', said George slyly, 'you could do it with murder suspects, boss.'

'The great British public', I said coldly, 'would object.'

'How come?'

'They wouldn't like bodies being stacked like dustbins at the side of the road. Just so you could drive past, giving your villain an airing.'

'I suppose.' He sounded unconvinced. 'So what are you going to do with Ian Richards?'

Ian Richards, the last of the Mohicans. Game, set and match. I'd met all Hacker's suspects now.

Ian Richards, twenty-six years, unemployed, professional

layabout and total waste of space. Admits fifty-nine burglaries (dwelling house) out of seventy-four on our books in the district around the old railway station.

Bedsit searched, fourteen items of identifiable property recovered. Lots of ducking and weaving as to where he sold the rest.

No solicitor; hints of deals with the fuzz. He was in the slammer, we were sipping tea: what deals? What could he possibly have to make it remotely worth our while?

Personally, I was marginally more interested in the fate of our injured canine colleague, duffed up by my miniature Lakeland thug prior to his rapid departure from the scene of the crime. An excellent runner as well as a sneaky fighter, Stalin.

Not that I was crying after Alsatians, much. I'd been forced to spend a considerable part of my morning saying sorry over the telephone to an affronted dog-handler and his aggrieved Headquarters boss. I was fed up with the sheer volume of toad-swallowing I'd done. They expect you to make no fuss at all when one of their German Shepherds gets enthusiastic and takes a lump out of some unsuspecting cop. Three hours' sleep hadn't exactly set me up for the day, either; stuff that for a comic song.

Besides, I'd lost my dog. He was out there somewhere, wandering the streets. And I was in no position to ask any favours, or launch what I really wanted – a massive missing-terrier search. One or two uniforms – the anarchists – had thought it was a hoot; promised to keep an eye open for an errant Lakeland dog. For the moment, it was the best I could do. Along the Superintendent's corridor, a faintly ominous silence reigned.

And now, along with a couple of drunks and a half-partner in a domestic dispute who didn't count, we had two genuine criminals in the cells. Both with ambitions to grass somebody up, providing the price was right. Such unoriginal minds.

'OK.' I stretched. 'Back to work. You've got Richards to cough fifty-nine breaks; let's see who else he wants to drop in the mire.'

'What about Anita Smith?' Andy closed his pocket book with a snap, and looked interested.

'All right, d'you and Malc want to give her another whirl, while George and I tell our Ian the facts of life?'

Number-one interview room is long, high-ceilinged and narrow, with wired frosted-glass windows through which you can see the shadows of the official iron railings at the front of the nick and an occasional blur of pedestrians passing freely on the street outside. Dispiriting, no doubt; evokes a healthy nostalgia among interviewees for the presently unattainable, the great outdoors. It contains one table, four chairs, the cabinet for our tape machine and a rust-streaked, cream-coloured radiator they could usefully employ in hell.

I wrenched at the cords and pulled open the tiny transom window to cool things down, December or not. Ian Richards followed the movement with his eyes. Too, too small and way beyond his reach. I was feeling tired, a bit worried, slightly down, with a touch of the nasty bastards all the way through.

We sat down, George in a tactical position in the rear. Ostensibly, he controlled the tapes, but the advantage was there. Sat behind the target, the very fact of his presence made Richards uneasy; the unknown quantity, seen only out of the corners of his eyes.

Two simultaneous tapes; check, set, switch on. Personal identities; caution; roll.

'Now, Ian; the investigating officers tell me you want to tell us more?'

'About what?' Broad local accent; boxing clever. The

hint of a whine. My first shadowy impression was correct, a slight figure; thin face. A starveling, almost: shell-suit, purple and black. Never would have thought he was a prosperous shopkeeper's son.

'Don't know, old lad: you tell me. More burglaries, perhaps?'

'I've told 'em all I know.'

'The ones you remember, or the ones you've done?'

'Both.'

'I doubt it, Ian,' George chipped in. 'Still, there's plenty of time.' He didn't feel generous either; you need your sleep when you're getting on. Richards, following the rules, was the only one of us who'd had a full eight hours.

So we skirmished for a bit. Saturday-afternoon sport; better than watching soccer on the box. Nothing too strenuous, just verbal bat and ball. Keeping the words moving, chatting away, even giving him the chance to offer a gem of wit. The confidence to make a smart remark. Then squash! *Remember, you're the one who's got the problems, pal*.

The art of trivial chat. One problem with taped interviews; the lawyers have learned our technique. It's nothing like the intimidating upper-middle-class bray they adopt in court – fake or not. The *I am a barrister* stuff.

Time was, they underestimated the fuzz. Put our successes down to a swift bounce round the cells, and some prisoners were only too happy to go along with the myth. Allowed them to keep their pride. Now the briefs have started to *listen*.

Not that I'm making too many claims for us: the knights-on-white-chargers guff. Just horses for courses: techniques for the times. Adapting to circumstances. Ever since the days of the Bow Street Runners and the time when Sir Robert Peel was verballing his own prisoners down in the cells.

'Come on, Ian. If you've got something to say, spit it out. Otherwise we're going home to bed.'

'Nothing gets you nothing, mister. What about bail?'

'Don't be silly.'

'Not opposing bail, Monday?'

'That depends on circumstances; not deals. I'm promising nothing.'

'What circumstances?'

'What the magistrates want. Sufficient sureties; reporting to the police, agreeing to a curfew. *Unlikelihood* of further offences, that sort of thing.'

'Clever bugger. All I'm asking for is a bit of help.'

'No deals. No threats of prejudice, no hopes of advantage, those are the rules, pal.'

'Switch the tape off.'

'You have to be joking.'

'Look, we both know the score. Admissions made, right? No promises, no threats, so it's legal. This is *information*. Give us a leg-up. Say I've been helpful, OK?'

Couldn't be better if I'd scripted it myself. I'd like to see some clever-clogs lawyer make something out of that.

'OK, so?'

'Eh?'

'You know: h-e-l-p, help.'

'Brenda Lawson; I sold her the gear.'

'The stolen goods?'

'You want jam on it, don'cha?'

'Yes.'

Jam today, and promises, promises of more tomorrow. Name, address and a list of property sorted out. House to search and an arrest for handling stolen goods.

And what about Alice Draper, then?

Too abrupt: his head jerked back as if he'd been slapped. Then he went white. He thought I was out to clear the books at his expense. One of the problems with a minor yob; he knows too many of his own kind, and they all go around telling each other tales about the wicked police; silly excuses for their own stupidity, mostly. Then they start believing in their own propaganda.

'You're trying to fit me up!'

And he stuck in the same groove, like a worn-out record whining and rasping, driving you mad. Alice and he had been innocent kids; she was dead and it was the worst thing to happen in his life. Ever since, he knew it; the coppers had marked him down. That Mr Hacker, the bastard, and now me . . .

I tried to establish a bit of confidence, digging patiently away in the slush and marshmallow of his mind. It was a long, unrewarding slog. Then, as quickly, as unreasonably as he'd turned hostile, he came across.

'Come on, Ian. Something to tell me, right? Information, that's what we said.'

'Well, y'know, don'cha; the abortion?'

'How do you know about that?'

'She told me, but I never let on. Never said to that bastard.'

'Superintendent Hacker?'

'Shithouse: wouldn't give him the time of day.'

'All right.'

'Thought he'd say it were mine if I said: pin it on me, the bastard.'

'Said what?'

'Alice . . .' The thin face twisted with an unexpected misery. 'She was all right. I gave her thirty-eight quid, it was all I'd got.'

There's a time to talk, and a time to keep it well

and truly shut. I flicked a glance at George, and we both waited.

'For the abortion. I gave her some dosh, but it wasn't mine, the baby I mean. We'd not – you know – for ages. But she was skint, and the bastard wouldn't come across.'

His favourite word; bastard Hacker, bastard – who?

'Ian' – very quietly – 'does this bastard have a name?'

Burglar, layabout, toe-rag, and suddenly he wept. Nothing to do with the unfeeling, oppressive CID. Alice, who'd played hunt the sausage with half the town, had left one grubby little criminal behind to shed real tears.

'She never said.'

He stared at me wet-cheeked, malevolent, daring me to sneer, his face a stark white mask. I could see it coming: one wrong word and I could win first prize. The Ian Richards belt in the mouth.

I stared straight back: no put-downs, but we weren't there to express our sympathies on behalf of the Queen. Do the job, walk away, do the next. Hearts on sleeves on duty not allowed.

Oddly enough, he appeared to be satisfied. He gave an infinitesimal shrug, then tonelessly, dragging out the words, he gave it his best shot.

'I've thought about it since, though. Thought about it a lot. Eric Goodwin, the garage creep; that's what I reckon.'

23

———•———

I got home about nine for a quiet brood. I hadn't felt much like a sociable drink, despite my promises of unlimited largess. Anyway, they were all tired: beer tomorrow, or on Monday, perhaps.

The wind was up and the whole house creaked and trembled, while the doors and window frames rattled like dry bones. A pre-war shack; not bad in summer, but not your upmarket seaside holiday home by any stretch. I built a fire, ate beans on toast and had a few of those harmful, solitary drinks. I was exhausted, but I'd no intention of going to sleep. I was stuck with the day's events, and uneasy, recurring thoughts of that damn dog.

Hacker and his prisoner had been in the Custody Sergeant's queue when I left the station an hour and a half before. Hacker with Goodwin, handcuffed, and an elderly DCI with a face like an open grave in tow. The Smiling Assassin, Silver's one and only mate, according to George.

I'd watched while Malcolm and Andy booked in our prisoner, Brenda Lawson. She was massive: a morose, middle-aged woman flowing out of a tight black winter coat, her ankles overlapping a pair of ridiculous high-heeled shoes. She had a lot to be morose about.

Ian Richards's handler of stolen property: Brenda the Lender, according to Anita Smith. One and the same. Receiver and loan shark; the possessor of a few bits of cheap stolen jewellery, a camcorder, a couple of pairs of binoculars and a small jade Buddha, for heaven's sake. Readily identifiable stuff.

Brenda in another guise; the kind lady who looked after the single mothers on Social Security, the merchant banker for OAPs. Eleven retirement pension books recovered and a fistful of Family Allowance and assorted DSS benefit books held as securities for her modestly priced loans. Ten per cent, apparently – per week.

And all found by usually clueless Malc when we searched the house: first he'd rattled it, then he'd unscrewed the panels of the bath to capture the evidence. Silly cow, she'd kept some sort of account book, too. Light reading for the boys, in due course. I should have been happy about that.

A silent moan, instead: insufferable Hacker. He'd come whistling over like a force-nine gale once Teddy had rung him at home. Joint decision to call him out, and I wondered if Teddy's motives were as murky as mine. Hard to tell. He didn't say much when I told him.

Just, 'Eric Goodwin, eh? Well. I suppose . . .' before he tilted back in his chair and scowled at the ceiling, looking as if he suspected it of planning to do him some personal injury.

Or perhaps he was inspired. Perhaps he knew his Hacker: the original knee-jerk-reaction copper, the man with one standard response in every set of circumstances – blue lights, sirens, and rip the bastards in! Superintendent Baring might just have been out to get Detective Superintendent Hacker's goat.

With a tiny whisper of a hypothesis that bordered on nasty wishful thinking, a totally daft *what if* at the back of my mind, I was hoping pretty much the same as Teddy, I suppose.

Risky, of course, spilling the beans like that. No alternative, so far as I could see. No legitimate way of keeping quiet about Eric, chasing the information ourselves; keeping it within the Eddathorpe family, so to speak. It was, however, courting a Hacker triumph if Eric Goodwin turned out to be our boy. Hacker was already busy with his zombie DCI, erecting a barbed-wire fence around any iota of credit.

Even so. I had a bit of a drifter in there somewhere, the merest smidgen of inspired unease. The sort of thing they ought to hammer out of you at the police training centre before they let you loose on the street. Imagination, inspiration; tea-leaves; the curse of the detecting class.

Mind you, I didn't see my way to arresting anybody for the killing of Alice, myself. Not yet. Not ever, to be honest, the way things stood.

I took a grip of my third large malt; thought about going back out. The uniforms had done the streets around the old railway station and goods yard; I'd had a wet and windy go at the beach. No Stalin; no bouncing, friendly Joe.

No excuses, either. I'd had a meal, a drink, a warm: if I wanted him back I was going to have to get out there and slog. Forget the murders, the burglaries, the politics and fat women in pop-button coats. I'd done what I'd been paid to do and more. Time to do something for me. Joe. A bloody pest, but he was my pest and I wanted him back. Wife; dog. If I kept on like this, there'd soon be nothing left. Three malt whiskies talking.

I stayed out till midnight, exploring back alleys, walking, whistling, calling. Made a nuisance of myself at the backs of terraced houses; a wandering breach of the peace. Nobody came out to complain. Some of them must have thought they'd got a raving nutter abroad, but it's amazing what you can get away with in the way of a racket when you're looking for a lost dog.

One or two people actually spoke; odd ones from the shelter of half-opened back doors, standing well back from the rain: purveyors of news about strays. Nobody could tell the difference between a Lakeland, an Airedale or a hole in the fence. But they meant well.

I thought up some interesting parallels as I walked: Mary Todd searching for her errant Sophie on the beach the day after I arrived. Her worries about the traffic: me and Joe. I gave the subject of Mary another wistful trot. Alcoholic wishful thinking, mostly. Besides . . .

Pregnancies: Alice and Angie. Well, no parallels there, perhaps; more like chalk and cheese. One aborting, dying; one very much alive, desperate to keep. A final parallel; a beauty. Me and Clive Jones. I was definitely the harder hitter, but one way or another we made a wonderful pair.

Then I wondered some more about Angie; picked up an oddity about her behaviour. I was doing well, it was only a couple of days after the event. I wondered how my schoolteaching wife had managed to meet me halfway through an afternoon session in the middle of the week. Skiving or sick? Well, I was the detective; something else I ought to find out.

The green Volkswagen was parked outside my gate. I saw it as soon as I turned the corner and started my dispirited trudge down the deserted street. It didn't click at first, then I got it: Mary Todd.

She had trouble getting out of her car as I came up. Something to do with the object clutched to her chest. Must be her dog. Then I saw the little Hunt terrier bitch with her face pressed against the rear window. I'm not often right, but I was wrong again. I could have cheered: not Sophie; Joe.

214

Head down, against the wind and rain, I thought, she thrust him at me. He was wrapped in a towel, legs safely trapped, and he struggled frantically to get at me, to lick me to death, to be free.

'Here,' she said, her voice oddly muffled, 'for his sake, not for yours.'

'Thanks.' I said fervently. 'He cleared off last night. Had an argument with a bigger dog. Thanks for bringing him home.' A strictly censored version. No need to spread tales of GBH, indecent assault, serious canine abuse.

'To be honest, I don't know why I bothered,' she said. It was only then I understood: the lowered head, the muffled voice. She was in tears.

'Come in, come out of this: it's the least I can do.'

Somehow, I chivvied her into the ranch, borrowed her keys, kidnapped her dog. I inveigled her into an armchair and mended the fire. And all the time, thick and insensitive as I am outside the job, I'd no idea what it was all about. I had missed yet another fairly obvious Eddathorpe point.

'That man!' she said. 'That bloody awful man; I don't suppose you're much better yourself!'

The lights came on: Hacker versus poor Eric. Not just her informing little bird; her boyfriend, partner, lover, common-law whatever-you-like. Overlooking the obvious: I really do think I'm in the wrong profession – sorry, *trade* at times. And now, thanks to my wandering four-legged disaster, an undeserved plum was ready to drop.

Even so, I wasn't giving her my full attention, yet. I was still happily warding off the irrational flying dog, who was busy bouncing chest high, growling with Lakeland pleasure and rushing madly around the room. Sophie flopped at her mistress's feet, looked hopefully at the reviving fire and gave the lunatic an occasional puzzled glance. The atmosphere was not conducive to an exchange of confidences: Joe was making it impossible to hold anything like an intimate chat.

I finally grabbed him on his umpteenth circuit of the room, thrust him into the kitchen and bribed him with enormous quantities of food. One of the major ways to that dog's heart is through his gut. I checked him over; he was slightly grubby, uninjured and nearly dry, which is more than anybody could say for her ruined towel.

I went over to the cupboard to get the malt, plagued with contradictory thoughts. I owed her and at the same time I wanted to pump her for anything she had to give. She was right: almost as bad, just as manipulative, as that bloody awful man.

'Where did you find him?' I handed over a substantial drink.

'On the beach.' No more tears, but she looked pretty ragged all the same.

'At this time of night?'

'Half, three-quarters of an hour ago. I went there to think. You know about Eric?'

'I'm sorry, yes.'

'It's so unfair!' She took a long pull at her drink: going down, it scarcely touched the sides. 'The one person who never even liked the girl. Little tart!'

'A bit of a Puritan, isn't he, Eric?'

'She was an embarrassment, working at the garage like that. Having it off with the boss.' The expression was so unexpected coming from her, so inelegant, that I caught a sip of whisky in the back of my throat and coughed.

She looked up at me quickly, her face heavy, sullen. 'All right, I know she was murdered. Just think for a moment about the grief she's caused my family, me. She was like a bitch on heat; my menfolk couldn't seem to leave her alone. That girl attracted her own trouble.'

My menfolk: divorced, and still ninety-five per cent Todd. Incestuous, said Teddy. Ambiguous, he could have added, in their relationships. Contradictory. Wheels within wheels, as well.

'Eric found her attractive too, didn't he?'

'Who told you that?'

'He – er – enjoys giving the girls the eye?'

'Most men do. Even you, Inspector; or do you consider yourself a cut above the rest?' I let that one pass. 'Eric is a shy man; he wouldn't have touched Alice Draper with a bargepole. He's got his standards.'

'How long have you and he . . . been close?'

'Been lovers, you mean?' She gave a tiny hiccup which might have been a laugh. 'A charming way to put it; Detective Superintendent Hacker wasn't quite so tactful. About eighteen months.'

'I assume your ex-husband doesn't know – otherwise he wouldn't have mentioned Major MacMillan in the way he did?'

'I haven't asked him. In any case, a spot of variety never bothered Richard,' she said with a trace of bitter amusement. 'I don't broadcast my private affairs to the world and we don't live together.'

'And Eric Goodwin is married, yes?'

'Separated; and in case you're interested, she was gone long before I came on the scene.'

Whoops! Another unwarranted assumption on the basis of my visit to Eric's office. Wife on the phone – just like Angie, perhaps.

'Mary – Mrs Todd . . .'

'Mary.'

'What happened this evening, Mary?'

'We were together at Eric's flat – watching television as it happens, when that – that man came round with some Chief Inspector or other, I forget his name.

'Superintendent Hacker was delighted to find us together. Gave a couple of nasty hints about Eric being a real ladies' man and said he wanted to talk to him about another very close friend, Alice.'

'And?'

She shrugged. 'One thing led to another and Eric lost his temper. He did it on purpose, I think.'

Hacker: on purpose, of course. He'd no intention of confining himself to a few questions, he wanted Goodwin down at the nick. So he'd scattered his corn and Eric, living-on-his-nerves Eric, had pecked. An hysterical scene, a swing at the cops and an arrest. A neat substitute for reasonable suspicion in Hacker's book. Afterwards, if it all went sour and he had to release his victim, he could justify the detention. Just about.

Victim? Was Eric Goodwin a victim, though? And were the ingenious Mr Hacker and his sidekick such a pair of stunt-pulling fascist brutes? Infringers of civil liberties? It's all very well, but I've never been able to let the scales come down with a bang, on either side. Arguments about ends and means, sure; but what about old Hacker, bastard though he was, genuinely trying to get a result and cutting his coat according to his cloth?

'Get him a solicitor?' I asked.

'Yes.'

'Charlie Pringle?'

'Charles? Certainly not. I've got a very experienced man from the county town. His firm handled my divorce.'

'There's a lot of difference between divorce work and crime,' I warned her.

She smiled humourlessly, 'Yes, I know. Charlie is all right in his place, but I've engaged a specialist in criminal law.'

'Not keeping it in the family,' I muttered, half to

myself. 'Tell me, why did Richard and Victor refuse to provide blood samples after they were arrested?'

'Do you really think I'm on your side? That I'm going to help answer your questions, after all the police have done?'

'The police', I said grimly, 'have been chasing the killer of a twenty-three-year-old woman, and I'm sorry to stick you in the front line, but Richard and Victor both—'

'Yes,' she said. 'Quite.'

'It isn't going to go away, you know, is it? She's going to stay dead and we're still going to keep on trying. Do you know why Richard and Victor refused?'

'I don't know but I can guess. Anyway, they weren't alone; there were five of them, from what I hear.'

'Six.' I said automatically.

'Five – your Superintendent's son agreed.'

So he had. But there were six refusals, still. One of the anonymous also-rans had given Hacker the thumbs down. Click: suddenly, it came together and I grinned at her. 'You're perfectly right,' I said.

'Richard and Victor', she said carefully, 'aren't criminals and they don't know much about DNA. Nor do I.'

'No.'

'But they are brothers, even though they have their ups and downs, and they believed that if one gave a sample it might incriminate the other. A similar test result.'

'Wonderful: Richard thought it might be Victor, and vice versa?'

'That's what I think.'

'All sticking together: happy families,' I muttered, 'but that doesn't account for the rest of them, unless . . .'

'A conspiracy theory? Rubbish, you're much brighter than that – Robert.'

'No.' I laughed. 'No, I don't believe in a conspiracy;

and yes, I do hope I'm brighter than that. I've been over this ground before. So, not Richard, not Victor, not Eric – a woman's instinct?'

She finished her drink and held out her glass imperiously for more. 'If I'm going to be a copper's nark, at least you can provide me with an excuse – the man got me drunk!'

I gave her a substantial refill. I wasn't going to recover this from the County Treasurer's coffers.

'Richard', she said, 'loves the idea of children. Do you know that? He'd do anything, literally anything, to have a child of his own. And Alice – well, at one point she was going to have a child, yes?'

Valerie, the second wife and the big vodka bottle. The interview at the house: Tricky Dicky's hint. Ah well, you live and learn.

'And Victor?'

She shrugged. 'Not a married man. I can see him falling out with the little bitch, but assuming she was trying it on about the baby she'd aborted, or about sex, he was more likely to laugh at her than kill. What had Victor got to worry about – the scandal? If you think that, you don't know the Todds!'

'Victor,' I said softly, 'a good Catholic.'

'Ho! You have been doing your homework. And Richard is a bad one, and I'm no sort of Catholic at all. So what?'

'Somebody got her pregnant, and somebody . . .' I paused deliberately. '. . . somebody refused to help her. Left her to scrape the money together for an abortion, all by herself.'

'Christ,' she said, 'I was right: policemen have got mean minds.'

'Not as mean as some people and their actions. Putting it bluntly, Mary, we just trundle along at the end of the parade to clear up other people's shit!' I was sorry as soon as I'd said it, but you do get fed up at times. The all-coppers-are-bastards bit.

Silly of me, diving for the trenches at the first shot, opting for immediate all-round defence. Another knee-jerk copper: circle the wagons, chaps!

'Is that how you see yourself?' she asked with what appeared to be genuine regret. 'Well, I'm sorry.' She took the rest of her drink and stood up. 'You've certainly stopped me feeling sorry for myself, and your colleagues can't touch Eric. He's done nothing wrong.'

'Truly, I hope you're right. Can I ask you something else?'

'Don't you think you've gone far enough?'

'Victor's new investment. He's pretty sore; he says Richard is out to queer his pitch because of plans for a new cash and carry – Cloverleaf Consortium, right?'

'Richard, in his perverted little way, was trying to watch out for me.' She paused to give herself time to consider, then she reached down and picked up her little dog. 'Although, I must admit, he'd chase his own advantage if he could.'

'What's Cloverleaf?'

'Nothing directly to do with Richard, but he owns the land. Not exactly green-belt: part of the long-term development plan. Cloverleaf want to build a cash and carry. Richard would do very nicely out of it, if it came off.'

'Victor seems to think he's trying to knock MacMillan and his business.'

'Not likely. Cloverleaf will have taken account of any tinpot opposition already. Nothing to do with me. I've already declared my . . . former association to the Council and stepped aside.'

'Is there a problem?'

'Environment versus jobs, that sort of thing. Constructing a warehouse, providing twenty-odd jobs, as against unspoiled hedges and fields. Then there's the local jealousies – you'll have heard?'

'Yes. Victor—'

'Has dropped himself in it. Twenty-five thousand pounds into Major MacMillan's scheme. A directorship too, for what it's worth. Had the cheek to suggest me as another investor. I can do without people looking after my interests, thanks!'

I was not about to offer, but I remembered some remnant of my manners, nevertheless. First she'd been upset, now she was hostile. And she'd done me more than one favour tonight.

'Thank you once again for returning Joe.' Not much; next to nothing, but I could try to sweeten the pill.

'Thank you for the whisky; good night.'

I saw her to the door, stayed on the step until she started the engine and drove away. Old-world courtesy? Tripe!

My empty, half-formed fantasy; and she'd helped me; and I'd been party to dropping Eric in the mire. Excuse: I'd only taken note of the suggestion, only passed it on. Could I be held responsible for the Hackers, the Victors, the Erics even, and their collective tendency to hurl themselves right into the horse feathers every time they took a hop, a skip or a jump?

24

I stayed in bed late the following morning, a token gesture in the general direction of the forty-hour week. Detective Inspectors get two rest-days in seven, the same as anybody else. That was the theory; it never used to work out like that.

I took another regretful turn down memory lane: Crime Squad detectives don't stay home. They do not sit around in grotty seaside bungalows with time on their hands. All that paid overtime, booze, excitement, ha, ha; sixty, seventy hours a week.

I couldn't kick the habit out here in the sticks, but I wasn't getting paid for anything any more. Inspectors' overtime payment was a thing of the past. Working my days off simply meant a few more hours in the book. Eventually, the credits would mount up; I'd have to take the time off. Probably at Christmas. In Eddathorpe. Counting the bank holidays, I'd get the best – correction, worst – part of a week. Then another bank holiday for the New Year.

Thoroughly disgruntled, I rolled out of my pit, took Joe for a trot, gave Angie a ring. I could add some spice to my existence: surprise myself by finding out what I had to say. I let the phone ring twenty-eight times: she was out. I made myself some brunch, drank three cups of coffee, and that concluded my official programme for the day. I looked at my watch; definitely not the magic hour: I couldn't even go to the pub.

I tried a spot of housework – unboxing and shelving several dozen books. I attempted to read and succeeded only in confusing myself with biology: deoxyribonucleic acid. Not much wonder I used to put up a zizz at the back of the class when jawbreakers like that were introduced to the CID. All that taxpayers' money being cast before non-scientific swine.

I gave it an hour before I packed it in. I had been an idiot: Hacker was a mug. Another fine mess, but I could almost excuse him: early days, back in 1989. I consoled myself with what one of the police instructors had said at the time: *Call it magic, lads: don't worry about the nuts and bolts, just be grateful it works!*

Afterwards, I cursed Buchanan junior and his remarks about DNA for a bit. I decided that my pronunciation, as well as my commitment to science, was less than perfect. Then I thought about going out to buy a wedge of Sunday papers: somehow it didn't appeal.

Why didn't I go and harass the DCs on duty? What a nice idea! Better still, find out if there was a result in the Silver versus Goodwin match. I drove down to the Factory: Joe stayed firmly in the car.

I sneaked into the custody suite around 11.15. The prisoner listing showed Ian Richards, Anita Smith, Brenda Lawson, yesterday's hero of the domestic assault, and another violent drunk. A slight change in the batting order. Eric Goodwin was apparently out for a duck, his name reduced to an indecipherable smudge on the board.

The Custody Sergeant gave me a knowing look. 'He's gone,' he said, 'released without charge. And I'm running this quiz: guess which Detective Inspector isn't exactly flavour of the month.'

'I can't think why.'

'Hacker's been having this conversation with our CI. The next time you have a bright idea about a murder, please keep it to yourself!'

'Is that right?'

'Absolutely: I was there. Right after the Police Surgeon left.'

'Police Surgeon? Hacker assaulted the prisoner, did he?'

The Custody Sergeant looked profoundly shocked. 'Mr Goodwin agreed to provide a sample for analysis; solicitor's advice. The Doc turned out to take the blood. No trouble, no arguments, as sweet as a nut.'

'Sergeant!' I said. Suddenly I loved the whole concept of DNA; I even loved the world – excluding one or two unimportant parts of it, anyway.

'Sir!'

'Might I be permitted to say what a splendid job you chaps do in very difficult circumstances down here?'

'Thank you, sir.' Ironically, he drew himself up to attention and tried to look suitably impressed.

'That's all right: carry on.'

'Devious bastards, the CID,' he said, resuming his usual position, gut propped comfortably against the charge-office counter and cigarette drooping from his lower lip at thirty degrees. He handed out a sly grin, expecting confidences. The word was out: Hacker had been done.

I said nothing and let him draw his own conclusions. Let them speculate as much as they liked. Devious was fine by me; stupid to gossip, though. Teddy Baring; me; two minds, each with the merest whisper of a malicious thought. But credit where credit's due: it was Hacker who'd walked into the revolving door, all by himself. Almost.

I went upstairs in search of confirmation; sure enough, Chief Inspector Derek Paget was more than willing to oblige. He ushered me into his office and delivered a mournful shake of the head.

'Mr Hacker', he said, 'is a bit displeased. His interview with your murder suspect did not go well.'

'He wasn't my murder suspect; he was a suggested line of enquiry. Mr Baring discussed the information with me and we passed it on.' We exchanged a look of total understanding. The whole art of the thing is never, never to laugh.

'Yes.' He dropped his eyes to the papers on his desk. 'I'm afraid Mr Baring did not escape censure, either. Detective Superintendent Hacker feels that any other . . . suggestions can be dealt with at local level. He asked me to pass *that* message on.'

'Well, yes,' I said. 'Thanks. I'll consult Mr Baring in future, of course – or you.'

I swear he shuddered. 'I think a word with the Divisional Commander would be best.'

'Right; thank you, sir.'

'No, no,' he said. 'Detective Inspector to Chief Inspector – no need for that. Derek, please!'

'Thanks, Derek.'

'Delighted. Just one thing – no need to go into anything specific, you understand. But do you have any other lines of enquiry on the Alice Draper thing?'

'One or two, Derek.'

'Yes.' He sighed gently. 'I thought you might.'

The CID office was deserted, but a scattering of hand-written statements on John Robey's desk showed he and his partner had been hard at work. Sunday morning, and half a dozen wrinklies had copped a witness statement. Nothing spectacular; your average loan shark, battening on your average victims in fact.

> I am in receipt of the State Retirement Pension and I live at the above address ...
> ... then, having fallen deeply into debt because ... a friend told me about a woman called Brenda Lawson who helped people like me. In desperation, I borrowed—
> ... She told me I had to repay her at ten per cent interest per week, plus at least five per cent of the original loan ...
> She took my pension book as security for the loan ... So far I have paid a total of – and yet I still owe her—
> She instructed me to meet her at the Post Office every Monday morning at – when she would return my book to me to enable me to draw my pension. Afterwards, outside, she took the book off me and I was forced to pay her a minimum of – each week ...
> I have had to pay interest upon the whole sum I originally borrowed for the past – weeks, despite having paid back part of the original loan ...
> I have examined a State Retirement Pension book shown to me by the police ...

I read each pathetic little screed right through to the end. I gave my undivided attention to the activities of Brenda the Lender for a good half-hour and set my imagination to work on the similar stories yet to come.

Pensioners, recipients of family credit, disability allowances, benefits from the DSS . . .

I made myself a promise: handling charges aside (and they were going to be good!), perfect statements were going to be assembled into an immaculate file.

Prior to us crucifying the bitch. Legally speaking, of course.

After that, for curiosity's sake, I snatched a selection of interview notes and half a dozen actions from four green filing boxes to confirm what my gut already knew. Then I searched out and examined a single house-to-house enquiry form addressed to Eddathorpe males between sixteen and sixty-five: *What were you doing on the night of 12/13 December 1989?*

No proof: poor Eric had, however, given blood – as sweet as a nut . . . So had Matthew Baring and all the also-rans with one solitary exception.

I checked and double-checked the exception; a distinct non-starter. I wasn't interested in *him* at all. Callously, I deserted Eddathorpe nick and adjourned to the Links Hotel, where, in company with Joe, I over-indulged our respective propensities for crisps and beer.

Naturally: the Job being just a job and not the Third Crusade.

25

——◆——

I was out of bed and my feet were seeking my Joe-infested slippers before I was fully awake. Trip the twit; another of his games.

'Gerroff!' I swung my left foot wildly and donated half my footwear to a delighted canine idiot, prior to stumbling off to answer the living-room phone. No modern bedside Telecom plugs at the ol' lonesome ranch.

'It's Paula.' She sounded strained, almost snappish. 'It's all happening, boss: right now. Three pantechnicons – self-drive hire, I think. He's shifting the lot!'

I looked incredulously at my watch. 'It's nearly one a.m. Are you sure?' No need for the who, what or where: sleepy or not, I knew.

'Dead sure; MacMillan's on the move. They're clearing out the warehouse, right now. What are we going to do?'

'Pay a visit; have you roused your DCs?'

'I've got two of 'em here; d'you want the rest?'

'Call George and get him to call out Andy and Malc. Meet at Retton Police Station, pronto. Send your lads to keep observations at the warehouse. Get some discreet uniform back-up. If MacMillan's lot try to move off, detain them!'

229

I struggled into my clothes, grabbed a torch, imprisoned the dog. I'd done it now: sooner be right than President, according to some famous Yank. CID version: better be right, or draw your big pointed hat, very soon indeed.

Teddy Baring, I thought, tucked up safe in his bed. Instantly – well, almost instantly – I thrust that one aside. Credibility at stake; sod off and join the Band of Hope if you can't hack it by yourself.

Cursing the lazy, weekend-loving, promise-breaking Met, I made a dash for the car. No solid evidence, no details of similar scams and here we were, charging off to do or ruddy die. Personally, I hoped somebody had blown up their fax machine. From Commissioner of Police to junior typist, my maledictions would have blistered paint. Reasonable suspicion? I hadn't got enough to nick poor Puss.

Half an hour later I took my first look at Superbarg Cash and Carry. The more I saw the happier I felt. Not a lot of old chapels open at 1.20 a.m. Not a lot of worshippers dashing in and out with sets of wheels and a forklift truck either, come to that. Incongruous: a bit of a boost to my morale.

Lights blazed throughout the building; three furniture vans were parked, one behind the other, outside and half a dozen men trekked steadily backwards and forwards loading the loot. MacMillan's BMW was parked coyly down a side street, a hundred yards from the scene of the action. Normal business activity? Not exactly, no.

Pirates: they even had a flag. The chapel railings were decorated with a red and white banner proclaiming massive discounts to the trade, putting to shame the modest carving above the double doors, *Primitive Methodist Chapel, 1885*.

Good job I hadn't sent for Teddy: he'd have done his

primitive nonconformist nut. The Victorian occupants, from bonneted old ladies to black-coated ministers, must have been doing back-flips in their graves.

George, Malcolm and Andy tackled the drivers; Paula's troops took the back. We marched in through the front door. The old chapel had been gutted inside and refurnished with high steel racks with narrow canyons between. Two-thirds of the bays were empty and a couple of men were busy tossing down plastic-sealed boxes of tea-bags. The wine, spirit and tobacco bays yawned bare. *Please, please* let the high-value goodies be stashed in the vans!

To the left of the main entrance a narrow wooden stair led to a first-floor gallery and a couple of crudely partitioned offices. He was waiting for us at the top.

'Good morning, Major. Moving house?'

'Get that damned woman out of here!' An opening salvo; quite impressive. Artillery, rather than Selous Scouts.

'Sergeant Baily's a little concerned about your business, Major; why are you clearing stock in the middle of the night?'

'Mind your own bloody business. Sheer persecution, both of you: have your jobs for this!' He was striving for ascendency and failing miserably. The outrage was almost shrill, the bluster overdone. His eyes shifted from me to Paula and back, looking for an opening, trying to sort out what he was going to say.

'Perhaps we could have a word in your office, sir?'

'No: you're trespassing. Get out!'

'Loading at two in the morning; using hired self-drive vans. I'd like an explanation, please.'

'None of your business. Urgent Christmas orders, if you must know.'

'Excellent; fine. Can we see the written orders, please?'

He glowered silently. I began to experience this little holiday in my heart.

'What about the delivery notes?' murmured Paula sweetly. 'Surely you've got them? The drivers will need to know where they're dropping the goods.' The glower intensified. No good for pantomime: a one-expression man.

'They'll want signatures', I suggested, 'to show they've made a full and honest delivery. I mean . . .' I paused to smile insultingly. '. . . you've had difficulties with inadequate deliveries from suppliers yourself. Or at least, that's what you told me the other day.'

'Twenty-seven thousand pounds in disputed invoices,' offered Paula helpfully.

'So you wouldn't want your customers to be suing you for the same thing,' I said.

'Right!' he snapped. 'I've had enough of this. If you've got a warrant, I want to see it. Otherwise get out.' Oh dear, warrant indeed. A box-watching crook; a second-rater, too. So familiar as to be almost sad: a mere pounder, after all. Lazy, or over-confident, he'd neglected the fraudster's classic line of defence: paper and more paper, in a big, confusing wadge.

'But I haven't said anything about searching your premises, *Mister* MacMillan. Why on earth would I want a warrant? Have you done anything wrong?'

He retreated to the door of the office. 'I intend to telephone your superiors – I warn you, if you come in here, I won't be responsible.'

'For what? Be reasonable, now. Only the other day you told me you were willing and able to pay for all your deliveries – remember?' I nodded my head encouragingly, trying to get him to nod along. His face, his neck muscles, his entire body stayed rigid. Obstinate bugger.

'All we want', said Paula, 'is some assurance that everything is all right. A bank statement? The paperwork covering tonight's transactions, perhaps?'

'Oy, mister!' A squat, balding man thundered up the stairs, pushed his way between us and stared aggressively at MacMillan. 'Your oppo downstairs is having a barney with the cops. They've taken the ignition keys for all the vans. We want our money – now. Me and my mates are drivers and packers; we didn't come all this way to buy a load of grief!'

'Hello, Mr – er—'

'Camber, Les Camber – are you a copper?'

'That's right. Where are you from?'

'Birmingham, pal. What's it to you?'

'There's a bit of a problem about the goods you're loading, Mr Camber; you wouldn't have a set of delivery notes with the customer's address, by any chance?'

'Not a smell; the feller downstairs, he employed us: sixty notes and a bonus at the other end, he said. No paperwork. It's him who's guiding this wagon train, pal.'

'Thanks: this feller, now – you know, the wagon master. Would you go and point him out to one of my detectives, please?'

'Why?'

I shook my head sorrowfully. 'Well, for one thing, I think you've been done. Maybe you're going to have to whistle for your sixty notes.'

'Bastards!' He treated MacMillan to a look of unadulterated venom, hesitated as if he was going to argue the toss for a few seconds, and finally slammed his way downstairs. A man promoting a lively image: a small, truculent human tank.

'All right,' I said, 'put up or shut up time. I'd like to see evidence that you can pay for the goods you've received on credit and I want you to provide details of the destination of the stuff you're shifting tonight.'

'Go to hell, both of you!'

Not the right answer: he'd missed the major prize. Arrested for obtaining goods by deception, cautioned, dragged off to Eddathorpe in company with his Brummie wagon master by Paula and George instead.

Six disgruntled drivers and labourers, casually employed, piled into a uniform van *en route* to a witness statement apiece. Somewhere along the way they'd acquired high and unjustified hopes of a police handout of sixty quid.

The bonus was something, all circumstances considered, that the lads were prepared to forget, said their spokesman. An altruistic lot.

Three fifteen a.m.; Charlie Pringle bustled into Eddathorpe Police Station like a cut-down version of the wrath of God, demanding Teddy, demanding me and generally stirring up the dust. Steadily, I inveigled him up to my office a step at a time while he yapped client and false arrest and police complaints like a shabby Pekingese.

He flung his disgraceful overcoat across the back of one of my chairs and prepared to impress.

'No delays; no police evasions or excuses,' he said. 'I want to see my client at once. Attempts to delay me will go very ill with you, Inspector.' For sheer priggish stupidity, I rather liked that.

'Are you sure,' I asked, 'sure you want to see this man at all?'

'Don't you dare to . . .' Seeing the expression on my face, his voice trailed away and a wary, almost apprehensive look crossed his face.

'What do you mean?' he said.

'This so-called major, Mr Pringle. Our information suggests he's got something like a hundred thousand pounds' worth of outstanding bills. We caught him doing a moonlight flit and he's probably conned your cousin out of another twenty-five grand. It's priorities I had in mind – conflict of interest, even. What about your local client, Victor Todd?'

'Oh.'

'Mr Todd is going to need your advice. He's a director, he's going to have to sort out the mess; decide whether he can continue to trade – try to recover some of his money, at least. Yes?'

And Victor Todd can pay his solicitor, mate. He won't be relying on the vagaries of Legal Aid. So much, for the sake of amity, that one needs to leave unsaid.

I did not like Charlie Pringle. I did not need to sympathise while he swallowed his pill. I didn't know how this was going to turn out; but I had this hackneyed motto in mind at the time: *To hell with the consequences, enjoy yourself while you can.*

As for Charlie, he had this big, illuminated pound note sign beaming from his eye.

'He's already instructed me,' he muttered. 'Those invoices . . .' He was looking for a way out.

'We-ll . . .' I let him simmer. 'Consider your information now. Absconding with the property, extraction of twenty-five thousand pounds from Mr Todd . . . Don't you legitimately suspect that he might not have instructed you in good faith? Might be using the law as a delaying tactic, getting you to issue bogus writs?'

'Oh my God!'

'I mean, consider the ethical position, the – er – Law Society . . .'

'I must withdraw. I must tell him so at once!'

'I'll take you down to the custody suite, Mr Pringle.' It's not often I've had the pleasure of seeing a solicitor move so fast. He even asked, politely, whether he could use a police telephone to contact his unfortunate, defrauded client, Victor Todd.

'Malcolm,' I said, 'is your pocket book up to date?'

'Yes, boss.'

'Can I have it for a moment?'

I wrote the instruction down carefully; then I signed, timed and dated it. I returned the book; he read the instruction, nodded and raised his eyebrows. He didn't look too surprised.

'Now,' I said, 'that's what I want you to do. You're obeying a lawful order, so you won't get into trouble if it all goes wrong.'

'It'll be a pleasure,' he said, with unexpected loyalty, 'but you didn't have to get me off the hook by writing it down. Anyway, what the hell is this one all about?'

26

![chapter divider]

Whoever he was, MacMillan knew the game. He'd taken the loss of Charlie Pringle in his stride, demanded the duty solicitor, and sat and dared us to prove that he was guilty of so much as spitting in the street. In the long run he was dead and he knew it, but then again, so are we all. It was the here and now which was providing us with the pain.

His wagon master – we all liked that one – called himself Paul Hurt. That was tempting fate all right. Despite rumours to the contrary, however, we're not like that. Mr Hurt with an address in the West Midlands: nobody's oppo, nobody's partner and in charge of nothing. Didn't know how those thick drivers and packers came to think he was somehow in charge.

Sure, he'd hired the vans; yes, he'd sorted out a few bodies to shift the gear and that was all. Major MacMillan gave the instructions; met him in a pub. No idea where they were going to take the stuff – he'd have got his instructions, probably, once they'd loaded up. Strange? Not at all.

We'd searched the premises: an unconventional business, you could say that. The sales and purchase ledgers hadn't been kept for months: one up to the coppers; a definite plus.

Hundreds of trade catalogues, letters, delivery notes, invoices – you name it – had been bundled together on bulldog clips and hung without rhyme or reason on nails on the office wall. We'd seized four or five out-of-sequence bank statements, the latest two months old, showing eight thousand seven hundred pounds in the business account. Few apparent payments to suppliers.

No stock lists, no till receipt rolls. Why? *An unreported burglary – sorry. A few hundred quid in cash and one or two documents adrift: odd, isn't it, what thieves will go for.* Yes, Julian, me boy: all those cute little rolls of paper missing; not something an ordinary thief would go for – a bit specialised: a bonfire for a bogus Selous Scout?

Item: eighteen thousand six hundred pounds in a briefcase locked in the boot of his car, together with his clothes, neatly packed in the matching pigskin luggage. Helpful, that. We also searched his Retton flat: swept and garnished, as empty and shiny-clean as the proverbial pin. Apart from the dustbin in the back yard – all those missing till rolls. Stinking, in more ways than one.

I could see it coming, though: police bail. This enquiry was going to be a long, long grind. The evidence was there, but it was going to take weeks, months to sort out. Postal enquiries; orders to examine bank accounts; statements from Land's End to John o' Groat's and all the time Julian Mac would be out on the street, laughing. Fighting off civil proceedings from Victor Todd. Probably flogging the stuff.

Who was going to stop him? The suppliers repossessing their gear? High Court injunctions? The good old Department of Trade Investigations Branch with a winding-up order? If they were in time. Very, very perhaps!

Then there was this small-town DI. Tying down an entire CID section on a commercial fraud. Taking flak from everybody from mousetrap manufacturers to distillers, not to mention every accountant and cowboy solicitor in the land.

Every one of them with a client; all of 'em demanding to know what *I* was going to do to recover their gear. The Commercial Branch, the Headquarters specialists, wouldn't touch this one with a bargepole now we'd dabbled our pretty little tootsies in the mud.

There's nothing, absolutely nowt to compare with the satisfaction to be derived from a really deep-down, hopeless wallow in gloom. While others continued the search, while Victor was shelling out six times sixty quid and having the vans unloaded, while he changed the locks, while MacWhoever and Unhurt slept in their respective cells, I gave it some mental hammer. Worst-case scenario, they call it.

'Mr Graham?' Two smartly suited strangers stood in the doorway: upmarket fuzz. I mean, we all had suits, but not like these. Top-quality wool worsted, hand-built; one in executive blue and the other in a very nice line in shadow-stripe grey. Somebody definitely knew somebody in the trade. They looked so young, so shiny, so squeaky-clean. Invented by a lady crime writer with a blue rinse. An instant assessment: more trouble. Just shows how wrong you can be.

'Yes? I'm DI Graham.' Not so much an admission, more a pre-emptive strike.

'Detective Inspector Rae sends his apologies, sir. Somebody must have left this on his desk on Friday night. Asks if you'll look through it and ring him straight away.'

'And you are?'

'DCs Hutton and Meadows; Fraud Squad.'

I took the thick buff envelope, crudely scrawled *D/I; HQ CID – Fraud*, and pulled out eleven faxed Metropolitan Police criminal descriptive forms, accompanied by photos and summaries of previous case histories. The cavalry had arrived.

Some idiot, some nine–five special in HQ Control Room had received the fax on Friday night, decided that the Fraud Squad were the exclusive recipients of information about commercial crime, and left the information to fester on a Fraud Office desk until Monday morning. You can't expect the élite to work at weekends, God bless us.

I leafed through my gallery of rogues: Rhodesian Special Forces, they'd claimed, mercenaries of one sort or another, and one real beauty – a rubber-cheque merchant claiming to be a former Superintendent in the British South Africa Police.

And there he was; the sixth man down. Major Julian MacMillan. Not a man to enjoy his photo being taken; looking as if they'd stuck his swagger-stick up his bum.

I looked at his pedigree on his CRO Form 74. I just couldn't help it, they must have thought I was barmy, but visitors or not, I gave the news an open, raucous laugh.

James Patrick Maynard, CRO 59569/56J; born 23.6.39, Bexhill on Sea. (And there was I plumping for Southend!) Convictions for Theft, False Pretences (an old one). Travelling on the Underground without a Ticket (Oh, really!). Deception (six separate cases). Fraudulent Trading and Conspiracy to Defraud. Last Conviction: Snaresbrook Crown Court, 10 June 1989, Obtaining Money by Deception – 30 months.

Circulated Police Gazettes (No. 5644 – 10 June 1983, item 419) for Obtaining by Deception – Modus Operandi – passed stolen cheques MP (XD Station) claiming to be a former officer of the Rhodesian Armed Forces, Selous Scouts.

Damn and double damn! I'd been a couple of years out.

Then came the crunchy bit; the part that topped the gingerbread with gilt, ice-cream, caviar and strawberry jam; enough to make the military grocer sick:

Extract From Police Gazettes (6004/92, item 13)

13. WEST MIDLANDS POLICE: Wanted on warrant not backed for bail. B Division (Belgrave Road) Conspiracy to Defraud (in company with associates obtained goods amounting to £130,000 on credit in respect of cash and carry business and absconded) James Patrick MAYNARD CRO, born Bexhill 23.6.39. Company Director. Description: 5' 8", medium build, brown hair (greying), thin face, sallow complexion, sometimes affects clipped military style moustache. Uses names John Mayes, James MacMillan, Julian Paul Hope-Prendergast: occasionally assumes bogus military rank. Convictions for Conspiracy, Deception etc. MPD(XD), Cheshire, Notts. and South Wales.

Wanted on warrant . . . no bail . . . with associates. What price Paul Hurt, or whatever he cared to call himself, now? Paula could have our boys safe on remand in Winson Green Prison with any sort of luck, while her fraud enquiries pursued their (fairly) leisurely way. My fingers itched for the Birmingham code, but I rang DI Rae first.

'Hear you've got a bit of a problem?' The voice on the other end of the phone was cheerful, young. I explained, thanked him for the Pony Express and never said a solitary word about needing help. We catch 'em, we charge 'em and it's down to us to do the file. Wrong again on this occasion.

241

'Thought you might like a hand,' said the voice on the phone casually. 'Couple of my lads for three or four days, once the West Mids take your prisoners off your hands? Get the statements rolling, get the bank sorted out?'

'That', I said fervently, 'would be great. I owe you, really I do.'

'Ah, never mind – we'll have a jar or two, some time. I'll tell you something, Bob; one good turn deserves another. You're a popular man around here.'

'Sorry, I don't understand.'

'Modest, aren't we? I'll give you a clue. *Hi ho, Silver and awaaaay!!!*' And the phone went down with a definitive crunch. Nothing succeeds like a popular catch-phrase: it was becoming the Hacker-baiting cliché of the week.

I replaced the receiver to face the two grinning DCs; they were obviously in on the joke.

Mixed emotions; in spite of having made one or two dissident friends, I had this uneasy feeling I'd also acquired a new disease. A sometimes-fatal political virus – Detective Superintendent's blight.

By this time they were all convinced that the Eric versus Hacker match had been an outright fix. With a reputation like mine winging its way from canteen to police canteen, Silver was soon going to hear a version of the latest lunchtime legend: Graham puts burr under saddle of masked avenger's horse.

I didn't have him clocked as the forgiving and forgetting type.

I travelled further this time, and met her in the Castle Tea Room in Newark, just off the A1. The half-timbered, olde-worlde borough where they served the super-helping of booze and dodgy fruit that finally nailed King John. More effective than Runnymede, I've always thought.

Pity they can't get our modern politicians to undertake a short, dyspeptic stay.

Traffic rattled the windows and Christmas-tree lights glistened wetly against the glass from the park across the road. It was getting dark. The café was three-quarters full of women with carrier bags and parcels and we were squeezed on a table for two against a cluttered rack overflowing with cloth coats, damp umbrellas and artificial fur.

'Why didn't you tell me?' I said.

She gave me a hint of a smile. 'Still looking after me, are you?'

'If you like.'

She concentrated on stirring her coffee, head down, eyes fixed on the rim of her cup. 'It isn't easy, you know,' she said finally.

'What?'

'Being the guilty party; your scarlet woman.'

'Ah, come on, now. I never saw it like that.'

'No?'

'Well, not now. I'm not exactly proud of myself, you know.'

'You can see both sides, can you?' A touch of irony there: never one to sit around and take it, Angela. Hope for her yet: she wasn't that far down.

'You haven't answered my question – and stop sending me up.' I smiled a bit, too. Encouragingly, I thought.

'It's nothing to worry about, the doctor says. High blood pressure; stress. He advised me to stay away from school for the rest of the term.'

'OK, Angie. No stress – I'll sort out the house, if you want. There might be a few thousand over from the insurance policies; we can split that, too.'

She jerked back her head in surprise, looking fixedly at my face. 'Sort out? What do you mean?'

243

'You can have the house,' I said carefully. 'Everything paid. We'll cash the mortgage endowment policy; I'll cash or sell the life policies – the ones I took out in your name as well as mine – and we'll do a fifty-fifty split of any excess. That's the deal, if you want.'

She made an involuntary gesture towards me with her hand, paused, and sought her handbag and a handkerchief instead.

'It's more than I asked for: you want to do that – for a clean break?'

'Yes, if it comes to that. There is an alternative,' I said.

And she said, 'What alternative?' And I took a deep breath and told her, burning the wreck of the odd seaside boat in the process, and she cried.

Embarrassing; stressful, even. I was never very good. Not the sort of thing to do in a tea-shop when it's three-quarters full, so we left and walked around for a bit in the rain. Inconclusive; no neat endings, beginnings, or anything concrete at all. But the coffee was good and far better value than the swill they dished out in that other roadside dump.

27

'Both the Girl Guides got bail,' said George the following morning.

'Didn't the Crown Prosecutor oppose?'

'For Brenda Lawson? Yeah, but you know the CPS; they sent this kid to do a man's job, once again.'

'Bail conditions?'

'Two sureties, each of five hundred pounds and report at the police station every evening at seven o'clock. Keep away from the witnesses, or else.'

'That's something, I suppose.'

'More than you think, boss. Andy wants a word with you.'

'What about?'

George looked smug, delighted and secretive all at the same time. Dangerous, in a man of his age – I thought he was going to burst.

'I won't spoil it for him.'

'OK, but it's not my birthday till June.'

Promises, broken promises: he just couldn't keep his big mouth shut. 'Early Christmas present,' he said. 'I think he's got you a watch.'

Andy Spriggs was apparently poring over the documents on his desk. A single involuntary flick of his eyelids as I came in gave away the game. He was behaving like the cat who'd got the canary, the cream and a smoked-salmon contract, all in one go. Why spoil it? Let him surprise his elderly, doddering DI. The simple pleasures are the best.

'Morning, Andy: you wanted a word?'

'Morning, boss. Brenda Lawson got bail. Ian Richards got remanded to Lincoln Prison.'

'Do him no end of good.'

'And her, if the CPS had got his way.'

'Please!' I looked suitably shocked. 'You can't send a lady to an all-male prison. Think of the scandal.'

'Can't expect the prisoners to entertain Fat Brenda, y' mean. One look at her and they'd all turn queer.'

'You'll never get promoted in Community Affairs: mocking the nutritionally challenged like that. Politically incorrect.'

'Sorry, boss: another career move blocked. Can I be a detective, instead?'

'Depends what you've got.'

'This!' He picked up Brenda's account book with a flourish, removing the beer mat he'd been using as a book-mark and laying the red Cathedral account book open on the desk.

'Very meticulous, our Brenda. No records of the stolen gear, of course. But she really loved keeping her accounts. Loans, securities, interest payments, defaults and sales. She should have been something in the City.'

'Most of them are,' I said gloomily, 'until they go to gaol.' He gave that one a minimal twitch of the lips. He wanted to get on.

'September 26th, 1989: A. Draper, 23 Selby Avenue – eighty pounds. Security – watch and cross-over ring. There we are; cash analysis, straight across the page.'

'Bingo!'

'There's more – cross-referenced, would you believe: March 1990: sales. Ring, one hundred and fifteen pounds; watch, seventy-five.'

'One hundred and ninety pounds on an eighty-quid loan. Lovely woman.'

'You're forgetting the weekly repayments, boss. Between September and December.'

'How much?'

He shook his head regretfully. 'Sorry, don't know. She's got a notebook for weekly payments and she does a roll-up cash analysis once a month. But her rough notes go back just over a year. The old stuff has probably been ditched.'

'Cheeky old cow. Flogging property belonging to a murder victim.'

Grateful. I hated the idea, but I was going to have to be grateful. Worse, I might even have to do a deal. After all the righteous indignation I'd deployed in the direction of that grasping old bitch!

'Silly old cow,' corrected Andy, oblivious to my Brenda the Lender plans, 'leaving a paper trail like that. Still, it's an ill wind.'

'Nice work,' I said. 'Smashing, in fact.'

The cracker-barrel philosophy, however, I could well have done without.

It was going to have to be Plan B for Brenda: revenge down the tubes. Held over, anyway, until such time as we'd persuaded her to be nice to us unctuous, untrustworthy cops.

She was, in George's language, a bit of an old jilt; an expression I'd never come across before. The face was vaguely familiar; the not-so Jolly Fisherman came to mind. Fifty-plus, plus, plus; pencilled eyebrows, a coat of enamel, and perfume you could use to slaughter ants. A too-short flounced skirt on a dress that looked something like the living-room curtains: kept a boarding house. Inevitable, really.

'You can call me Hilda,' she said, ignoring George and giving me the eye. Potential cradle-snatcher, I decided: over-ambitious, too. Despite my personal intimations of mortality, I wasn't quite that hard up; not yet.

'Thanks, Hilda. I'm Bob, this is George; he's a Detective Sergeant.' Any problems, and it was going to be his virtue up for sale, not mine.

'Yes, but you're in charge, aren't you?' She leaned forward in an unnecessary imitation of a Hugh Heffner Bunny Club dip, treating me to a trip round her heavily powdered boobs. Twenty years ago, it might have been fun.

She herded us into her private sitting room; all silver-framed photographs and Dralon suite, and stood between us and the door. Silently, I made this bet; there were summer visitors – *husbands* of summer visitors – whose nearest and dearest wouldn't allow them a second holiday beano with Hilda and her all mod cons.

She'd captured us and that was that. A minimum Danegeld of coffee, biscuits and a nice long chat. Seaside winter widows are by far the worst, but she was a taxpayer too and if she wanted value for money the least I could do was oblige – up to a point, anyway. If she wanted a sex slave, however, she'd have to make a bid for George: sacrificed in the line of duty, we could tell his wife.

Give Hilda her due, she was out for a bit of fun. A pretty mundane existence out of season and a sixteen-hour day between May and September, if she was lucky. Feuds with seasonal staff, a house full of buckets and spades, plastic ray-guns, brawling kids and marital spats. All for ninety quid per head, per week; children under twelve half price, babies free. In the space of three-quarters of an hour we learned all about the seaside holiday trade. Not much wonder they go abroad in winter; revenging themselves on waiters in foreign parts.

It was nigh on impossible to stem the flow, once the captive audience was in place. The whole art and skill lay in dropping our questions in between the flow of useless information. By the time we left, we could have qualified as *Mastermind* contestants in Guest-House Skills, Hilda's Grandchildren, Unemployable Slobs as Seaside Staff, and Marriage Guidance Counselling for Beginners. We grew to recognise her practical interest in sex therapy without being told.

George acquired this stunned expression, while I felt as if my brain had been vacuumed and the bits shredded before being emptied into the nearest dustbin. I'd have killed anybody who'd said it at the time, but she probably meant well.

I had three or four good attempts at getting her, keeping her, to the point.

'Brenda Lawson,' I said. 'Four or five years ago; she sold you a Gucci watch.'

'A funny woman. Do anything for you in some moods. Believes she's doing good, you know: concentrates their minds.'

'What?' Somehow, I just couldn't resist.

'You know what I'm talking about: I don't want to speak out of turn, but you wouldn't be here otherwise, would you?'

'Sorry?'

'You know, about all this loan business.' She sighed and shook her head. 'You don't have to go round the houses with me. Ask away and I'll tell you what I can.'

'What do you mean, it concentrates their minds?' Whatever it was, I wanted some of that.

'Lending them money; charging interest and making them pay it back. Then they realise the value, she says. Of budgeting.'

'She does it for their own good?' George's voice rose an octave.

'Oh, yes. Easy come, easy go with some people, she says. Makes them think.'

'A philanthropist,' I muttered.

'A social worker,' said George.

'Now, boys; there's no need to be like that. Live and let live, that's my motto.'

'Yes,' I said desperately. 'She sold you a watch?'

'I haven't got a lot of jewellery, you know. A little, but good. Paddy, that's my late husband – he wasn't Irish, mind you – Paddy bought me a few good pieces. I could go anywhere in those, he used to say. Funny, isn't it, calling a boy Patrick, when he was as English as you and me?'

'My grandfather was Scots.' I could hear myself saying that. The woman spread a kind of virus of inconsequentiality around. She could have turned Einstein into a bingo freak.

'Oh, yes? You'll know the Buchanans, then: the father's Scotch. But I shouldn't say that, should I? You should say Scottish . . .'

'Brenda sold you a murder victim's watch!'

I'd got her undivided attention at last.

'Gracious! Is it valuable? You know, like something belonging to a famous murderer – Crippin's walking stick, or something.'

'I don't think so. It's evidence; I need it for a while.'

'I paid for it, you know; fair and square.'

'Yes.'

'Well, it's mine, then, isn't it? You're not going to keep it, are you?'

'Can I see it, Hilda?'

'I don't want you to take it away. Not if it belonged to somebody famous.'

'It belonged to Alice Draper.'

'The car-park girl?' She looked disappointed; not famous enough, apparently. She struggled to her feet in a flurry of over-upholstered thighs; the armchair was both too soft and too low. 'I've got it here somewhere.'

She left the room and George sipped his coffee with an injured air.

'*This is George; he's a Detective Sergeant,*' he said bitterly. 'You tried to lumber me, boss.'

'Thought you might appreciate the mature type,' I replied shamelessly. 'Hilda could do a lot for you.'

'Hilda could do a lot for the Army, the Navy, the Air Force and most of the RNLI,' suggested George.

There it was: the green and gold box. She placed it on the coffee table and watched me like an elderly, disreputable hawk while I picked it up. The genuine article this time, no doubt about that. The watch was coiled around a central velvet-covered pedestal: the trademark, the maroon and green disc, nestled in the centre, five variously coloured discs lay in slots on either side and one was fitted to the watch itself. Alice had handed over her property intact. Gucci label, Gucci symbol, Gucci watch.

And a neat stick-on label inside the lid in black and gold. Santa's gift to good detecting boys: the jeweller's name and address.

'Thanks, Hilda, thanks very much. I'll need a statement from you. I'll have to borrow this – I'll let you have a receipt.'

'A cheque,' she said flatly. 'If you're taking it away I want a cheque for a hundred and eighty quid.'

'Who d'you take me for? The last of the big spenders? You paid Brenda seventy-five, second-hand.'

'Replacement cost, one hundred and eighty and I want your cheque – I won't cash it unless you keep the watch for good.'

'I'll never get authority for that.'

'OK. It's my watch – I'll keep it and produce it in court whenever you want.'

'Hilda; it's evidence – evidence in a murder enquiry.'

She lowered her head and looked stubborn, then she spoke slowly, patiently, as if she was dealing with a retarded child.

'This Alice girl, she handed it over as security; right?'

'Right.'

'Then she welshed on the deal.'

'No, Hilda. Alice Draper was murdered before she could reclaim her watch.'

'Same thing. She handed it over: Brenda got it legit.'

I nodded. This one had a master's degree in barrack-room law. So much for the goofy old jilt.

'She sold it to me, so it's mine. Although I'm a very co-operative person,' she said, giving me this look, 'I wouldn't like to disappoint you.'

She was right. Brenda might be making unlawful loans, but she had a good title to the watch and when she sold it she passed her title on. I couldn't snatch it. I could probably get an order from a crown court judge, but I didn't want to raise a fuss. No fuss, no Hacker; that was *my* motto.

George, fascinated, made some sort of choking noise and she treated him to a slow, speculative smile. He wilted and she returned all her attention to me.

'You want the watch; I want a guarantee – something negotiable, Bob, not a receipt. A consolation prize. Just in case you want to hold on to your evidence, after all.'

'And you won't cash it, unless I fail to return the watch?'

'You can do me a receipt on the back.'

I could hardly believe I was doing it, but I reached into my pocket and I wrote out the cheque. Inconsequential? She was about as inconsequential as a steel-toothed trap. I was, I promised myself, going to take extraordinarily good care of that watch.

She got her guarantee, endorsed with conditions on the back. Then I took a statement and pocketed the box. Gottim. Well, getting close; providing the jeweller and his records turned up trumps.

I had another cup of coffee and dunked a couple of ginger creams. Why not? They could be costing me a hundred and eighty quid. We parted with mutual expressions of esteem. Highly qualified on both sides, I suppose. One thing was certain; Brenda the Lender had missed the boat. She could have entered into a flourishing partnership there.

Once outside, the reaction set in. For one thing, George was too happy; I had this problem with George.

'Fancy paying for it!' he said with an ambiguous leer. 'You double-sixed Hacker and now she's double-sixed you.'

Shrewd, but I wasn't making any compromising comments to the constabulary press.

'The things I do for the Queen,' I snarled instead, patting the pocket containing my chequebook and staring at the blank, uncompromising surface of Hilda's firmly closed front door.

'The Queen won't be all that grateful,' prophesied George.

28

George, I knew, was still barking up the wrong tree. Malcolm Cartwright, keeping his tongue firmly between his teeth, had guessed. George was the problem – another problem, and I couldn't make up my mind. I was going to have to have a chat with Teddy Baring about my Detective Sergeant before I made my move.

In the meantime, the whodunnit was going to have to wait until I'd taken another look at Paula's residual sporting activities at the end of the MacMillan-Maynard chase. The hunt was over, so to speak. The expert butchering of the carcasses remained. Not a pretty metaphor, eh? Well, if you wanted to be a vegan, you shouldn't have joined.

No doubt about it, the Commercial Branch had done us proud; the two DCs had chiselled a VDU link out of the HQ admin boys and Teddy Baring had found us a computer-literate PC to work the magic box. Paula had a cosy little incident room buzzing, all of her own.

The enquiries were being indexed, the printer was churning, and the requests for suppliers' statements were winging their way to disgruntled, overworked plods in eighteen forces out of the forty-three in England and Wales. The Scots with distillers on their ground were probably cursing us as well. The one nice thing about a fraud; you can usually involve some other poor bugger in the boring bits, from time to time.

Paula and her mob were feeling chuffed and I was happy they were happy, to coin a phrase. Personally, I would not have felt quite so euphoric if I'd been grinding my way through a couple of hundred witness statements involving orders, invoices and delivery notes. Not to mention taking telephone calls from Victor Todd every five minutes: now there was a man with a brand-new whinge! No more complaints against the police – it was *Sergeant, oh, Sergeant Baily, what am I going to doooo?*

She was on the phone to Victor when I walked in. Teddy would have approved; she was oozing Christian charity by the bucket. Nothing like forgiving the odd defeated enemy: it frequently makes 'em feel so much worse.

'Sorry', she was saying, 'I can't come over right now. If they want to come and see me afterwards, I'll put them in the picture if you like . . . Yes, I'm afraid you do have to tell them . . .

'Yes, Customs and Excise do have special powers: they *can* prosecute for failing to send returns, or they can demand up to three times the value of the unpaid VAT . . . Yes, yes . . . I don't think I'd let your brother swear at them, if I were you . . . Oh dear!'

She replaced the receiver gently and smiled at me in a thoughtful sort of way. She reminded me of Madame Defarge; without the knitting, of course.

'Richard', she said, 'is helping Victor out at Superbarg. The Customs men have arrived.'

'Nice to see families coming together in a crisis.'

'Richard *is* the crisis.'

'Together with the National Insurance, the Inland Revenue, the suppliers, the bank, the High Court, the county court, the bailiffs, and the little dog with his leg cocked up against his doorpost outside . . .'

'Yeah.'

'Yeah . . . All this, and we get paid as well.'

We both sighed.

'You already know about MacMillan,' I said to Victor, once we'd got rid of the men from the Customs and Excise Investigations Branch. 'His real name is Maynard and he's been remanded in custody for a job he did in Birmingham last year. Hurt is an associate; he buys and sells dodgy stuff – West Midlands wanted him, too.'

'What happens now?' Victor Todd was slumped in the office chair, while Richard, very much the elder brother, was perched on one corner of the desk. He and the lads from HM Customs and Excise had not turned out to be friends.

I shrugged. 'Hopefully, they stay locked up, while we prepare a case. Then we take a trip to the crown court.'

'Was MacMillan ever in the Army?'

'At one time – he was a corporal-cook in the Army Catering Corps.'

'Thanks!'

'What are you going to do?' I was curious all right. Richard and Victor, the new dynamic duo. All they needed were the masks and capes.

'Do a stock-take; talk to my accountant. We'll do our best to sort it out: Richard's promised to help. I'm a director of the bloody thing, I just can't walk away.' Victor Todd, responsible citizen. Oh well.

'True.'

'Besides . . .' His face brightened. '. . . you did recover my eighteen and a half thousand quid. That's some return out of my twenty-five.'

'Not exactly, Mr Todd. We'll bank it, of course, and

put it into an interest-bearing account for the time being, but I doubt if it's yours.'

Richard shook his head. 'Come on, Vic, you're not thinking straight. The Inspector's right, it's not your money. It belongs to the company. You're just a share-holder; a sort of unsecured creditor. You'll have to join the queue, like everybody else.'

There is nothing, absolutely nothing, to compare with being the bearer of good news. For one thing it makes people amenable to suggestions they may not otherwise entertain.

Richard and Victor. Together: taken by surprise. A burst of diplomacy, a touch of sympathy, and I got my reward. A pair of noddy-doggy heads. One or two arrangements, a promise of confidentiality, a few soothing words, and I'd hammered another nail in my killer's nice new shiny coffin. Definitely my killer: all mine, now.

It had been a doubly profitable afternoon. Especially the tête-à-tête with the Customs officers at Superbarg, the original reason for my visit. Coppers are a surprisingly ignorant lot. I'd no idea that businesses have to retain their VAT invoices for at least six years. Jeweller's business in this particular case, that is.

She was crying again; I could tell by the way her voice kept going up and down and the odd little pauses in the conversation over the phone. Tears: she knew I couldn't stand tears and I knew she wasn't doing it to create an effect. It had been going on for – an exaggeration – hours.

'I know you,' she said, 'only too well. You and your sentimentality. But you're as tough as old boots about some things: proud. And this is a baby, Rob; you can't send it back.'

258

I'd tried soft, I really had. Maybe that was what was worrying her so much. It just wasn't me: she'd had nine years' experience of Steamroller Rob and perhaps I was lacking a bit of the the old street cred. That's why I reverted to type.

'*A puppy is for life, not just for Christmas!*' I quoted. 'Is that it, Angie, your slogan? If so, don't trust it. You can't run your life on gloomy car stickers pushed out by the RSPCA. Lots of Christmas puppies do very, very well.'

'I can't rely on happy ever after, either, you fool. I've got to do the thinking for all of us. You've got an awful memory for what it was really like.'

'*Boring?* That's what you said at the time. Oh, and unpaid housekeeper, I think that's what you also said.'

'You see? You remember everything, Rob. You'll remember whose baby it is – every single day. Maybe you won't say anything; maybe you'll try to – to love her. What's going to happen when you don't?'

'Angie, Angie, listen to yourself: one moment I've got an awful memory, the next I'm dragging things up and remembering only too well. You're making excuses. What do you *want* to do? Get back together, or what?'

Or what?

Silence at last.

We were both terrific at the questions: how would we feel about the baby, about each other? What about the nosy coppers and nosy coppers' wives; what would the neighbours say? What about her job? What about my job? What about the house? Where would we live? And as for answers, came there practically none.

I tried for something trivial, unexpected: what about coming to the dance on Friday? Lots of humming and hawing, even there. Another burst of what will the old women of both sexes say? Sod 'em. Sodom and Gomorrah, come to that, but not the sort of thing to say

259

aloud. No jokes, in the delicate circumstances, down the plastic and wire.

So; no answers at all, really. Except to the question we never bothered to ask. Answer enough, then, in my opinion: to the one about Clive Jones.

Frankly, my dear, neither you nor I appeared to give a damn. To hell with Clive! One very muted cheer for that.

29

——•——

I couldn't read George's expression. Shock? Disbelief?
Wondering whether he was going to sink without trace,
along with his crazy DI? Or perhaps he felt some
measure of distaste, arresting a fellow clansman, if that's
the word.

All coppers are supposed to be bastards: lock up
their granny for the price of a Superintendent's nod.
The conventional wisdom, the received opinion, and
who are we to deny it? Surely, nobody could possibly
feel the slightest reluctance in doing their public duty,
could they?

And yet . . . Put it this way: if you'd been party to
locking up one of her relations, how would you feel when
you went home to dish out the glad tidings to the wife?
And that was precisely what George was going to have
to go and do. *By the way, dear, funny thing; I locked up
your cousin today!*

Teddy and me, we'd both given it a gentle bat around
before we jumped: duty versus propriety, injured feelings
and what would the defending barrister say? But George
was the other supervisory rank: the Man, in both senses
of the word.

Therefore we went out together and stuck Charlie

Pringle under arrest. *Charles Francis Todd Pringle, I am arresting you for the murder of Alice Draper on the twelfth or thirteenth of December 1989. You are not obliged to say anything . . .*

Back at the Factory, they both still looked as if I'd hit them with a brick. I suppose I'd better make this admission – I had a bit of a knot in the belly myself. Not that I couldn't prove it in the long run: I was well on the way. Not that I felt too uneasy about knocking off a solicitor: I'd done that before.

A touch of old-fashioned stage fright, to tell the truth. It's supposed to give you an edge: maybe and perhaps. All I know is that I still get it, even after eighteen years, and whenever I start an important interview it screws up my gut.

Anyway, could I really prove it? Absolutely? At that particular moment, no. Reasonable suspicion: enough and more than enough to make the arrest, but as for copper-bottomed, scientific proof: hold your breath and wait.

I *knew* the forensic lads would back me up, some time in the future, weeks ahead. When they'd finished chopping molecules, putting them in gel, sticking them to a membrane, radioactivising, X-raying and comparing to their hearts' content. DNA? It was still a mystery to me. So far as I was concerned, schoolboy biology terminated abruptly when they made me chop up a frog.

Maybe Hacker felt the same. I certainly wasn't wallowing around in my ignorance alone; 1989, and he'd played around with the new biological toy. A brand-new technology and he hadn't thought things through. Literally, he'd been out for blood. Nothing too ambitious; he hadn't had the resources or the backing to do a town of forty-five thousand people.

Especially – especially when the rumours of inter-necine strife had spread. The world's first DNA enquiry, circa 1983–89, had ended up in battle, murder and sudden death. And that was only among the cops; metaphorically speaking, of course.

So it was caution, caution all the way for Hacker: suspects only; nothing high-profile for him. Then six of his victims had refused to play and he'd left it at that. There but for the grace of God and an idle Sunday-morning read . . .

Which brings me to my second admission: I hadn't got around to submitting anything to the laboratory, either. It would have given the game away. I just couldn't have stood Hacker's hysteria; Silver's screams of mortification, rage. Not to mention the way he'd have come raving down, cock-up in hand, in an effort to ruin a victory and snatch up another glorious defeat.

So Charlie and I faced one another, with George in charge of the tape machine and ready to chuck the occasional verbal grenade if things got rough.

I cautioned him again for the sake of the tape and he looked back at me with a mixture of fear and malevolence. He moved uneasily on his chair, took his glasses out of his top pocket and adjusted them carefully on the bridge of his nose. Then he took them off again and dumped them on his side of the desk. There was nothing for him to read.

I began cautiously, batting my way in. Name, address, date of birth, occupation, why he'd been brought to the nick. Trying for the occasional concession, agreement, looking for a 'yes'.

'Cards on the table, Charlie,' I said at last, with that bogus intimacy of cop and crook. 'I'll tell you about it. Tell you what you did.'

'I'm innocent,' he said. No bluster; none of the threats. Innocent; and he wasn't going to sit there dumb. A better man than I'd expected, in his way. Hating but rational. I could describe his line.

'You probably got to know Alice Draper in the spring or summer of 1989: around the time she had her bust-up with Richard Todd, or shortly afterwards, she started an affair with you.'

'I had known Miss Draper', he said softly, 'for some years, in the sense that she was the girlfriend of a client of mine, Ian Richards. That's all. You inhabit a fantasy world, Inspector.'

'A casual acquaintance, then. Until the summer of '89?'

'A casual acquaintance. Never anything else.'

I gave him the slow, disbelieving smile, and took out the boxed Gucci watch.

'I recovered this,' I said, 'from a woman named Hilda, who had it from a loan shark who accepted it as surety for a loan.'

He stared at the box on the table, then he lifted his eyes enquiringly and shrugged.

'Alice Draper wanted a loan so she could get an abortion. She hocked her watch, an emerald ring, scraped together her own few quid, got thirty-eight pounds from a friend and got her abortion on 29 September 1989. Cost: two hundred, plus VAT. How would you rate a two-hundred-quid termination, as an upmarket piece of work?'

'Fascinating.' He ignored the crack.

All right, my lad, try this for size.

'The abortion took place one week after you got married: the good Catholic boy to the good Catholic girl. Right?'

'You contemptible pig!'

'It takes one to know one, so they say.' Ice skating, again. Trading insults; not what they want to hear at crown court. But a spot of provocation never did any harm. *It's the oppressive conduct what gets a copper the evidential chop, guv: surely, he can make the odd comment in self-defence?*

'It was your baby, wasn't it? Why wouldn't you pay for the abortion: too mean?'

'No.'

'You admit it, though?'

'No. That's typical. I want to go on record as saying that you are twisting what I say.'

'So, you refused to pay for the abortion out of principle – religious scruples, in fact?'

'That's a new low, even for the police.'

'All right, Charlie; let's go back a step. You went to bed with Alice, didn't you?'

'No.'

'Then why did you buy her this?' I tapped the top of the box. He lowered his eyelids and smiled, the merest lifting of the lips. Contempt. I waited.

'All you have done is show me a watch and made a series of unsubstantiated allegations. Defamatory remarks.'

Come on, Charlie; you can do better than that. Threats of defamation? What about Crown privilege, mate?

'At the risk of sounding facetious, Charlie, would you like to open the box?'

He stared at me blankly; he didn't get it. *Double Your Money*, that daft sixties-revival TV game show where they answer questions and open boxes – I must be getting really old, and Charlie must have been too snobby to watch common people at play. But he opened the box.

'A genuine Gucci,' I said. 'Not like the one Dicky gave her. Name and address of the jeweller inside.'

It wasn't much; you could hardly call it a movement; nevertheless I knew. I'd got in there; under his guard for the first time.

'You know what I'm going to say next, don't you?'

'That I bought her the watch?'

'Is that an admission, or am I twisting it again?'

'No doubt you've got the jeweller's copy of the receipt, addressed to me.' His voice rose a notch; enough to notice. The more I got down to cases, the more he hammered it home: the pseudo public-school voice.

'And the credit card counterfoil, and there's a statement of your account on its way.'

'Very well, I knew Alice well enough to buy her a present.'

A throw-away admission in a dismissive tone, looking down his nose all the time. So what? he was saying; totally unimportant that he'd lied; that he'd just contradicted himself.

'Valued at one hundred and seventy-two pounds at that time. A sexual relationship. Right?'

I was gunning for him now. His shiny suit, his shabby coat, his supercilious airs: one hundred and seventy-two quid. *A fortune to you, Charlie-boy*.

'Yes. I would like to point out that I was one among many. It was not necessarily my child and I certainly did not kill her.'

'Spoken like a true professional, Charles.'

He glowered.

'Right, we've established that you were bedding Alice, yes?'

'You're a crude, unpleasant man, aren't you?'

He must have been reading my mail.

'What do you want to call it; making love, then? Precious little love about it, wasn't there? She was a bit on the side – pick her up, buy her a watch, drop her when it suited. How long before the wedding bells, Charles?'

'You sadistic bastard.'

'Never mind the compliments: tell me about this love

266

affair of yours. Sensitive attorney meets damaged flower?
Come on!'

'I knew Alice Draper, I went out with her occasionally.
I bought her a present and I do not have to put up
with this!'

Very true, but he didn't seem able to help himself,
somehow.

'You knew Alice, you had sexual intercourse with her,
you bought her that watch, you ditched her and she was
pregnant at the time. Yes?'

'She had other . . . boyfriends. It was not necessarily
my responsibility.'

'But you knew about it?'

A tiny nod.

I spoke for the benefit of the machine. 'Mr Pringle
nodded, indicating that he knew that the murder victim
was pregnant. How did you know?'

'She asked me for money.'

'For the abortion?'

'I refused. It's not something I wanted on my conscience.'

'I beg your pardon?'

He rocked back in his chair and closed his eyes.
'You obviously don't understand: I didn't want to be
responsible for the death of a child.'

Yes, I could understand, oddly enough; but love and
understanding weren't part of my brief. Not just then.

'So, would you have paid for her to keep it?'

'It was not necessarily mine.'

'She told you it was yours, didn't she?'

'She probably thought I was a good bet.' Evasive;
wriggling. He was right; he'd got a conscience in there
somewhere. All I had to do was dig.

'But you abandoned her, instead?' I could be slip-
ping away from him here. The little burglar alarm

was tinkling a warning somewhere at the back of my brain.

I was hacking away with this bloody big chopper, when I might have been using a stiletto. And yet . . . I was getting to him; he was still trotting out the replies. A miracle in itself. Easy, easy, nevertheless. *Catch more flies with sugar than you'll ever drown in vinegar, old pal.* And the old, repetitive clichés are the best . . .

'OK, you were engaged to be married and Alice was a bit of a tart. She'd got form for it, hadn't she?'

'She was promiscuous, if that's what you mean.'

'And you were tempted; you weren't the first and you won't be the last, Charlie. Unfortunately for you, she turned sour – she landed you with this pregnancy tale, but you didn't fall for it. Right?'

'More or less.'

'What happened then?'

'Nothing.'

'Of course it did – you got married to your fiancée for one thing. What's your wife's name, by the way?'

'Keep her out of this!'

'Carole, her name's Carole,' said George.

'So you married Carole – and pathetic Alice scrimped and scraped to get rid of your child. That's what happened next, Charlie.'

'It wasn't necessarily—'

'Yours. I know. But afterwards, she kept after you, didn't she?'

'No.'

'And on the night of that – what's the name? – the Song and Strut Ball, as they call it, you arranged to meet her.'

'No.'

'And you did meet her, and she tempted you again, yes?'

'No.'

'And you had sex. Afterwards she tried to get money out of you – blackmail, was it? *Repay me for what I've been through, or I'll drop you in it with your wife?*'

'No, no, no! You're making this up; you have absolutely nothing against me. All these lies!'

'You had the opportunity, Charlie – look at this.'

I handed him the house-to-house enquiry form I'd dug out: one of thousands. Addressed to Eddathorpe males; *What were you doing on the night of 12 December 1989?*

He put his glasses back on. 'Yes, I was out. I went to a legal dinner.'

'Yep, a Christmas binge; thirty miles away. The Society for the Prosecution of Felons; a quaint legal survival of the olden days. But you don't prosecute felons any more – the lawyers and big-wigs get together and make speeches and drink themselves daft. You didn't get home until after two a.m. Opportunity, Charles.'

'I don't see you bringing a couple of crown court judges, lots of barristers and the magistrates' bench to ask them offensive questions: they were there too.'

'If they were busying themselves with pregnancies and Gucci watches, Charles, I'll oblige. Just let me know.'

I ought to stop that: puts people's – juries – backs up, too many smart remarks.

'There must have been dozens – hundreds – of local men out that night.'

'True.'

'Well, then?'

'Not all of them are solicitors, Charles. Not all of them knew Alice and only one of them represented six – *six* – of Superintendent Hacker's suspects.'

'So?'

'You naturally represented your relations, Richard and

269

Victor Todd. You advised them not to undergo blood tests, didn't you?'

'I was acting in the best interests of my clients.'

'And in the best interests of Keith Baker, Ian Richards, Alex Buchanan and an out-of-town indecent assault merchant called Miller, who was just dragged in to be interviewed on the off-chance?

'They were all your clients: and guess what? Of all the persons asked to do a test, they were the only ones who refused. All on your advice.'

'What's the point of all this? I warn you now; you will not bully me into forgoing my rights. I'll not be submitting to one of those grossly unreliable tests!'

I grinned at him while he shifted uneasily in his chair. 'That's exactly the point. You gave your clients some horror story about the unreliability of blood testing for DNA. Deliberately, to save your own skin.'

His lips scarcely moved. 'And why should I do that?'

'Because of the contents of this very popular book, published in 1989, as it happens. The story of the world's first murder conviction based on blood samples revealing the identity of a killer through his unique genetic code.'

I threw down a copy of my Sunday-morning reading, Joseph Wambaugh's *The Blooding*, on to the table. The story of the notorious Leicestershire double murder enquiry, successfully concluded in the midst of one hell of a cop-on-copper row, in 1988.

'Right now the lads are searching your house and I bet you've got one of these at home. Am I right, Charlie?'

He looked at me and into me and through me, and when he couldn't make any progress he finally ripped his gaze away.

No reply.

'OK – I think you've read this book, or something similar. All about deoxyribonucleic acid, the chemical

270

basis of life. You knew that each individual possesses a unique genetic code, that blood can be matched to sperm and that the chances of two people possessing an identical genetic code are hundreds of millions – billions – to one.'

I was pushing my luck and I knew it; nobody seems to have made up their tiny forensic minds about the odds. Lots of conflict about the reliability of the test. Defence barristers may still want to give it a whirl. Never mind; it was mongoose versus snake, and the mongoose wasn't going to have to jump. Just tell it how it was.

'You killed Alice and you had unprotected sex with her, not long before she died.'

'Why should I – why should anyone prevent others from taking a DNA test? Such advice would be irrelevant. You said it yourself, individual characteristics are unique.'

Still that voice, those elocution lessons doing their best; wavering a bit now.

'You read the newspapers. And the bones of the murdered Russian Tsar and his family have been identified by referring to the blood of their living relations, even after seventy-five years.

'You share grandparents with Richard and Victor Todd. If they had been successfully tested, they would have shown up as innocent. But their genetic make-up would have shown sufficient similarities to the unknown killer to put us on the track of a Todd relation – you!'

Silence.

'You stirred up Richard and Victor; made them think they were protecting each other by a refusal. Instead, they didn't know it, but they were protecting you.

'Then you had a bit of luck – duty solicitor to some of the other suspects. So you muddied the pond a bit – got them to refuse a blood test, too. Just in case Vic and Dicky's refusal stuck out like a sore thumb.'

More deathly hush.

'Oh, Charlie, come on, now. You and Hacker, both: you were obsessed with matching the semen found in the body against suspects' blood. And look what I've got: one, two samples of blood from Richard and Victor, for what they're worth. Then, from a hairy overcoat – sample number three.'

I placed two vials of blood and a sealed plastic packet of shed greasy hair on the desk between us. Victor and Tricky Dicky: a favour or two, a bit of a chat – and they'd become my willing volunteers. Useful, but not conclusive, I would have thought.

But Bob's your uncle and Fanny's your Gran! If you put the blood samples side by side with the material obtained by Malc, our amateur gentleman's gentleman. The man with the clothes brush and the funny (not very lawful) instruction written in his pocket book – *Go and brush the hairs off Charlie Pringle's coat*.

'We could have sorted this, you know; back in '89,' I said. 'Cleared Richard and Victor; hooked you up, if you and Superintendent Hacker hadn't been so obsessed by samples of blood.

'Hair, for example, could have nailed you if he'd done his homework: genetic material, just the same. We can take that from people in custody, whether they object or not.'

He was still waiting; I hadn't managed to turn the key. So I kept up the chat.

'Lawyers and their gobbledegook: cops and their assumptions. Intimate samples: *blood*. It obsessed you both, didn't it? And all because of that first, famous case where they took thousands of samples from volunteers. Silly, isn't it?'

He looked at me with a curious expression. If I hadn't known him better I could almost have plumped for respect.

Then, deliberately, struggling for a shred or two of dignity, he spoke.

'I would like at this stage', he said, 'to take independent legal advice.'

It was something I'd have chosen to do from the start.

The lawyer who represents himself has a fool for a client.

You bet.

We had the booze-up: an unedifying affair composed of jolly drunks, boastful drunks, depressives and steady old soaks. Halfway through the evening they stood Joe on the bar and tried to get him interested in beer, but he backed off and knocked over Sandra Lawrence's glass of cream sherry. He took an instant shine to it, the expensive little sod.

George, surprisingly, was the least satisfied of us all. He had this bee in his bonnet: Charlie was unlikely, in his opinion, to get his just deserts. He wasn't out to hang him: life imprisonment would do.

He had this theory, however. He'd started developing it the moment we walked out of the Drapers' front gate. We'd told them; they'd thanked us. Old Man Draper had cried. Happy Christmas, folks. And that's the bit which had probably got to George. A touch of guilt: it was his wife's cousin once removed who'd done it. Banging him up on a permanent basis was George's idea of an adequate response.

Me too, I suppose. But I could see Charlie and his defence from a long way off. From the moment the big-city smoothie smiled at me and said, 'My client

273

wishes to put the whole of this matter before you, Inspector.'

Which translates easily into the vernacular: *We're cooking up a pretty good story here, Jack.*

I bought a few rounds, Keith Baker bought one: I even slapped him on the back. Paula was gabbling management-speak like the Chairman of ICI; even Malcolm was happy, detecting his first murder all over again. We all deserved a break. We had, as Andy put it, booted a bit of bot over the past couple of weeks.

But George had his theory. He too could spot Charlie coming. It made for a depressive drunk.

'Shysters', he announced loudly, after his seventh pint, 'are all the same. They all stick together, even the Crown Prosecutions lot, and when Charlie gets stuck in with his tale of woe, it'll be reduced to manslaughter. Commiserations from the judge and a fiver out of the poor-box, I shouldn't wonder.'

'C'mon, George!' Andy had him by the sleeve. 'Sod 'em all; we've scored. Nicely banged up and ready for crown court. The boss isn't worrying – leave the problems for another day.'

I bought another round on the strength of that. No, I wasn't worrying, but Charlie'd have a good try: Alice Draper's promiscuity, the improbability of the child being his, an allegation of blackmail . . . trying to scare her . . . minimum force on her neck . . . an almost accidental death. Almost. Charles Francis Todd Pringle, Solicitor of the Supreme Court.

'Come on, George, sink your pint. If you can't take a joke, you shouldn't have joined!'

It echoes, echoes somewhere, does that.

30

———▶————

Friday afternoon: it was getting dark and I took a stroll from the Pirate's Haven and the Fun Castle at the north end of the Esplanade, to the Jolly Fisherman and the raw earth where they'd excavated the floral clock at the south. The sea was flat calm, grey and chill, the cafés and amusement arcades were still shuttered and lights were coming on in the houses. A solitary newsagent's shop glistened with tinsel, while a troupe of illuminated reindeer stationed on a traffic island pulled a bloated, battered Santa Claus in a polystyrene sleigh at the high-street junction.

My town: I felt a bit like that. All I needed was the star, the stetson and the low-slung gun. Not the happiest image in the circumstances: I was in trouble with the Lone Ranger's horse. One murder, detected, paled into insignificance when set against Silver's dented pride.

Teddy Baring was fielding the flak and enjoying his revenge for Hacker's treatment of his son. Thou shalt not cross Teddy: another eleventh commandment, brought down from the specially engineered Eddathorpe mount. And Silver had only just found out. New friends; new enemies and a spot of careful cherishing, just like I've said.

I turned down the steps and on to the beach, releasing the dog. He scooted over to the wet sand at the edge of the waves and sniffed cautiously, then he barked. Not your hardy winter swimmer, Joe.

I began to wander back along the sand towards the slip where I could regain the Esplanade, *en route* to the ranch. Time for a drink, a bit of a read, a shower, before I climbed into my ever-so-slightly tight dinner suit and put on an appearance at the Eddathorpe coppers' Christmas bash. Angie had said she was going to come. Booked herself into a hotel. Funny girl.

Funny situation, too. I – we – had put ourselves on offer, all right. Estranged wife turns up for good night out. At the high-profile police event of the year. Expectations aroused, a burst of the wagging tongues, and I might be sorry for this in the morning. Oh well.

I'd done it on impulse, and the more I thought about it, the sillier it seemed. A bit of manoeuvring, a cautious coming-together to test how we felt, OK. A spot of courting on neutral ground. But this – I must have been mad. She must have been crackers too. Bloody Christmas, I thought; setting us both off.

I remembered my last police event. Jonesie taking a dive in the first round. The embarrassment. Ye gods! What on earth had possessed Angie to agree to come to another coppers' carnival after that?

And what about me? What were my new neighbours going to say, if I didn't get a result; if, after all the public parading, she cleared off again?

What were they going to think of me if she stayed? Getting bigger by the day: how many policemen, how many policemen's wives, were incapable of counting up to nine connubial months? And I despised myself; I'd always taken pride in not caring a single, solitary damn for any outsider ever pupped.

'Hellooo, Inspector!' A formidable, Burberried figure loomed in the gathering dusk. 'Call your dog; I don't want them running away again.'

Sophie and Mary Todd. Joe trotted meekly beside me and cocked his head on one side with a slightly supercilious air. A member of the team; the dog who always did what he was told. In other words, biological shut-down. He wasn't quite so interested in the little bitch, once her season was over.

'She's pregnant,' said Mary Todd.

Exactly how, what – no, she meant her dog.

Not the moment for effusive congratulations, or cordial hopes it was going to be a boy. What the devil do you say?

'I hope she'll be all right.'

'She's healthy; a litter will probably do her good. Remember our agreement, that's all.'

Agreement? Not exactly an agreement, I recalled. Dragooned into looking around for good homes. It would be like trying to place the offspring of Attila the Hun.

'Ought I to congratulate you?' she said.

'Well, she's coming to the dance, but . . . Oh!'

'Cross-purposes?' She smiled. 'Well, I do believe you're human, after all. I was talking about your recent professional success. About which I have mixed feelings, by the way.'

'Your ex-relation by marriage? Yes, I suppose you would. Alice Draper's brought you a fair amount of trouble, one way or another.'

'Yes,' she said, 'living and dead. Charlie – well, he'll have to stand up and answer for himself, but what about his wife? What did she ever do to deserve this?'

I shrugged and shook my head. Not exactly a unique point of view. Villains with families, people to care about them, whatever they'd done. What was I supposed to do about it? Be sorry – uneasy, anyway? But it wasn't going to change anything. A wholly unproductive line of thought.

She looked hard at me for a second or two, as if she could read my mind. Abruptly, she changed her tack.

'So, you're going to the Divisional dance,' she said. 'So are we.'

'You and Eric?'

'Yes: former murder suspect rubbing shoulders with the police. Tut, tut.' Maybe she was taking the mickey; if so, she wasn't making much of a job.

'No reason why he shouldn't go, Mary; he's in the clear. Everybody goes to everything in this town, so I've been told.'

'That's right, with whoever they can raise. Beats being lonely, wouldn't you say?'

'Er – yes.'

'I'm not embarrassing you, am I, Inspector? Surely not: you must have wondered about us, what we find to keep us together in this dreary little town? Why I see Eric; why Richard and Valerie and Victor and all the little Eddathorpe cliques keep bumping up against each other socially – and in other ways. Going around in ever-decreasing circles, perhaps?'

'Why does anybody live anywhere?' It was the best I could do. What was this? A fit of the out-of-season blues? I was totally out of my depth.

'We're all here because we've settled for second best – did you know that? Settled for a shabby, inward-looking little world on the edge of the sea, but it's better than nothing at all, so we stay. And everybody goes to everything, because there's nothing else.'

'Well,' I said weakly, 'it's not such a bad little place.

As good as you're prepared to make it, depending on your point of view.'

Remember this, old son. You could get a job sticking mottoes on matchboxes if ever you gave up the coppering game. Until, of course, your new employer went broke.

'Ah,' she said, 'an Eddathorpe fan.' It was the second time I'd been accused of that. 'You ought to enjoy yourself here. Save me a dance. I'll see you tonight.'

'Yes; see you tonight.'

I watched her walking briskly across the sands. Burberry flapping, stepping out and giving it some swank; Sophie, a trifle reluctantly, in tow. A big, healthy girl: a possibility becoming indistinct in the dusk; a bit of a fantasy. Not so much a might-have-been; in truth, a never-was.

My aggressive little shadow trotted sedately beside me, giving me the occasional anxious glance. The importance of potted philosophy, nostalgia and sentimentality paled beside the attractions of regular meals. I made my way towards the slip, watching the Esplanade lights and the moving shadows of the occasional pedestrian silhouetted on the prom.

Eddathorpe; not exactly the hub of the universe. Unlikely to become the millionaire playground of the East Coast. Full of cliques and back-biting and malice and bearing a distinct resemblance to everywhere else.

Unbidden, thoughts of Buchanan junior and his opinion of fairy tales drifted across my mind. Precious few virgins around here. Little chance of finding the ideal maidenly lap. In any case, the occupation was lacking in excitement. In the interests of mere survival, unicorns were going to have to retrain. And Angie was not second best.